In and Out of the Shadow
An Autobiographical Novel

Born in Cobh, County Cork, Liam Nolan worked as a shipping clerk with the Cunard company before emigrating in 1953 to London, where he joined the BBC. He began his broadcasting career with Radio Luxembourg, and on demob from National Service he worked on *This is Your Life*. He wrote television and film documentary scripts, and he became anchorman on BBC radio's *Today* programme. He later anchored *Sports Report* and became BBC radio's athletics and boxing commentator. He returned to Ireland in 1970 and presented *The Liam Nolan Hour* and many other radio and television programmes. He covered the Munich and Moscow Olympics for the BBC. His books to date include *The Hills Hid Us Well* (about the Resistance), *The Pain and the Glory* (a biography of the composer Smetana), *The Small Man of Nanataki*, *The Forgotten Famine* (about the Ethiopian famine of the early '70s), *The Square Ring* and *Islanders*.

LIAM NOLAN

IN AND OUT OF THE SHADOW

MOUNT EAGLE

Published in 1998 by
Mount Eagle Publications Ltd.
Dingle, Co. Kerry, Ireland

ISBN 1 902011 05 8
(original paperback)

10 9 8 7 6 5 4 3 2 1

Published with the assistance of the
Arts Council/An Chomhairle Ealaíonn

Cover design: Public Communications Centre, Dublin
Typesetting: Red Barn Publishing, Skeagh, Skibbereen
Printed by ColourBooks Ltd, Dublin

For all my family,
but particularly for Liamy

Tears and Penny Dinners

"CHALK AND FUCKIN' cheese -- that's summer an' winter in this hoorin' place!" the old man said. He had matted hair on his face, a greasy cap and a raggedy, soaked overcoat. The words came out of him in a croak.

He wasn't talking to me. I was just a small boy trying to make myself invisible as he stepped backwards into the entrance to the railway station, trying to back away from this depressing winter day. He was talking to himself.

The wind was blowing cold rain across the harbour from the south-east, blowing it right in under the cast-iron-and-glass canopy. It reached halfway in the passage that led to the concourse where the ticket office and the paper shop and the bar were.

"I hate the winter," the man moaned. "It's killin' me."

The sole of one of his collapsed boots had separated from its upper and, even cowering there against the wall, I caught a glimpse of scrunched-up dirty toes pushing through holes in a black sock. There had to be toe-jam in there. The man raised his foot off the ground and shook it, the way a dog does after peeing against a lamppost. A stream of dirty drops poured out of the boot, adding to the spreading pool forming around his feet.

7

"*Christ!*" he said.

There was a stench from him which the wind blew in my direction. I retched, heaved, but felt sorry for him.

"Rain an' cold an' fuckin' wind," he said, beginning to swing his soggy arms, trying to get some feeling, some warmth into them. "No one gives a tuppeny shit . . ."

I was sure he was crying.

". . . least of all that fucker up there in his palace . . . Bishop . . . *Bollocks!*"

I moved away then, frightened. I had never heard anyone talking of Bishop Roche like that.

I watched him from near the ticket office, his filthy form a silhouette against the light of a darkening afternoon. Every now and again he'd turn and look inwards, and I pretended then to be interested in something, anything, else. But when he turned around again to look outwards, moving his head backwards and forwards in a kind of rocking movement, I couldn't take my eyes off Routum.

I had this awful, indescribable feeling about him. *For* him, really. It wasn't a pain, or even an ache. More like a fist twisting slowly inside my chest. A bit like the way I felt every year when Uncle Willie went back to Dublin after his summer holidays with us in Cobh, a torn-asunder, empty, lonely, sorrowing feeling. Except that in the case of poor old Routum there was no loneliness. Not in me anyway.

None of us knew anything about him, not even how he got his nickname. All we knew was that his real name was Sanders. Six days a week he went around the town selling the Cork *Evening Echo*. He dressed in rags and slept rough. We never knew where he came from in the afternoons or where he went to at night. We didn't know where he ate or what he ate, or even if he ate.

When Routum went through the streets in the late afternoons and evenings, up and down the hills of the town, you'd hear that croaking voice shouting, "Ek-wa . . . Evenin' Ek-wa!" And always, too, there were the taunts of the youngsters who

8

ran behind him, mimicking his shout and calling out, "Routum! . . . Routum! . . . Routum!"

They did it for the thrill they got when he turned and tried to chase them with a pathetic shuffling excuse for a run, his broken boots flip-flopping, the papers dropping out of the bundle held under his arm. Some of the taunters threw small stones at him, and when I saw the tears that poured out of his eyes and into the hair on his face as he shouted at them and made his attempt at a chase, I felt like crying, too. But I did nothing. I was too much of a coward to stand up for him.

I gave up going out when it was "Ek-wa" time. I got too upset. But when I heard his "Ek-wa" call as he came along Roche's Row or up Harbour View, I went out with the few coppers Mam gave me and bought the *Echo* from him. I tried to make up a little for the cruelty of the mockers by saying, "Thank you, Mr Sanders."

He never acknowledged it, never showed in any way that it meant anything to him, just took the pennies in his dirty hand, peeled off an *Echo* from the bundle, gave it to me, and walked on, croaking, "Ek-wa . . . Evenin' Ek-wa!"

Years later, when he died, a huge number of townspeople turned up at his funeral. Among them were boys-turned-teenagers who carried a deep guilt for the things they had done to him. They knew that they had stripped him of any dignity he might once have had and made of the last years of his existence a time of anguish and distress.

I wondered all sorts of things, like, why did they call him Routum? What did it mean? Why did it make him cry? And was Bishop Roche really a bollocks?

"Ah, sure 'tis a happy release for the poor divil," Mrs O'Brien who owned the sweets and vegetables shop on Roche's Row said, "and I have no more to say on the subject."

But regardless of whether or not Mrs O'Brien, or anyone else for that matter, had any more to say on the subject of Routum, the *memories* weren't ended by the assertion. You couldn't switch them on and off like a light. And if you were only a boy with a limited amount of living under your belt, you also had only a limited number of *memories*, too, to play around with. It wasn't as if a gigantic maelstrom of occurrences and happenings and details and emotions were all jostling for attention whereby some, because of the sheer multiplicity of numbers, the colossal volume, crowded out the others. Thought replacement was away far off in the future for me.

So Routum and the wet winter day in the station, and all the other grim afternoons and evenings when a taunted tramp wended his way through our town, remained clear in the mind, as sharp and painful as all of yesterday's sorrows.

* * * * * * * *

The winters seemed to come in from the sea. They were grey, dark, cold and wet. Everything seemed to change, even the foghorn on the Spit lighthouse. In hot, hazy summer its sound would be long and lazy, but in winter it filled your heart with sadness. It became a mournful sound, a sound of warning, as of impending death – the way the howl of Buckleys' mangy hound Riff did. It always put me in mind of small rusty ships, rolling dangerously out there in the murk.

And in winter, when ships came down river from Cork, their lights fuzzy yellow blobs in the rain, the red eyes of their portside navigation lamps the only hint of other colour as they passed the waterfront, they seemed reluctant to leave the shelter of the harbour. Many nights I stood by a window on the top floor looking out, watching for the pilot launch to slip out from the camber on the Holy Ground to take the pilot off, and when that was done, still watching as the ships inched out past Whitegate towards Dog Nose buoy, and then south to the open ocean.

But it was the wind which made the real difference in winter. It caused women who would otherwise stop for a chat instead to hurry past after a shouted, "The east wind is a fright to God, isn't it?"

The other women wouldn't pause for a discussion, just a confirmation: "God, girl, it goes right through yeh – and I wouldn't mind but my eldest fella hasn't a shoe to his feet. They'd have yeh skint."

Standing outside the door of Tom Darcy's shop at the bottom of King Street one Saturday night waiting for my mother, I heard one woman saying to another, "And that bleddy thing up in the Town Hall had the gall to send me a bill for the rates! Where in God's name would *I* get money for rates? Jesus, Mary and Joseph! . . . He can *wait* for his bleddy rates, then! . . . Excuse me a minit, missus," and she came out and looked at me.

"Come 'ere, aren't you one of the Nolans?"

I said I was.

"Billy Nolan, isn't it?"

"Yes."

"Well, stop your ear-wiggin' now like a good boy, and go after your mother. She's along at Tom Hanlon's, the butchers."

I looked into the faces of the two women before I hurried away and saw worry and something I didn't understand then – the pinched appearance of people who were struggling.

"If only we could get free of the flu and the colds," the woman who had spoken to me continued to her companion.

"Cod liver oil and malt – I *swear* by it."

"If I could *afford* it . . . God bless."

I looked back as I went down past Madigan's and saw the first woman stepping out of Tom Darcy's doorway and fighting to raise an umbrella. It blew inside out.

When we got home, my hands were so cold they had turned blue, suffused with red. They looked really ugly because the chilblains had thickened the fingers and made them look like lumpy sausages.

I held them out towards the fire in the dining room grate, but my mother immediately said, "For God's sake keep your hands away from the fire! Otherwise those chilblains will burst

11

and you'll be crucified. And I'll have no pity on you if that happens because, God knows, I've warned you often enough."

Winter was mean. It was as if it had a spiteful will of its own and deliberately searched out ways to make people suffer hardships, and it didn't matter whether they were young or old. Wind gusts lashed icy rain straight into your face as you rounded a corner, or blew books out of your grasp, or tore your cap or beret from your head and sent it spinning away into a puddle to land with the inside downwards, under water.

When Gerald Taaffe, the only child of one of the local guards and a bit of a bully, saw this happening to me one stormy afternoon and laughed, I wanted to howl out loud and long at the injustice and the accompanying misery. I hoped he'd break his leg. I even started to pray that he would.

A week later I saw him being blown off his bike by a violent gust of wind that hit him as he passed the cathedral. Instead of feeling pleased, I felt very sorry for him because his glasses fell off and broke, and his knee was cut and bled, and the blood ran down into his grey stocking, and his blubbery lips trembled as he tried to fight back the tears and failed.

I wheeled his bicycle home for him. Nux McCormack said the next day that I was an eejit to do that after the way Taaffe had mocked me.

"You're an eejit! You shoulda left him there. Or laughed out loud and said, 'Serves you right! Now, maybe you won't be so smart in laughin' at me the next time my beret flies off.' Why didn't you?"

"I don't know," I said. "I couldn't."

"Ah, you're only a soft oul eejit!"

That winter I got a brand new oiled sou'wester with warm ear flaps, a new pair of shiny wellingtons, made in Cork in the Dunlop factory close to Ford's, and the use of one of my father's old yellow ARP capes. He'd been issued with a new one. With the front of the sou'wester turned up to channel the rainwater off my head back on to my shoulders, the total-ly rainproof cape reaching well down beyond the tops of my wellies, and the wellies themselves capable of keeping out anything liquid, I could walk out and dare the rain. And I did.

The town being built on the side of a massive hill, all the streets other than the ones down at the waterfront consisted of slopes. I liked standing in the gutters (we called them shores) in the teeming rain and pretending my wellingtoned feet were dams, causing a back-up of muddy torrents to form foaming, churning reservoirs. On days like that, I liked to think of myself as Gulliver. But I kept private stuff like that private.

That was the year we went into Sully's class. To us he was a west Cork giant with a huge head of blue-black curly hair turning grey. He wore manager's suits, striped shirts and black polished shoes. He lodged in King Street, was unmarried, and pushed a gleaming Raleigh bike up the hills to school every morning and freewheeled back down in the afternoon when school was over.

Sully was one of three lay teachers in St Joseph's National School, which was run by the Presentation Brothers. Tom Cooney, a smooth, quiet-voiced and precise man given to wearing what was then called nigger-brown suits was one. He had neat, short, flattish, black hair, and a smile that fell somewhere between effeminate and menacing. The other one was Spud Murphy.

Cooney taught first class, and to anyone who seemed to have difficulty settling down, he'd say quietly, "Do you want to go into Mr Murphy's class, boy?"

Nobody wanted to go into Spud Murphy's class. To be asked was a threat in itself. If you were any way smart, you'd skip second class anyway, which was probably another way of saying that only the slow boys, the ones with learning difficulties, had to spend a school year under Spud Murphy's harsh regime as he noisily hoicked and hanky-spat greeners all day every day.

13

His voice was high, harsh and piercing. He was a small, squat, bad-tempered individual with a bullet head and bristly grey hair. He wore black suits, white shirts, black ties and laced boots. *Boots!* . . . He wore silver-framed grannie glasses and looked a bit like Heinrich Himmler, whose face we knew from pictures. And he had the letters P.C. after his name. It meant, we were told, that he was a peace commissioner.

"What dat?" Nux whispered.

By the time we came to Sully's class, we were into the second half of our time at "the nash". Sully was really enormous, and on that first morning he stood to one side of the blackboard, licking the tips of his fingers as we filed meekly into the room. His face was so big, I reckoned you could make three of our sized faces from his! The flesh on his face was nut-brown from sea-wind and sun, and brilliantine fought a losing battle with his hair, trying to keep the gigantic mop from springing out of combed waves and forming into a thousand unruly question-mark curls. Then he spoke, or rather roared, his first words at us.

"You bloody, hairy clodhoppers!"

We'd never heard a teacher curse out loud, and we looked nervously at each other and shrank and moved our bums on the hard shiny benches of the desks.

After a pause spent bending over from his great height, hands on hips, eyes exaggeratedly open as he gave each one of us "the look" and searched our faces, he straightened up and walked towards the window and gazed out over the rooftops towards Spike Island. A sibilant rustle of whispers went through the room, and he let it carry on for several seconds before suddenly whirling around and roaring, "You lopsided bosthoons! I'll raise hollywhite hairs and nobs on the first of you god-damned savages I catch carrying on in my class! Is that clear?!"

"Yes, sir," came the meek response from 27 frightened pupils.

"Is that *clear*? Holy mackerel! What are ye – a bunch of

cissies? Let me *hear* ye! . . . Now when I ask again, 'Is that clear?' I want to hear ye *shouting*, as if ye *meant* it, 'Yes, Mr O'Sullivan!' . . . Right – is that *clear?*"

You'd have heard the answer all the way down to Millwood's pub.

"That's better," Sully said, and then, miraculously, he smiled, his head nodding in satisfaction, and from that day until we left his class at the end of the year he never again roared at us.

But the smile wasn't the only surprise he delivered to us on that first day, or indeed in that first hour. He walked behind the blackboard and bent to open a press beneath the window ledge. Out of it he took a wooden-headed golf club and walked to within three or four feet of the front row of desks.

There were brass studs in the uncarpeted bare board floor. Sully lay the head of the club in such a way as to cover one of the studs. Then he shuffled his feet until they were about as far apart as the width of his shoulders. He followed that by very carefully wrapping the fingers of his left hand around the grip of the club, then overlapped part of that hand with the fingers of his right hand. Not a word was spoken.

After what seemed like minutes of immobility and concentration, and keeping his left arm stiff and straight, he very slowly swung the club head back off the stud and brought it all the way up over his right shoulder. It came down in a blur of speed and clicked over the stud where the head had rested earlier.

To our utter astonishment, he swivelled and followed the imaginary flight of the imaginary ball, even to the extent of taking his right hand off the club's grip to morry-ah shield his eyes against the sun.

But the real question that was troubling all of us was, was that golf club going to be used against *us*? And if he was going to hit us with it, would it be with the head or the grip? Surely not the heavy end? That'd brain you. And what part of the body would he attack?

15

He straightened up abruptly and walked back to the press where he deposited the club. When he came back from behind the blackboard, he was again licking the tips of his fingers.

"Now, you great mutton-headed parallelograms, I want the six best handwriters in the class to come up here and sit at the front, because I have a little job for ye."

Nobody moved.

"Great leaping left leg! Can none of ye write in a legible hand? What kind of a crowd of isosceles triangles have I got here at all?"

He didn't wait for an answer, but picked up a piece of chalk and walked to the blackboard where he wrote out the words "I wandered lonely as a cloud." Then he turned to face us and said, "All right, take out your exercise books, all of ye, and copy what I've written on the board in your very best writing. Take your time, don't rush it and don't scribble – and no ink blots, you squirmy little isopods!"

He gave us a few minutes grace to get out our exercise books and pens with the new Wyvern nibs, and presently began to move from desk to desk examining our efforts.

"Blithering flaming cows, man!" I heard him say to someone in the back row. "Do you call that handwriting? My God Almighty, a baboon would do better with a bloody crowbar, or a shovel!"

I half turned to see who he was talking to, but he said, "Mind your own business, you fathead!" He selected his six handwriters and sat us along the front row of the class. He flipped the board over. On its reverse side we saw the following:

Cobh Charitable Coal Fund

A meeting of the above will be held in the Town Hall at 8pm on Thursday.

(Signed)   Hon. Secretary

"Now my fine calligraphers," he said, "I want each of you

16

to write out those lines, exactly as you see them there, on each of ten slips of paper that I'll hand to ye. Write magnificently! And no mistakes, or I'll knock yeer thick blocks off with my number three iron!"

One thing was certain – we had never heard words like some of the ones he used, and we didn't know under God what they meant. "Isopods", "calligraphers", "isosceles triangles" . . . what kind of language was that? And what was a "number three iron"?

And what, in God's name, was the Cobh Charitable Coal Fund? That was something else we'd never heard of. But this was no time and he was no man (at this point, anyway) to ask questions, particularly as he was working his way across the head of the classroom very carefully counting out ten four-inch slips of lined paper for each of his chosen six to write on.

"The Unholy Half Dozen" he called us: – Danny Murphy, Barney Cullen, Nux McCormack, Johnny Moynihan, Mickey O'Brien and myself.

At the back of the class Gerald Taaffe, Brodduck Walsh, Paddy Waxer and a few others started whispering jeering comments at us, and, using elastic bands as catapults, they fired hard pellets of chewed, rolled-up paper which, if they hit an exposed part like the back of your neck or the tip of an ear, stung sharply. When one of the missiles zipped past my right ear and hit the back of one of Sully's hands, he jumped, stood tall, looked at the floor where the pellet had dropped, glared tight-lipped towards the back seats by the partition and said through thinned lips, "If I catch any of you cross-eyed, buck-toothed gittherygogs trick-acting, be the Holy Jehosophet you'll get a lathering the likes of which you'll never forget! Is that clear?"

This time he didn't have to ask for a repetition of the answer.

"Yes, Mr O'Sullivan!" the entire class shouted in unison . . . and the mocking crew and pellet firers sat cowed and sullen-faced, knowing the threat was no idle one.

Sully's classroom was on the second floor of the grey, pebble-dash school, at the western end of the building, next to, but separated from, the convent school next door. The front of St Joseph's Boys National School looked due south towards Spike Island and Roche's Point and, ultimately, the Bay of Biscay. While we were busy writing out the meeting notifications, Sully went again to one of the southward facing windows and looked out over the school yard, over the slate roofs of the houses, towards the sea which dominated the town and shaped its history and its destiny. I stole a few quick glances at him and wondered what he was thinking about.

We were about halfway through the writing chore when we all heard the door of Brother Eugenius' classroom along the corridor opening and banging shut. Eugenius was the head brother, the school's principal, and as such commanded respect from the other teachers no less than from the pupils. He was the boss.

Sully and Cooney and Spud Murphy and Brothers Prudent ("Puddens"), Emmanuel ("Brutus"), Linus and Cormac may each have been boss in his own individual classroom, but Eugenius ("U-Boat" or "the Boat") was the boss of all bosses.

The sound of U-Boat's door opening and shutting electrified Sully into action. With astonishing lightness of foot for such a big man, he raced from the window to the blackboard, whipped it off its supporting pegs, turned it around so that "I wandered lonely as a cloud" was again facing the pupils.

Just before the door was knocked on from the outside, he whispered fiercely to the six of us in the front row, "Get those papers off your desks, quickly!"

When U-Boat, chalk dust already visible on the front of his black soutane, came into the room, we all looked from him to Sully and back again. U-Boat's glasses were glinting, his bald pate shining.

"Ah, hello Brother Eugenius! I was just having a preliminary chat with this fine group of cawbogues here and seeing what their handwriting skills were like." Sully's voice came out sounding like something filtered through whipped cream, and the smile on his face was as big as a slice of watermelon.

U-Boat nodded to him, looked across the rows of faces, and said, "Hello, Mr Sullivan" (very few ever gave Sully the O in his name). "Welcome back to school! And tell me, what was their writing like?"

"Not bad, not bad at all, Brother. Of course there's room for improvement."

"There's always room for that."

"Yes. Some of these amadhauns, when they write on the page, make it look all to one side like the town of Fermoy."

"Yes, yes, I know what you mean . . . Well," (to us) "let ye take heed now of what Mr Sullivan tells ye, and remember that handwriting is a very important part of yeer education. There may be one or two boys here hoping to win scholarships, but ye'll have no hope at all unless the handwriting is good and neat and clear. Remember that."

"Yes, Brother."

U-Boat turned back to Sully and said, "Can I have a word with you?" and walked up to the corner window which looked out on the back of the school where the lavatories were and beyond them the Plantation, and beyond that again English's field. We remained more or less quiet, thinking about the things that had already taken place and we not yet an hour in the new class, and wondering what the future held for us under the charge of this unpredictable giant who came from near the border between County Cork and County Kerry.

"All right so," we heard the head brother say as he walked away from Sully, "that'll be grand . . . And, ye fellas, don't forget what I told ye!"

He was hardly out the door when the blackboard was reversed, and the Unholy Six finished writing the notices for the Cobh Charitable Coal Fund. It was the first of many times we wrote such notices.

* * * * * * * *

As the autumn was killed off by the incoming winter, we saw more and more of the many complex sides to Sully's character. Lost was the roaring giant of our first hour in his class. Often at the height of a rainy gale beating at the school's windows, he would stop teaching and stand there looking out, and then turn to us and talk to us about poverty, the misery of people who were cold and hungry, who didn't have enough to eat, who had only rags to cover themselves with.

We knew him to buy boots for really poor boys in the class out of his own pocket and to pay for shoe repairs for others. After the late masses in the cathedral on Sundays, he collected for the St Vincent de Paul, and he made slightly but unmistakably disparaging remarks whenever we were targeted by the collectors of funds "for the black babies".

"There are enough needy cases in this town who could do with your pennies," he'd say, without malice but with deep compassion.

And when Dave Sliney and Johnny Moynihan walked all the way in from Cuskinny in the lashing rain, he said, "You two are *wonderful!* But, you know, God Almighty, ye needn't have come to school on a day like this. No one would expect you to. Take off your boots and put them under the hot pipes to dry out, and sit there yourselves. You must be famished with the cold."

There was a great stillness about him the day he said that, and he went again to the window and stood looking out. After a while he turned back and said to all of us, "I'll defend any of you to the last if your parents think it is too bad a day for ye to come to school, a day like this. And I'd cheat the rolls if necessary to defend ye against the schools attendance officer, Guard Cahill. And I'll deny I ever said that!"

He was no plaster saint. He was no softie, either. While he didn't roar at us the way he did the first morning, that didn't mean he wasn't capable of becoming cross. We learned to recognise the difference between the simulated anger and the real thing. He had a temper. It was a lip-pursing, soft-voiced affair of disturbing quiet and shattering seriousness of purpose. But it only ever showed its presence if he thought he was being lied to, and that was rarely.

When Brodduck Walsh, accused by Sully one morning of not having his homework but of slacking, said that the only reason he hadn't done the written part was "because I was up half the night, sir, readin' the stories in the algebra," Sully pretended he hadn't heard him properly and asked him to repeat the excuse for the class. Sully had to turn away and walk behind the blackboard to conceal his laughter.

And when Nux tucked a copy of the *Irish Press* down the arse of his pants to protect his bum from the ministrations of Sully's cane following a spectacularly wrong series of answers to mental arithmetic questions, Sully pretended to be unaware of what was going on as Nux winked unashamedly at us. The resounding thwacks from the cane sounded horrendous.

Sully carried on with marvellous surface seriousness which was betrayed by the laughter in and around his eyes. He pretended to be amazed at "your capacity to bear pain, boy". And then, with a glorious bit of pantomime, he "discovered" the secret. He sent a red-faced Nux back to his seat, and late in the afternoon gave him a sixpence for scoring the winning goal in a schoolyard soccer challenge against the college.

* * * * * * *

One freezing morning Father Egan came to the class to talk with Sully. He was perceived in the town as a gentle and saintly man whose black suits – his clericals – and timeworn raglan-sleeved raincoat only just managed to retain a semblance of blackness. The green of old age and hard wear shone all over them.

"Boys," Sully said, "ye all know Father Egan. He's in charge of the Cobh Charitable Coal Fund."

Father Egan stood holding his soft hat in front of him and didn't take his eyes off Sully as the master spoke.

"Father Egan, some of these fine hoboes have been doing good work for the fund, writing the notices for the meetings. I'm sure they'll continue to help. Ye will, won't ye, boys?"

"*Yes*, Mr Sullivan!"

"*O'* Sullivan!" Sully said, and he laughed as he turned to Father Egan.

So this was the head of the Cobh Charitable Coal Fund? I couldn't understand why they called it that name at all. There wasn't a knob of coal to be had in the town – not for the ordinary people anyway. Very little was coming in. Just a few Kelly boats, grimy, black and old-fashioned, ploughed slowly across from Barry in south Wales. But most, though not all, of what they brought was for the railways, the gasworks, the hospitals, a few factories – and the ones who were rich enough never to have to go short of anything.

The British, we were told, needed their coal for themselves and the "war efforts", and so many colliers had been bombed, torpedoed, shelled or sunk by mines, they couldn't spare ships to send coal to Ireland, a country which wouldn't even let them use its ports – ports like Cork Harbour.

So, apart from the big nobs who lived out the High Road or on the Low Road, and presumably the bishop and maybe the priests, the only ones, we believed, who had coal fires on winter wartime evenings were the families of the harbour and river pilots who brought the ships up and down from Cork. Sometimes Con Lynch, whose father was a pilot, had to go straight home after school in order to go down to the pilot boat camber to collect a bag of "black gold" which his father had managed to scrounge from an obliging ship's engineer.

I went with him once and helped him push the heavily loaded baby pram up Harbour View and along Roche's Row to his home. For helping him, he gave me a huge lump of coal which I ran all the way home with, broke it into small pieces with my father's claw hammer and put it piece by piece on the fire where it reddened and sparkled among the sodden sods of turf.

Everyone knew there was hoarded coal in the town for favoured customers, and I often stood watching small queues of distraught mothers standing in the rain at the coal sheds waiting to plead in whining voices, only to be told, "I'm sorry, missus, we haven't a shovelful."

"Bleddy liars, that's what they are. Sure I *know* it goes out the road every fongin' week!" I heard a Glenanaar woman saying in angry desperation.

So when Sully turned to Father Egan that day in the classroom, I was ready to hang on every word the priest might utter.

"Thanks, Liam," he began. That was something else we had never heard before – Sully's first name. "Boys, I want to thank all of you who helped Mr O'Sullivan with your efforts for the Cobh Charitable Coal Fund. Mr O'Sullivan is the charity's secretary. I don't know what we'd do without him."

He turned to Sully who inclined his head and smiled embarrassedly, muttering something inaudible to us.

"The fund's committee works on behalf of the poor," Father Egan continued. "I won't forget ye in my prayers. And don't *ye* forget *me* in yeers. I suppose ye still pray, hah? . . . Ah, sure ye do – ye're good lads . . . But how can you pray to a Jesus you don't know? Hah? Can anyone answer me that?"

There was total silence, and Sully looked at the backs of his fingers. What's Father Egan getting at? I wondered. What kind of a riddle is that?

I glanced at Danny Murphy. He just shrugged and made a puzzled expression with his mouth. Sure didn't we *know* what Jesus *looked* like? About average height, with a long, brown, silky-looking beard and moustache, he wore a kind of big white blanket wrapped around him. He had brown eyes and was quite good-looking – you could see that from the big pictures of him showing off his Sacred Heart. What more did we need to know?

And sure it would be impossible to actually *know* Jesus. I mean, he was *God* for God's sake! And he was crucified when he was only 33, and that was hundreds and hundreds of years ago! So what was Father Egan going on about?

Father Egan answered the question himself.

"You see, boys, we *can* know Jesus, because he's amongst us," he said. "I'll explain that for ye. There's terrible need in the town, terrible poverty altogether, people who are really, really poor. And we must never forget the poor. Remember what the Holy Bible said about the poor? . . . No, I don't suppose ye do. We Catholics are not very good as regards the Bible. However, in Proverbs we find these words: 'He that hath pity upon the poor lendeth unto the Lord; and that which he hath given will he pay him back again.' And in Saint Matthew's gospel we get: 'For ye have the poor always with you; but me ye have not always.' You see, Our Lord Jesus Christ is in our midst, always, and at all times, and Christ is in every poor person walking the streets . . . Well, boys, I didn't come here to preach a sermon – I came here to talk to Mr O'Sullivan about committee matters. But if any of ye would like to come down to the coal fund's shed on the Holy Ground after school to give us a hand to help the poor, the Lord will reward ye. God bless ye all now."

"Charity?" I'd heard Mrs Smith in No. 4 say to my mother. "Ah, for God's sake, charity begins at home!"

I wasn't able to disentangle that, but I knew enough from the tone that it was dismissive of the notion of organised charities and special collections and all that kind of stuff, and while my mother didn't immediately give Mrs Smith's opinion her whole-hearted support, there had been enough in her silence to suggest that, at a time of pegged wages, rising prices, scarcity and general tension, the idea did have a certain appeal for her.

Which is why I didn't call in home before heading straight for the Holy Ground with seven others from Sully's class.

Turf and logs, or blocks, were the only fuels we had to

burn in those years, and the turf which was delivered by the town's coal merchants, Murray's, Coleman's and Paddy Harrington from Top o' the Hill, was useless muck. It was wet and soft-soggy, and you had to pour paraffin oil over to get it to even smoulder.

"There's bleddy farmers down there in Kerry makin' a fortune now outa turf," Danny Dinan said. "Cute hoors, keepin' all the good, hard, dry stuff for theirselves and sendin' all their oul shite up here to us – gawbeens that we are for *buyin'* it."

On Harbour Hill we passed the pathetic rouged woman who lived down below and opposite the priests' terrace. She was incontinent and dribbled, leaving a trail of drops on the pavement behind her on dry days, and had a cruel nickname – "Dirty Bitch".

On Harbour Row, we passed poor shell-shocked Bill Buckley. As usual he was rambling on unintelligibly about guns and bangs. His belongings were tied in a handkerchief which in turn was tied to the end of a walking stick which he carried over his shoulder. He was dragging an empty gin bottle along the ground behind him, the piece of white hairy string that was tied to the neck of it wrapped around his wrist. His dog slunk along behind that. Among the similarities between Bill and "Dirty Bitch" was that Bill dribbled, too.

Normally we might have stopped and tried for the umpteenth time to make sense of Bill's ramblings. The only word we could ever pick out from the sounds that poured from him – other than "guns" and "bang" – was "Jutland".

How come no one from the church or the St Vincent de Paul seemed to bother about Bill or "Dirty Bitch"? Or about that poor half-crazed woman near the Holy Ground whose husband used to beat her up, kick her, continue to make her pregnant and repeatedly kick her in the stomach even then, in that filthy, sour room in the condemned house?

"Father Sheedy or Father O'Connor go down there? Not at all, girl! Catch them! You hafta be jokin'. They're far too 'grawnd' for that. They wouldn't even *walk* in Harbour Yoo! And as for his nibs up in his palace, the bishop – when do you think was the last time he was ever beyond The Bench, or even up in Glenanaar?"

"Still, all the same, you'd think at least the *guards* would do somethin' to protect that creature from that . . . that . . . *thing* of a husband of hers, wouldn't yeh?"

"Sure she won't give evidence against him! Every time he's brought to court she either refuses to say an'thin' against him, or else cries an' pleads for 'im, an' all they can do is charge 'im with bein' drunk an' disorderly, an' fine him five shillin's or half a crown. If he was mine, I'd *knife* 'im, the rotten article!"

A lot of it was over my head, but I couldn't help hearing what was being said or seeing some of the people who were being spoken about. Were they so far gone, and so far down, that they were worthless? That there was no point in *anyone* trying to help them?

But Father Egan did.

I let the others get ahead of me on Harbour Row and stood for a while looking in the window of Miss Dillon's trinket shop. When I walked on, the lads were almost out of sight by now. O'Sullivan's grocery and provisions stores was doing brisk business as usual, Maisie all go and smartness. Stella Donovan's shoe shop had mainly women's shoes in the window; no interest there. Jack Lynch's house had his insurance agency office on the ground floor, and just a few doors away was the house where Mr Lotte the tailor had his business.

By the time I got to Kane's big grocery shop almost at The Bench, the others had disappeared, and when I looked into Phipps' shoe repair shop, the deaf-and-dumb man was working away at his last. Fifty yards away, close to the bottom of East Hill and at the start of the Holy Ground, was the Cobh Charitable Coal Fund's shed.

* * * * * * * *

26

The two big doors were shut, but when I knocked on them there was the sound of a bolt being pulled on the inside, and one door was opened by a man I didn't immediately recognise. For the first time in my life, I was looking at a priest who had taken off his Roman collar. It was only when he said, "Ah, there you are, grand, grand," that I recognised him as Father Egan. "Good, good, in you come."

He was wearing a faded blue collarless shirt, braces and black trousers. It was a shock to see a priest dressed, or undressed, like this, sleeves rolled up and traces of turf dust around his hair line and around his eyes. Two naked electric light bulbs hanging down on long flexes threw light on what was going on. The seven other fellows were already at work.

"Just take it as it comes now, men. Don't let ye pick out the sods at all. And on like the wind with ye, we've no time to lose."

However he had swung it or whatever strings he had pulled, he had managed to get a few lorryloads of the good quality dark, dry, hard turf for his beloved poor.

"The Lord will reward ye," he said any time we seemed to be slowing down.

"I wonder if *he'll* reward us, though?" Nux whispered as we took off our satchels, overcoats and scarves and hung them on the nails on the back of the doors. For the next two hours we toiled in dusty darkness and I, for one, at the beginning anyway, felt twinges of envy of the "poor" who were to get this good fuel. But that dwindled with the sense of adventure there came with short-pants boys being "allowed" to do men's work in filling the bags and working for a charity.

The fleas put a different complexion on that, and on us. The turf seemed to be alive with them, and they began to bite when they transferred themselves to our clothing and then to our skin, where the little, brown, shiny-backed buggers sensed blood and went after it. The sound of bare flesh being slapped and small yelps of "Gotcha!" began to punctuate the puffing and grunting silence of our manual labour to help the poor.

27

"Father Egan doesn't seem to be bothered by the fleas at all," Nux whispered to me after about an hour.

"Maybe priests are flea-proof!" I suggested.

He burst into ill-suppressed giggles, and Father Egan, across by the far wall and dripping sweat, said, "Are ye having a grand time, boys? It's always good to have a laugh. Let ye get the laughing over now, though; we have a lot of work still to do."

For some inexplicable reason the face of Routum came to me in that dark place, and I wondered: is *he* Christ? But that seemed impossible, even crazy, and maybe a sin, so I dismissed it from my mind.

But what was going to happen when we got home? Anyone who "had fleas" was labelled "dirty".

"Keep away from that fella. I believe he's walking with fleas!" was something I'd often had said to me. But, Holy God! Now all eight of *us* were walking with them! I tried to convince myself that my mother would be swayed by the argument, "But we *all* got them, and they were got helping the poor."

At five o'clock Father Egan opened both big doors of the shed, and there they were, waiting – his beloved poor. They had hungry faces and were staring with avaricious eyes. They weren't pleasant to look at and they smelled awful. Father Egan appeared to be oblivious to this.

"Well, we're ready for ye," he said to them. "Hello, John! How's the old cough?"

"Not bad now thanks, Father."

"Good man, good man . . . And you, young lady, is your mother any better?"

"A little bit, Father."

"Grand, grand. Tell her I'll be around to see her tomorrow, will you?"

"Yes, Father."

I recognised the girl and knew that Father Egan's promise to visit her mother would entail a walk through a slimy hallway and into a room where the rats ran out only when a stranger walked in. He'd be lucky if he didn't throw up from the smell. In the houses of the very poor, rats that die beneath the floorboards are left there to decompose. It was a house I crossed the road from if I had to pass it.

The poor's priest got those who were outside the shed to form an orderly queue, and in less than ten minutes every one of the bags it had taken us an hour and a quarter to fill were distributed.

As the last limpy-legged man left, his bag of turf balanced on the frame of a rusty pram whose wheels had no tyres, Father Egan turned to us and said, "I suppose ye're all jaded now? Of course ye are, of course ye are. Why wouldn't ye be?"

He got his jacket and collar off the nail on which they were hanging.

"Ye did a great job, a great job, and ye'll be in my prayers tonight and mentioned at mass in the morning. All right? Good men! Let ye run home now because it's getting late. Goodbye, men, God bless ye."

"The *poor!*" Mam said. "What do you think *we* are – the *rich?* Where have you been until this hour? Look at the cut of you; you're filthy! Your face and hands and coat and shoes and socks – how do you think I can wash your stuff and get it dry in this weather, not a breath of drying on the line, and only old wet turf and a few blocks to burn."

"But it was for the poor, Mam."

"Charity begins at home," my mother said, echoing Mrs Smith. Then, almost immediately, her hand flew to her mouth and she said, "Oh, My God! That was a *terrible* thing to say! That was awful! God forgive me! I didn't mean it. God love them, some of them haven't a *tráithnín* to their name . . . But I wish you'd tell me when you're going to do something like that. You can fill turf bags in your old rags, not in the only decent clothes you have to your name.

"Go on now, go in and wash your face and hands properly before your daddy comes in, or he'll have a fit if he comes home and finds you in that condition."

29

After that it was all right to go down to the Holy Ground to help Father Egan with the turf-bag filling – provided I called in home first and changed into what my mother called my "old duds". And I looked upon and thought about the poor in a different way, and thought often about what Father Egan had said was in the Bible – that whoever pitied the poor "lendeth unto the Lord", and that the Lord would pay him back. I wondered how, or with what, or when, he'd pay *me* back. Would I ever get a bike like Uncle Willie's? Hardly, I thought. Still, you'd never know . . .

I never got a bike like Uncle Willie's.

But I got into trouble over the poor.

* * * * * * * *

At the back of the cathedral, next to the Guides' Hall, was the Penny Dinners Hall. Along a little way from it was the Bon Secours convent, and Sister Fidelis and the other sisters from there, severe-looking women with crinkly white wimples encircling their faces, handed out hot meals at lunchtime every day in winter in the Penny Dinners Hall to the poor of the town who cared to walk up there with a penny in their fists. The odours of food that wafted out as you passed the door made the mouth water.

Sometimes, on the way home after school, I'd stand for a while and watch as farmers from the back of the island delivered cart-loads of vegetables – potatoes, carrots, parsnips, mangolds, yellow turnips – to the PDs. What usually caused me to walk away was the language the men used to their horses.

"*Come* on! . . . *Hup*, yeh bitch! . . . Come *on!* . . . Yeh *hoor* yeh!"

I hated that. It was all wrong to speak to poor dumb animals that way. And so close to the house of God, too!

The queues started forming outside the Penny Dinners Hall at noon, and the penny-clenching poor waited patiently in rain or blustery gusts or knifing east wind, all but drooling at the prospect of hot soup, stew, currant buns and tea. Some of the poor boys from "the nash" went there as a matter of course, and I envied them on days which were wet and the walk home seemed interminable. Inevitably there came a day when Nux and I succumbed to the temptation to go in and partake.

We stole in in the middle of a queue, kept our heads down and our eyes averted, and were convinced that we hadn't been spotted, but had been accepted as genuine "poor boys".

"Yes, he came in with the McCormack boy. They both kept their heads down and made no eye contact, took the meal and wolfed it down. I thought you should know, Mrs Nolan. It's not right, you know, especially with his father working." Sister Fidelis was like that – direct and opinionated.

My mother was mortified.

"Disgracing me and your father and the rest of the family! I won't be able to hold my *head* up! *Ashamed* of yourself you ought to be – and a plate of hot beef and dumplings waiting here at home for you! How could you *do* it? How *could* you?"

The three swipes around the back of the neck with the damp dishcloth were unerring in their accuracy and stung like the devil.

My mother wasn't finished yet.

"Taking the food out of the mouth of some poor little divil whose father is idle, or dead! Get on upstairs out of my sight! I'll never live this down, a boy from a respectable family . . ."

And then, astonishingly, she was crying uncontrollably there in the kitchen, and never in my life had I felt so terrible about anything I had done. Causing my mother, Mam, so strong and so proud and so protective and so loving . . . to actually *cry!*

Up in my bedroom at the top of the house I knelt down by the double bed and blessed myself.

"An Act of Contrition: O my God, I am heartily sorry and beg pardon for all my sins . . ."

When I saw Nux the next day, he told me that Sister Fidelis had visited his mother, too.

"What did your mother say to you?"

31

"Oh, she gave me down the banks . . . By the way, what did you think of the dinner?"

"I liked the currant buns. What about you?"

"I thought the soup tasted like horse's piss."

That was the first and last time we went to the Penny Dinners.

I didn't much like Sister Fidelis from then on. I thought she was a sneak to report us, even though she was probably right.

Storm in the Night

WHEN DANNY DINAN came to deliver the milk midway through the morning and banged the knocker hard and urgently, my mother called out to me from the kitchen, "Be sure you close the glass door now before you open the front door. And bring him in, don't leave him outside in the rain. He must be drenched."

It was a gruesome winter Saturday in December of 1942, and the rain coming in from the sea was being hurled at the town by a driving southerly wind, one of those days which made our town look dingy, frowzy, windswept and neglected, a town anchored to the past in a winter that was harsh, bitter and treacherous. Because no houses stood on a level with and in front of the Bellevue Terrace house where we lived near the top, we got the full brunt of south-east, south, or south-west gales.

Danny, two large cans of milk held in his wet, red-blue hands, stood on the step, blinking against the rain that was streaming into his eyes from his hair.

"Terrible day, isn't it?" I said as I held the door open for him to step into the hall and then closed it behind him.

"Oh, Sweet Jesus, don't *talk* to me!" he said. "You wouldn't send a dog out in weather like this."

My mother opened the glass door an inch or two and asked, "Have you got the lock on the front door?"

"I have," I said.

"He has, missus," Danny confirmed.

"It looks as if the rain is in for the day, Danny," my mother said, coming into the little area between the doors where the wind had blown rainwater in under the flap at the bottom of the hall door and left a little pool on the lino.

"The rain is bad enough, God knows," Danny said; "it's that bloody *wind*. It'd skin yeh, and it's gettin' stronger. There's slates off everywhere."

I had gone down to Higgins and Wall's earlier for the *Examiner* and was looking forward to reading it now that it had dried out in the kitchen, draped over the back of a chair in front of the range. Of course I'd have to hand it up if either Mammy or Daddy wanted it.

I sneaked a look at the entertainments notices for the Cork cinemas. They were high on the left hand side of page 2. While Danny Dinan and my mother exchanged bits of gossip out by the front door, in the kitchen I read that *Million Dollar Baby*, starring Ronald Reagan and Priscilla Lane, was the film due to start next day (Sunday) at the Ritz.

The notice for the Savoy said, "Definitely Last Day", *Gone With The Wind*. There were to be two showings, and the seat prices ranged from 2/6d (Back Circle) to 4/9d (Grand Circle). Well, you could always dream.

The Pavilion had *Beau Geste* (Gary Cooper and Ray Milland). *Green Eyed Woman*, starring Rosalind Russell and Fred Mac Murray, was next week's attraction at the Palace, and Ronald Colman and Douglas Fairbanks Jnr. were the stars in *The Prisoner of Zenda* at the Assembly Rooms ("De Ass*ems*" as Corkonians called that comprehensively unlovely fleapit picture house).

I wasn't all that interested in the Opera House, but read what was on there, anyway – a play called *Quiet Week-End*.

When Danny Dinan left to call to Mrs Duggan next door,

my mother came into the kitchen and said, "I want you to go out to Carrignafoy after you've had a bowl of hot mutton broth, and get a couple of bags of blocks. Will you do that for me, will you? That damned old turf is all wet, what there is of it, and we need a nice warm fire in the dining room."

I said that of course I would, and she gave me a hug, pulled me to her and ruffled my hair.

"There's a good boy," she said. "I'll give you the price of the pictures."

"Mammy, Mammy, can I go with him to get the blocks, and then *I* can get the price of the pictures, too?" Norma, who was two years younger than me, asked.

"No you can't, Norma," my mother said, "the weather is too bad – you'd get your death of cold, and anyway your shoes and coat are still wet from last night. And besides, you're too young for the pictures."

But Norma wasn't going to be fobbed off that easily. "Please, please, *please*, Mammy, can I go? Ah, *please* let me go!"

"I've said no, Norma, and that's all there is to it," my mother said. "I'm driven to distraction as it is trying to dry all the clothes. Now go in and keep an eye on John and Margaret and make sure they stay away from the fire. There's a good girl."

Norma stuck out her tongue at me and said, "Yah-yah, yah-*yah*-yah – Mammy's pet," and ran out the hall as my mother threatened to give her a skelp with a dish cloth.

While my mother was setting the table, I went back to reading the *Examiner*. Christmas was only 13 days away. Ever since the time I had come across my mother crying by her bedroom window in September 1939, the day she told me that the Germans had invaded Poland, I had been fascinated by the war. I scanned the paper now to see if I could pick up any more information on the way things were going between the Allies and the Axis. I didn't understand all of what I read, and the columns of unillustrated print were frequently too long to hold my attention right to the end of the bigger stories. But the headlines were often enough to give me mental pictures.

The Tunisian battle was being waged in "a sea of mud" which, it was made out, was worse than that they had had to contend with in World War I. I found that hard to understand because I thought of Tunisia as being all sand and ferocious heat – so how come they were fighting in a sea of *mud*? It was puzzling, but there wasn't time to read further down this long article in search of an explanation.

There was a story about a proposal by the Swiss government against the shackling of prisoners of war. I couldn't believe it – prisoners of war were being held in *fetters*? Some German official said the Germans were giving the proposal "sympathetic consideration". Meanwhile, the British and the Canadians (*Canadians*?) intended taking the shackles off German prisoners.

The president of the USA, Mr Roosevelt, had told congress the previous day that by the end of the month there would be a million US servicemen overseas.

A report from Lagos in Nigeria said that 58 people ("so far") had been killed in an accidental explosion in the harbour on the Tuesday. And on page two there was a little story from the Reuters news agency which said that Radio Paris had gone off the air shortly before midnight and was still silent.

That prompted me to see what Radio Éireann was scheduled to broadcast that night. The only thing that caught my attention, because I thought it was so daft, was a programme listed for 7.25 – "Irish Dancing for Children". How in God's name could they put *dancing* on *radio*?

I didn't get any further with my reading because my mother had poured out a bowl of her special soup for me, and put an Abernethy's skull loaf and Mitchelstown creamery butter ("Go easy on the butter or we'll have only marge or dripping for the rest of the week") on the table.

"Get that into you now, and go off then for the blocks before it gets too dark," she said.

When I went out with the pushchair about twenty minutes

later, the wind was streaking in savagely from away out beyond Spike Island. The afternoon was already darkening under the grey lowering cloud.

I was wearing my new black sou'wester, its strings tied tightly under my chin, the warm flaps close against my ears, shutting out the sound of the wind, giving me a sense of security, or safety, or something like that. I went up to the top of Bellevue to where the hill levelled out and the wall was low, and I was hit by the full strength of the wind sweeping in unimpeded from the sea. I was glad to have it at my back when I turned in through the big iron gates that led past Queenie Meade's house, and up the avenue between the swaying, tortured trees. But because of the earflaps, I was spared hearing the winter creak of naked branches. I reached the lodge at the top end where the McCarthys lived and went out past Kellihers' house on the back road, past Hanlons' farm and the football field, down the slope past the New Cemetery, where I was blown across the road by a wind gust, along past where Daisy Sullivan lived next door to the Caseys, and down part of Cuskinny Hill to the bungalow near the corner where they sold the blocks.

The two bags were lifted on to the pushchair for me by Mr Ryan, and I began the long trek home. There was no one on the roads, and the wind-driven rain was miserable. By the time I reached our house, I was soaked – except for my head (the sou'wester was great) and my feet (those wellies were really great).

"Are you famished, son?" my mother said when she answered the door, and before I had a chance to reply she felt the shoulders of my raincoat and said, "My God, you're wet through! Run upstairs quickly and get those wet clothes off you! Get a towel out of the hot press and make sure you dry yourself all over or you'll get your death."

"What about the blocks?" I asked.

"Don't mind those. *We'll* get them in – upstairs now like a good boy, and do what I told you."

* * * * * * * *

About an hour later I was still in the top front bedroom, alone. After getting out of my wet clothes, drying myself and putting on dry pants, socks, vest, shirt and gansey, I lay on top of the bed with the light switched off, listening to the sounds of the gale sweeping in the harbour. The shutters had been closed earlier, probably by my mother, and I lay in the darkness.

After a while I got off the bed and went to the window nearest to me, opened the shutters and looked out. Every few seconds the glass of the window quivered and rattled when the roaring wind gusted and hit the house. The noise, the force, were terrifying.

I stood there, transfixed, with thoughts of wind and waves and ships, and sailors and Granda Jim and Uncle John, and fear and drowning and death, all mixing together and mesmerising me.

When my mother called from the bottom of the stairs two floors down, I heard her as from a very long way off. I didn't take in her words, didn't connect them, whatever they were, or her voice, with her calling *me*, and so didn't respond. It was as if that voice calling out were in a different existence; or as if it were a background sound, and therefore not yet an interruption.

Mentally, I was out there in the harbour, in the storm, in the midst of the rearing oncoming seas. I was imagining, visualising what it must be like in a boat or on a ship on a night like this.

Another squall unleashed itself against the front of the house. It hit the window so hard that I took a step backwards, fearful that the glass was about to smash inwards and maybe pierce me with sharp shards hurled by wind-force. But the glass held, and I moved forward again and put my nose against the pane and looked out as hard as I could.

Although I couldn't see anything much, I knew for certain that mountainous seas had to be breaking heavily out there in the blackness. The paper had said that high tide in Cobh was due at 9.42. It was now somewhere around 6 o'clock, which meant that the tide was flooding. Those waves would be howling in from the screaming vastness of the dark, lonely Atlantic.

"I won't call you again!" my mother shouted, her voice closer now that she had come up as far as the kitchenette. "Come down at once. Your tea is ready."

"All right, Mam, I'll be down now," I answered, leaning over the banister rail on the landing.

"What are you doing up there anyway in the dark?"

"Just looking – looking out the harbour. And thinking."

"Looking at *what?*" she said. "There's nothing to see in the dark."

"I'll be down in a minute so," I said, trying to build into the tone of my voice an unasked "Can I stay here a little while longer?"

"All right," she said. "And while you're at it, say a prayer for Uncle John and Granda Jim."

I stayed on the landing, straining to hear the sounds of her going back downstairs. The old chestnut tree in Allens' at the back of the house hissed and swished as the wind tore through its denuded branches. Just as I was about to go back into the dark bedroom, a limb cracked off the tree and clattered down into the backyard and, by the sound of it, carried a loosened stone from the top of the wall with it.

I decided to shut the bedroom door when I went inside. I had to slam it hard against a powerful draught that whooshed up the stairwell as someone in the kitchen opened the back door to see what had fallen into the yard. The trapdoor to the loft lifted noisily out of its seating and then banged down again, leaving a two-inch gap at one end. The noise up there among the rafters was alarming. I'd have to get the sweeping brush or the mop and stand up on a chair and manoeuvre the trapdoor back into place. But later. Not now.

The wind rumbled and moaned in the chimney, and I made the sign of the cross as I approached the window, and said, "Thank you, Jesus, for letting me be safe in the house, and please, Jesus, protect my Granda Jim and Uncle John tonight, and all the sailors at sea."

I could see a few fuzzy, blurred, yellow lights on Spike Island and due south, out beyond that, the timed red and white sweeps of the lighthouse on Roche's Point. We had been told (it was part of the sea lore you grew up with) that Roche's Point light was visible up to 15 miles away.

Over to the left from where I was standing at the window, in fact south-east from the terrace, the Spit lighthouse on the corner of the Spit Bank, where the navigation channel coming in from the sea turned sharp left through 90 degrees and ran westwards past the waterfront, was also throwing its red and white beams into the howling night.

I had often rowed around the Spit through sun-shot waters in summer and had been in picnic-bound punts when we tied the painter to one of the mussel-encrusted supports and tried a bit of fruitless hand-line fishing for half an hour or so. It was impossible now in the fury of this December night to conjure up images of sun-shot water or summer days.

Out beyond Spike, indeed out beyond Forts Camden and Carlisle it seemed to me as I struggled with the perspective, I saw the navigation lights of a ship coming in. There were two white lights, one above the other, and a red light to the right, a green one on the left, and every now and then the lights were obscured by rain and spindrift. She must be about three miles out from the town I reckoned, but she was well inside Roche's Point. Maybe she was running for shelter? Steering by the leading lights ashore, she would have come in past Harbour Rock buoy.

As I stood by the window with the gale driving furiously in from the sea and rising all the time, I tried to figure out *exactly* where the ship was, tried to figure out how big she was. She was certainly much bigger than a trawler, and bigger than the

Kelly boats, and bigger than the smart little *Kerlogue*, the 300-ton diesel coaster which put-putted busily in and out of the harbour every so often.

But however big or small she was, she was taking a desperate hammering in this storm, pitching and rolling in heavy seas.

I was thinking of this when a movement of lights down at the boat harbour on the Holy Ground caught my attention. They formed a small triangle – a white one on top, red and green lower down. The pilot launch! Going *out*? The lights kept the form of a triangle for seconds only while she was broadside on to the waves.

I watched her masthead lights leaping and waving crazily, until she turned and headed out towards the mouth of the harbour. Then the only coloured light visible to me was the green starboard light, moving up and down erratically as she plunged into wave troughs and then came up to start the whole process over and over and over again.

Suddenly I became very frightened – frightened for the men on that small boat – and for a minute or two couldn't bear to watch and backed away from the window until I came up against the door and stood there with my back to it, the palms of my hands pressed hard against the cold, green, hard-gloss paint.

Over the mantelpiece above the empty fireplace a large picture of the Sacred Heart hung from a nail. I couldn't see it in the darkness, but I knew it was there, and I prayed to it now: "Sacred Heart of Jesus, please protect them, please keep them safe, please . . ."

After a while I went back to the window. Something high up in the chimney banged, and then banged again, and settled into a pattern of slamming noises.

The rain was hopping off the window panes, and I could only barely make out, pinpricks of light out beyond the Spit where the pilot launch was butting her way towards the distant ship.

41

When the rain let up for a few minutes I could see the ship's lights, and, as I watched, the green starboard light disappeared from view, leaving the red port side light clearly visible on its own. She had come about and was now facing across the harbour entrance, bow to the east, stern to the west. She was broadside on to the seas, and it must have been very uncomfortable aboard her.

I had a new fear now – if she kept on steaming in her new direction, she was in danger of running aground on Dog Nose Bank. In this storm she'd be wrecked.

A frightful feeling of helplessness took hold of me, made me catch my breath. A sob tore itself out of my throat. There were men out there in awful danger, and here was I, and all I was doing was *watching* – watching and dreading, and *doing* NOTHING.

I wanted to run downstairs to the lavatory; wanted to shout something, anything, a warning; wanted to alert someone; wanted desperately to leave that window, and at the same time didn't want to stir from it.

I put my hand between my legs and squeezed my thighs tight, holding myself in in case I went in my pants.

Something came sliding down the roof and shattered against the wall across the road. The wind gusted harder than ever, the rain hit the glass of the windows with a pitiless hammering.

I started to cry, and I couldn't stop . . .

And then, out beyond Spike Island I saw another small cluster of red and white lights in that huge black space of sea between the island and the ship. The cluster was moving towards the larger vessel – the Port Control boat! The pilot boat and it were closing on the ship, which seemed to have shifted back a little from where I'd seen her a few minutes earlier.

Suddenly the whole of the ship's side was lit up as her floodlights were switched on, and I saw them then, the enormous tricolours painted on the black hull above the water-

42

line. The word ÉIRE was in huge plain white letters. She was one of Irish Shipping Ltd's vessels.

That immediately brought Granda Jim's name and face and voice into my mind; Granda Jim who looked so like Spencer Tracy; Granda Jim of the World War I photograph standing, hand on sword, looking so proud and dignified in his Royal Navy officer's dress uniform; Granda Jim who, in his sixties, went back to sea in World War II as a chief engineer in the fledgling Irish Shipping Ltd ships – obsolete, rusted old tubs, bought, patched up, and sent back and forth across the U-Boat infested Atlantic when British ships would no longer carry supplies to Ireland.

Then I began thinking of the two launches out there, and of Mr Duggan from next door. He was wireless operator on the Port Control launch. Pretty soon I was thinking of Connie Lynch and Crab Walsh and Rowdy Ellis and Tony Nash, all of whose fathers were Cork Harbour pilots, and I wondered which pilot would, any minute now, have to step off the pilot launch and on to the swinging Jacob's ladder and climb up the side of the ship's hull.

I thought of Pat Higgins, too, because his father was a motorman on the pilot launch, and then I wondered where Granda Jim was tonight, and Uncle John, who was a chief engineer with British Tanker Company. And that made me think of torpedoes, and explosions at sea, and drowning men blackened with oil, hands up, beseeching, and gulping-gulping-gulping, choking-choking-choking . . . *dying*.

Remember, O most tender Virgin Mary, that it was never known that anyone who fled to thy protection, implored thy help, or sought thy intercession was left unaided . . .

43

Hazardous Boarding

ONE DAY IN 1912 a 352-foot long steamship of 3282 tons gross tonnage named *Withernsea*, was completed by Earle's Shipbuilding and Engineering Company Ltd in Hull.

Over the next twenty-five years, she was sold on five times and renamed four times, becoming the *Bathampton*, the *Ardenhall*, the *Northborough*, and finally the *Vassilios Destounis*. One day early in 1941, the ageing, now Greek-owned ship was attacked by German aircraft off the Spanish coast, abandoned by her crew, and left to drift on the high seas. A group of Spanish fishermen from the port of Aviles on the north coast of Spain, west of Santander, managed to get her into Aviles, and received £80,000 for the salvage.

This was the same ship that I watched from my bedroom window at 9, Bellevue Terrace, Cobh, on that ferocious December night in 1942 – except that by then her name was *Irish Poplar*.

Irish Shipping Ltd had purchased her in April 1941 for £142,000 from the Greek owners whose ship she was when she was abandoned in Biscay following the air attack.

When war broke out in 1939, Ireland had no ocean-going shipping fleet and was dependent mainly on British ships to carry its imports of food, and virtually every other commodity needed for existence. War changed the situation dramatically. De Valera's declaration of Ireland's neutrality, and the refusal to make Ireland's ports and airfields available to Allied forces, enraged Churchill.

In a letter he had written to America's President Roosevelt, Britain's prime minister said,

" . . . *we cannot undertake to carry any longer 400,000 tons of feeding stuffs and fertilisers which we have hitherto conveyed to Eire through all attacks of the enemy. We need this tonnage for our own supply and we do not need the food which Eire has been sending us.*"

Britain, involved in a war from which Ireland had chosen to stand back, and requiring all its own ships to fulfil its own needs, and having those ships constantly under attack and being sunk in the Atlantic by German U-Boats hunting in wolf packs as well as by German war planes scouring the ocean, could no longer be relied upon by Ireland to carry Ireland's desperately needed supplies.

Ireland was suddenly in urgent and desperate need of its own deep sea fleet so Irish Shipping Ltd was set up in March 1941. The company's main objectives were to acquire, operate, and maintain a deep sea merchant fleet so that the country's economy and people could survive the war. Trying to find ships to buy, however, proved hugely difficult, which is where the abandoned and subsequently salvaged *Vassilios Destounis* entered the picture.

A Wexford master mariner, Captain Matthew Moran, and two other officers, were sent out to Spain to inspect the now 30-year-old ship where she lay in Aviles Harbour and to take official delivery. To their dismay, they found when they boarded her that almost everything that could be taken away had been removed, even her wireless equipment. The ship was in a serious state of disrepair and neglect, she wasn't seaworthy, and she needed to go into dry dock; but the nearest one was on the south-west coast of Portugal. Moran and his two fellow officers arranged for running repairs to be carried out at Aviles. Captain Moran had taken delivery of the *Vassilios Destounis* on 9 April. In June she was still lying at Aviles. As the Spanish authorities refused to allow the Irish crew to travel to Aviles, a Spanish crew was mustered. Not long out of Aviles she had to put into the port of La Coruña for engine repairs. They didn't arrive in Lisbon until mid-August, and the ship went straight into dry dock, where the mainmast, eaten away by rust, collapsed during loading and had to be replaced.

It was 1 October before she eventually left Lisbon for Dublin, arriving there on the 9th.

The *Irish Poplar* thus became the first in the fleet of obsolete old ships, which were either bought or chartered, to become Ireland's lifeline during the long hazardous duration of the war.

She paid her first visit to Cork on 10 March 1942, with a cargo of 6000 tons of grain from St John. Now she was in the harbour again, light and in ballast, out there in a southerly gale, waiting to pick up her pilot and the Port Control inspecting officer.

* * * * * * * *

In 1942 Cork Harbour had 17 licensed pilots employed in the port. Ten of them worked the outer and inner harbour; the other seven were river pilots.

The Cork Harbour Commissioners, perceived by many to be an elitist and autocratic body, made up of local business and establishment figures given to making pompous statements which reflected the Commissioners' own sense of self-importance, had the responsibility for the overall running of the Port of Cork.

All of the pilots were experienced and qualified coastal navigators, and their job was to conduct ships into and out of the port through the various navigation channels and approaches. In the days before the development of radio communications technology, Cork Harbour pilots, in common with pilots all over the world, waited for incoming ships in pilot cutters. In Cork Harbour's case, the waiting area was close to Roche's Point. By 1942 ships requiring pilots could radio ahead and arrange to pick up a pilot at a pre-arranged place.

That was what had happened on the evening of 12 December 1942, when the *Irish Poplar* came into Cork Harbour in ballast. The pilot on duty for her arrival was Pilot Patrick Lynch (Con Lynch's father). Pilot Lynch lived at 8, Roche's Row, almost opposite the Church of Ireland church, and only a few hundred yards from St Colman's Cathedral. He was a pale-faced, quiet, serious man.

The pilots and their families formed a fairly loose-knit community in Cobh. They didn't live next door to each other, or even in similar houses, nor did they all live in the same street, or even in the same area. But they shared common experiences, common hopes and aspirations, and common knowledge of Cork Harbour and the job for which they were employed. They knew the reality of common dangers. They knew about ships and the sea. They knew about tides and winds and weather of every sort. And they knew how the ferocity of the elements could show up and punish with fearsome treachery and, sometimes, finality, any mistakes of judgement.

* * * * * * * *

The pilot launch, with Pilot Lynch on board, left the boat harbour at the eastern end of Cobh at about 6pm in the teeth of what was described variously as "a raging storm" and "a howling gale". The weather was vicious, exhausting and frightening.

At the helm of the launch was James Horgan, also a pilot in his own right. He lived on Harbour Terrace. The boat's motorman was 45-year-old John Higgins. He lived with his wife and two children in Connolly Street, just along the road from the boat harbour.

Horgan, squat and powerfully built, balanced and braced himself against the boat's violent pitching and rolling. Streaming water deluged the windows as the pilot launch, slewing wildly, made sickening descents into wave trough after wave trough, having occasionally almost stood on her stern, or smashed her bow into the face of an oncoming wave. Horgan was steering for the mouth of the harbour. Neither he nor Lynch knew at that stage that the vessel they were going to meet was the *Irish Poplar*.

On the bridge of the *Poplar*, Captain J.F. Taylor, from Preston in Lancashire, was complying with an official order. He had received a signal to "go to Dog Nose buoy for examination". His ship could not go to the anchorage without first being given clearance by the Port Control examining officer. Dog Nose buoy, a lighted conical buoy about a mile-and-a-half northwards of Roche's Point, would be the rendezvous point.

On this vile night there had been no question of picking up the pilot at Roche's Point. It would have been highly dangerous and improper. So, in darkness, rain squalls and gale force wind, Captain Taylor had had to rely on using the leading lights (which were placed near the head of White Bay, and near Fort Carlisle) and the uniform system of buoyage.

Taylor, a veteran mariner of 30 years experience, had done so successfully.

Arriving at Dog Nose buoy, he let go the starboard anchor and swung the ship around. The seas were now smashing into her starboard side along the full length of the hull. Having paid out 65 fathoms of chain, and finding that the ship was dragging, he hove the anchor again and steamed up to the buoy. He knew how to handle ships, but he could feel the shuddering vibration of the hull under the impact of the hammer-blow seas.

In the pilot launch *Carraig an Cuain* – a 25-footer built in Baltimore and not long in service – Horgan and Lynch screwed up their eyes, trying hard to see through the rain and spindrift which made visibility alarmingly bad. The boat was being pounded and buffeted by the gale and the huge waves.

They could feel rather than hear the engine over which John Higgins was bent, listening and watching closely. He, too, felt, through the soles of his boots, the pounding and grinding and vibration of the engine and the shuddering of the small hull every time the launch smashed into a wall of water.

He had to be extra careful where he put his hands whenever he needed suddenly to steady himself against the boat's savage movements. There wasn't much room, and there was too much hot oily metal and moving parts to allow any carelessness, any lapse of concentration.

It took all of Horgan's strength and skill to keep control of the launch. Like his fellow pilot Patrick Lynch, he had vast local knowledge of the sand banks, shoals, rocks, currents, channels, tides, sea marks and land marks of the extensive waters of Cork Harbour. They knew every conical, can, lighted and unlighted buoy in the harbour, what their shapes and positions indicated, and every beacon and post placed there as aids to navigation. They had had to study them, learn them and live by them.

Now with the Spit light behind, over to the westward they could see some of the sparse yellow lights of Spike Island. Horgan had to deal with advancing waves of the kind which leave even the most experienced seamen convinced that no boat could ever climb them. There are frightening moments in storms at sea when all you can do is hold on very tight, and pray, when your craft goes up, up, up, and there are seconds at the top, which seem like minutes, as she hangs, balanced and breathless, on the crest, before falling down, down, down, shuddering and crashing into the trough. Ordinary conversation-level talk would have been useless. The wind had taken on a solid roar, and between its noise and the sound of the pounding waves smashing against the launch's hull, the only way they could communicate with each other was by shouts and gestures.

When they first got a decent view of the ship outside Spike Island at Curlane Bank, she was facing south, her stern to the north. She was very high out of the water. The upper part of her rudder and part of the lethal-looking blades of her propeller were exposed.

The climb up the Jacob's ladder tonight would be long and perilous. Horgan knew that just getting the launch alongside and positioned so that Pilot Lynch could get on to the ladder would be extremely hazardous, given the kind of seas that were running and the ferocious strength of the wind. He and Lynch would need all of their long experience, judgement and seamanship.

They would have to be critically accurate in their gauging of the rise and fall of the launch in close to the side of the ship. Adjustments would have to be made for wind strength and wave pattern, and relative speeds. Lynch would have to judge precisely the moment at which to step off the launch, out over whatever gap of surging water there might be between the hulls of the two vessels, in order to begin the climb up the streaming red and black riveted hull of the old ship; up, with the rain beating across and down on him; up, with the ladder swinging in and out from the hull, as well as from side to side; up, while the gale tried to rip him off the steps of the ladder and hurl him spinning into the sea.

Disaster at Dog Nose

ON THE BRIDGE of the *Poplar*, Captain Taylor was aware of the approaching launches.

The gale that was blowing into Cork Harbour from hundreds of miles of open ocean was producing waves of between 20 and 25 feet high. Captain Taylor was concerned about the safety of his ship. It was wallowing, broadside to the sea. He wouldn't be able to relax until they were safely at anchor, but before that could happen, he first had to pick up his pilot and the Port Control officer, who would give the permission to proceed to the anchorage. He could see the lights of their launches coming closer by the minute.

He had decided to bring the ship about, swinging her bow to the east, to give the launches a broad lee, using the vessel as a giant iron wall to shield the two small craft from the worst of the wind and the breaking seas – the wave crests were toppling over, and there were dense streaks of foam along the direction of the wind.

Abaft the bridge, a small knot of seamen, crew members, stood, hunched against the weather, near to where the top of the Jacob's ladder was secured and where the pilot would come aboard. The ship's third officer, Horace Curtis, was the deck officer.

* * * * * * * *

When the *Poplar's* floodlights were switched on, illuminating almost the entire length of the ship as well as a goodly segment of the heaving surface of the sea close to her port side, Horgan and Lynch on the pilot launch got a view of her that was similar to the view a submarine captain might have got just before an attack – they could see the red boot topping, the black hull above it studded by lines of round-headed rivets, and above that again her buff-coloured upper works with, rising up straight and thin and old-fashioned, her single perpendicular funnel. The big tricolours in green, white and orange painted on the ship's side, together with the word ÉIRE in enormous white lettering, stood out prominently. The launch was dwarfed by the huge bulk of the empty cargo ship.

Horgan manoeuvred the pilot launch into position to make the run to get her alongside. Pilot Lynch readied himself on the starboard side. A couple of fenders swung with the motion of the launch, buffeted by waves. Horgan concentrated. His task now was to get the launch as close as possible to the Jacob's ladder and hold her steady there long enough for Patrick Lynch to lean out, and step on to the lower rungs.

By Horgan's reckoning the ship still had some way on her, moving eastwards. As he wrestled the launch closer to the *Poplar*, he was conscious of the Port Control launch's lights about 200 feet off, but he was focusing on the dangerous manoeuvre he was involved in. There was a howling bedlam of sound.

Keeping an eye on Lynch's state of readiness, he worked the launch closer and closer, carefully judging his angle of approach, something made doubly difficult by the seas that were running and the corkscrew twist they imparted to the launch as she rose and fell. An error of judgement could be disastrous.

And then, Lynch was swiftly leaning out. He took firm hold of the rope ladder, steadied himself for a millisecond and stepped off the launch just as she began another slewing drop into another wave trough.

Pilot Patrick Lynch was on his own now. For both men this was a sigh-of-relief time, thank-God-for-*that*-time.

When Lynch reached the top of the Jacob's ladder, someone extended a helping hand as he stepped aboard. He went straight to the bridge and introduced himself to Captain Taylor. He noticed that the engine-room telegraph was at STOP, and he asked the captain to leave it like that.

Taylor complied unhesitatingly. An experienced ship's master, he knew that he was required to follow the pilot's instructions – even though he, as captain, retained ultimate responsibility for the ship's safety.

As they had neared the *Poplar*, Lynch and Horgan had agreed that, given the fearsome weather conditions, the launch would return to Cobh as soon as Lynch was safely aboard the ship. "Take her back in," Lynch had shouted. "I'll signal if I want you." Horgan had nodded an acknowledgement. Although under normal weather conditions, both launches would stand about 200 yards off to await signals, tonight's weather conditions were not normal.

On the pilot launch, Horgan put the helm hard a-port and asked John Higgins for full speed ahead. Then suddenly, to his amazement and anger and alarm, the Port Control launch drove in hard against the pilot launch's port side.

On the deck of the *Poplar*, Able Seaman Scanlon was watching what was taking place. His memory of it would be that the Port Control launch came in slowly when approaching the ship, stopped about 15 feet from the pilot launch, and "then came in suddenly".

Horace Curtis, the third officer of the *Poplar*, saw it this way: The Port Control launch "drove in at considerable speed" from 20 or 30 feet off, and hit the pilot launch "a considerable thump".

The *Poplar's* boatswain, Able Seaman Patrick Ahearn, was also looking on. The way he saw it was that the pilot launch

53

was leaving the ship when the Port Control launch "threw it back against the *Poplar*". He heard James Horgan shouting, "What the hell are you trying to do?" A lot of shouting went on between the two boats in the space of a few minutes. There was what Ahearn called "a quarrelsome argument". He thought "the two boats were definitely locked together".

The Port Control officer, Chief Petty Officer Frank Barry, would later deny that the Port Control launch had come alongside the pilot launch at excessive speed.

What is beyond dispute is that the Port Control launch *did* come alongside the pilot launch and, with its helm hard a-starboard, jammed the pilot launch against the ship's side and held her there. Chief Petty Officer Frank Barry jumped from his launch on to the pilot launch, and from there got on to the rope ladder and went aboard the ship and headed straight for the bridge to meet Captain Taylor.

No one on the *Poplar*'s bridge was aware of the alarming developments on the ship's port side.

On the pilot launch, Horgan, his boat's engine now racing flat out full ahead, was screaming at the Port Control launch to get away. But with the Port Control launch's helm still hard a-starboard, and her engine, too, going ahead, there was no way the small boats could force themselves away from the towering hull of the *Poplar*.

Able Seaman Ahearn on the deck of the ship shouted to the coxswain of the Port Control launch to reverse his helm, to put it hard a-port.

Horgan shouted to John Higgins to switch the launch's engine to full speed astern. He shouted to the crew of the Port Control launch to do the same with *their* engine. If it wasn't possible to get away from the side of the ship going *forward*, then perhaps, just perhaps, reversing might work.

Fear now drove the men on the launches into a frenzy of activity. The *Poplar*'s boatswain saw one man on the bow of the Port Control launch trying desperately with a boathook to push off from the pilot launch. Another man aft was pushing equally desperately with his feet.

Those on the *Poplar*'s bridge were ignorant of what was happening on the launches, and Chief Petty Officer Barry went about the business of clearing the ship for entering harbour. He got through his duties within a few minutes and gave the clearance to Captain Taylor to proceed.

The engine-room telegraph was still showing STOP. The wind on the ship's starboard quarter was increasing in violence. Still more or less broad-on to the seas and wind, the ship was rolling uncomfortably. The visibility was worsening.

On the launches, the tactic of reversing the engines, as well as propelling the boats astern, enabled the crews to move them, by James Horgan's estimate, six or seven feet out from the ship. When he glanced up, he could still see members of the *Poplar*'s crew looking down.

Able Seaman Ahearn thought both launches were fouling one another, and that they were locked together. He said later, "Coming to the exhaust, the ship's floodlights showed me the launches apparently moving away from the ship. I took it they were all right, and I diverted my attention elsewhere."

At that moment they were anything but all right.

Ahearn said the bows of the launches were out from the *Poplar* at an angle of about 30 degrees. But with their engines in reverse, they were going further and further astern towards the high overhang of the *Poplar*'s counter.

On the ship's bridge, Pilot Lynch walked out to the exposed port wing of the bridge and looked down and astern. There were heavy rain squalls at the time. He saw no sign of the launches, didn't see or hear anything unusual. He checked the compass once more. The ship's head was north-north-east. He signalled the engine-room for half speed ahead. It was he who gave all the orders (relevant to the ship's navigation) from the time he arrived on the bridge until the ship was at anchor.

For Horgan and Higgins on the pilot launch, and for Petty

Officer Frank Lloyd (coxswain), Leading Seaman William Duggan (wireless operator), Seaman Frank Powell (motorman) and Seaman Patrick Wilshaw (crewman) on the Port Control launch, it was a worst nightmare come true.

Horgan didn't know the ship had restarted "until we got down along the ship's side and were near the stern abaft the exhaust".

The men on both launches began to shout and scream at the tops of their voices.

Michael Scanlon on the *Poplar* heard them. He got the impression they were yelling to the *Poplar*'s bridge. Able Seaman Ahearn, the boatswain, heard them. The last shouts *he* heard were, "Stop her! Stop her!" He said he didn't think they meant to stop the *ship*.

But as the ship moved inexorably forward, gathering speed, and the launches went steadily back along her hull, terror took hold of the men in those small wooden boats. They continued to scream upwards, desperately, to the men on the deck of the ship; continued to roar at them, "Stop her! *Stop* her! *Stop* her!"

As Horgan said later, "We both drifted astern along the ship's side. We were singing out to stop the ship. At that time there were two or three sailors on board the *Poplar* abaft the bridge. Both our crews called out to them to stop the ship."

They kept up their shouting and screaming against the bedlam for as long as possible. They were in terrible danger, and knew it. The ship's propeller was now turning with fearsome power, its blades slashing into the water, making their awful kerr-*umpf*, kerr-*umph*, kerr-*umph* noise, which got faster by the second. The water thrown up by the blades was atomised and blown away by the gale.

"We were yelling at the top of our voices," Horgan said. "I can't say if they heard us . . . At that time the launches were well lighted up by the floodlighting of the *Poplar*."

Later he said, "I think the sailors ought to have heard us yelling out . . . If there was a proper look-out on the ship, they

56

could not have failed to have seen us. Our only danger was from the propeller, and if the ship's engines had been stopped, both launches would have been safe. There was nothing to prevent the ship's anchor from being dropped, and it would have put us out of all danger."

But no one on the bridge heard the anguished shouts of the men in the launches. And the engines were not stopped. And the anchor was not dropped. And the *Poplar* steamed away towards the anchorage.

When the ship's propeller sliced the wooden boats, cutting them as though they were constructed of balsa, and sent them straight to the bottom of Cork Harbour, the six men on the launches were thrown into the roaring waves in the darkness somewhere between Dog Nose buoy and Spike Island.

The huge seas and the shrieking gale swallowed them up. The *Poplar* steamed on, leaving them, insignificant blobs in the darkness, bobbing for a short time in the howling storm.

* * * * * * * *

Petty Officer Frank Lloyd, the coxswain of the Port Control launch, was 45 years of age. He lived near the bottom of King Street. He had a wife and a young son, and his mother lived with them at No. 7.

Leading Seaman William Duggan was also aged 45. He was the Port Control launch wireless officer on duty that night. Married, but childless, he lived with his wife at No. 10, Bellevue Terrace.

Youngest man on the Port Control launch was the motorman, Seaman Frank Powell (23). He lived at No. 9, Plunkett Terrace.

The fourth member of the Port Control launch's crew was 27-year-old Able Seaman Patrick Wilshaw. Unmarried, he lived with his parents at No. 21, The Mall.

"Hail Queen of Heaven"

WHEN I GOT out of bed at about a quarter past eight on the Sunday morning to go to 9 o'clock mass (the children's mass), I went over to the windows and opened the shutters. The wind had moderated somewhat during the night, but it was still blowing hard and still raining, and there were small puddles of water on the floor at the bottoms of the windows. It was a dark, grey, threatening morning, and lights were still showing on the pier at Spike Island. Roche's Point light was visible in the murk, and you could just pick out the tiny intermittent red and white flashes from the lighted buoys.

The Irish Shipping Ltd vessel was at anchor not far from the Spit. I was puzzled by the unusual number of lights blazing on her.

When my mother came in from first mass, her eyes were red rimmed, and her mouth had a heart-breaking collapsed look about it.

"What's wrong, Mam?" I asked.

She couldn't talk, couldn't answer me for a minute or two. Her shoulders were heaving. She took off her coat and hung it on the end of the brass rail to the left of the range, untied the knot of her headscarf and wiped her eyes with the corner of it. Then she pulled a chair back from the kitchen table and sat down heavily. Shaking her head in anguish she said, over and over again, "Poor Willie Duggan, poor Willie Duggan." Then, making the sign of the cross, she said, "May Jesus have mercy on him. May Jesus have mercy on *all* of them."

"Why, what's wrong?" I said. "What happened? Who's 'them'?"

"He was prayed for at mass," my mother said. "They were *all* prayed for."

"But *who*?" I asked. "You said they were 'all' prayed for. Who are you talking about?"

"Willie Duggan," my mother said, "and all the other men on the Port Control boat and the pilot boat. They found poor Willie's body last night down by the Deepwater Quay."

"Was there a collision or what?" I asked.

"Oh, Billy, I don't *know*," my mother said. "No, there wasn't a collision. It's something to do with the *Irish Poplar*. She ran them down or something, and some say the men were cut to ribbons by the propellers. Oh, God, isn't it terrible?"

She began to cry again, burying her head in her hands, and I didn't know what to do, where to turn, what to say. I brushed my teeth at the sink, and when I finished I turned to see her standing by the range, one hand to her mouth, the other, palm open, propping her against the wall.

"All of them lost except one," she said. "And he'll never be the same again. How *could* he?"

Neither of us heard Norma coming down the stairs or into the kitchen. She was in her stockinged feet, having left her shoes downstairs with mine and John's and Margaret's, all for Daddy to polish. It was something he did lovingly and with great care and pride every Saturday night, and when he had them all done, he lined them up in perfect formation against the wall in the hallway just outside the kitchen, ready for us when we came down to go to mass on Sunday morning.

Norma was standing by the kitchen door now, her eyes wide and troubled.

"What's wrong, Mammy? Why are you crying?" she asked, her small face furrowed and worried looking.

My mother sniffed and hurriedly wiped her eyes, and tried to pull herself together. But sobs which she was unable to stifle still convulsed her, and Norma ran to her and clutched her and tried to put her arms around her. In an unconscious acting-out of the things my mother did automatically for all of us, the eight year old held Mammy tightly and said in a manner meant to be soothing, "There, there, you'll be all right."

That broke my mother up, and she pressed Norma to her and just cried and cried.

I couldn't take it. I ran out of the kitchen, grabbed my sou'wester off the hook in the hall where it was hanging, got my raincoat from the back room where it had been left to dry overnight and ran out into the sad, dreary, wet, windy morning. Tying the strings of the sou'wester and buttoning my coat, I walked across to the wall on the other side of the road and looked out at the *Poplar* riding at anchor down by the Spit. So many lights! Apart from that, she looked normal – a long, high, ship with a thin perpendicular funnel, and two masts with derricks on them.

On the way along Roche's Row I hurried past Con Lynch's house, in case it was his father who had been the pilot last night and was now dead. I wouldn't know what to say to Con.

During mass, you could hear the wind blowing outside and around the cathedral. Its noise was drowned out only when Staf Gebruers played the organ, but whenever he stopped, you could hear it again.

There was no sign of Pat Higgins or Con Lynch, both of whom were in my class at school. No sign, either, as far as I could tell, of any of the other pilots' sons – Tony Nash, or Rowdy Ellis, or Crab Walsh or John Chandler.

There was a ghastly seriousness in the faces of Brother Eugenius and Brother Prudent, and in the faces of Mr O'Sullivan, Mr Cooney and Spud Murphy, and in the faces of Sister Paul and Sister Eucharia across the nave with the girls from the national school and the pension school. Over in the side aisles (the men's on the left, the women's on the right), that same seriousness was mirrored and was at its most aching fullness when Father Egan, with his saint's sad expression, spoke in the pulpit about "the terrible tragedy last night out there" (he spread his left arm wide) "in the harbour".

As he spoke, my mind kept wandering. I remembered some of the pictures of ships and boats and the sea which I had seen in an art book my father had taken out on loan from the town library. In one dark picture by an Irish painter named Danby, there was a wrecked and sinking sailing ship, masts and canvas gone, the hull heeled right over on her port side, only the forward portion of the ship visible. Two men clung to a broken spar in the sea, about to be engulfed by a breaking white-topped wave which had already up-ended one of the ship's boats. The bow of the ship was teeming with men, and others clung precariously to the bowsprit and the jagged-ended, broken jib-boom, the raging seas directly beneath them.

I used to get drawn right into Danby's picture, imagining myself among the desperate people hanging on, soaked through, terrified. What were they thinking, "Is this the end?" or "God forgive me for the sins of my past life," or "I wonder what the moment of death will be like?"

In the church, with Father Egan talking, it all came back to me as I drifted in and out of what he was saying, in and out of listening to the high wind screaming and whooshing around St Colman's on its exposed site facing Spike Island. I looked at Father Egan and tried hard to concentrate on what he was saying: words like "sorrowing" and "loved ones" and "mourn" and "grief" and "healing".

Twice he stopped, overcome, his chin down against his chest, and it seemed each time that he wouldn't be able to carry on. We sat mute and numb, trying to deal with something enormous, something too big. And Father Egan, that

61

most ordinary and compassionate of men, didn't seem to have any answers, just seemed to be stricken, and wondering, and wounded like the rest of us.

No one's eyes were dry when he eventually left the pulpit, moving slowly like an old man, hands folded in front of his breast, head leaning to one side as if pulled over and down with the weight of sorrow. Staf played the introduction to "Hail Queen of Heaven," and in that church on that morning at that time, I truly heard the words for the first time. Oh, I'd been singing the hymn for most of my young life, by rote, the same unthinking way we'd sung out the seven-times tables.

But now . . . now my eyes filled up and I ached inside when everyone in the church, with last night's harbour deaths so much in the air, sang:

Hail Queen of Heaven, the ocean star . . .

No stars seen last night over the ocean.

Guide of the wanderer here below . . .

No guide in the wild stormy darkness.

. . . Save us from peril and from woe.

They weren't saved!

I was crying.

Mother of Christ, Star of the sea,
Pray for the sinner, pray for me.

Star of the sea: pray for *them*!

Nightmare Swim

WHEN THE PILOT launch, with the Port Control launch still jammed alongside her, went in under the overhang of the *Poplar*'s stern, the exposed parts of the blades of the ship's propeller were thrashing the sea and driving the vessel forward.

Just before the pilot launch went under, James Horgan and John Higgins jumped on to the Port Control launch, but she, too, was being sucked, forced, in towards the propeller blades.

The noise was indescribable – noise of quickening propeller pounding the seas and sundering the boats, noise of the shrieking wind, noise of crashing waves, noise of men screaming.

The pilot launch was gone within seconds. Then the Port Control launch.

Horgan, when he came to the surface, choking and gagging and spitting out water, looked all around him to see where he was relative to the ship. The *Poplar* was well clear of them and going away. He heard shouts in the darkness, recognised Willie Duggan's voice and the voice of John Higgins. There was someone else as well, whose voice he couldn't identify. He thought it might have been Petty Officer Lloyd's.

"Try to keep together!" Horgan shouted, but his words were carried away by the gale as he was first smashed by a breaking wave and then sucked under the surface again. He was struggling to resurface, struggling to shed his boots which were dragging him under, struggling to get his heavy coat off, struggling against the rising panic, struggling to keep calm, struggling to clear his mind, struggling against the force of the storm.

Struggling to stay alive.

Each time he was swept to the top of a high wave he could see the lights of the *Poplar* moving steadily away as she steamed towards the anchorage. She was lost to sight – everything was – when he went down into the troughs. He shouted the names of John Higgins and Willie Duggan and the others. He strained to hear if there was any answering call. Nothing. All he heard were the sounds of the storm.

The lights of Spike were about two miles away. He started praying and swimming at the same time, but he was fully clothed, the tide was flooding, and he was at the mercy of a southerly gale with the wind gusting at up to 50 miles an hour.

He thought he was going to die.

* * * * * * * *

In the silence and darkness of the *Poplar*'s wheelhouse, Pilot Lynch devoted all his concentration to his job. By 7.20pm he had the ship safely at anchor. The gale was roaring out of the south.

* * * * * * * *

He wasn't sure how long it was, but thought that it was an hour and a quarter to an hour and a half after he'd begun trying to swim towards Spike Island that James Horgan's bootless feet touched ground. He thought at first he might be imagining it. He was so exhausted that he found it impossible to differentiate between reality and imagination. He had swallowed what felt like gallons of salt water, and his throat was sore, his stomach full and sick. He didn't know why he hadn't drowned.

His arms felt so heavy that he thought he might never again be able to raise them, and his legs were like a couple of colossal weights hanging out of the trunk of his body. But yes, his feet *had* touched bottom, and he clawed and hauled himself into shallower water, and then ashore and away from the sea, inch by agonising inch.

Then he gave up and lay in a collapsed heap, retching and gasping for breath, his head reeling, the hard ground beneath him feeling as if it, too, were rising and falling and surging with the same rhythm and motion as the sea.

Eventually he forced himself, staggering and weak-legged, to reach the nearest building that showed a light. He knocked. It seemed hours before someone opened the door to him. He stood in the light flooding out from the hallway. He couldn't speak, just stood there, drenched, shivering, almost unconscious on his feet.

When they brought him inside, he could barely control his thoughts. Eventually it came out of him in confused dribs and drabs, until he sank into haunted wordlessness. They got him to the island's sick bay where he was given medical attention. At the same time, the first phone calls were being made, alerting people to the fact that a frightful thing had happened near Dog Nose buoy, and that there might still be men in the water out there in the howling darkness.

* * * * * * * *

The phone calls from Spike Island were the first intimations that anyone (including those on the bridge of the *Poplar*) got that something had gone terribly wrong with the two launches.

Once the news got around that they had been sunk and their crews thrown into the sea, a search operation was mounted. A Department of Defence steam launch was dispatched immediately to the *Poplar* from Spike Island, and then began searching for survivors.

They found none.

Searchlight crews on Camden fort, Carlisle fort, and Westmoreland fort on Spike Island swept their beams over the harbour waters for hours on end, cutting sharp white swathes in the darkness in the hope of picking out anything in the sea that might be a man swimming, or someone clinging to a piece of wreckage – or even a body. They saw nothing. Just huge waves, breaking seas.

Marine Service vessels set out from Haulbowline. Their searching yielded up no living thing, no piece of floating debris from either launch, no piece of flotsam.

The Ballycotton lifeboat was called out. Under renowned Coxswain Patsy Sliney (awardee of the Lifeboat Institution's gold, silver and bronze medals), it took four hours to reach Cork Harbour, a journey which in normal circumstances would be covered in an hour and a half. Coxswain Sliney said it was one of the worst nights he had ever experienced.

The Garda Síochána were alerted at their Cobh headquarters across the road from the Naval Pier; members of the LDF, Maritime Inscription, LSF and army were mobilised to keep a sharp look-out along the shoreline.

The crew of the *Muirchú*, which was anchored in Cobh Road between Haulbowline Island and the Deepwater Quay, was instructed to be on the alert for anything unusual.

Ensign James Barrett was the duty officer on the *Muirchú* that night. At about 10.15, with the tide ebbing and the stern of the vessel down channel, Barrett noticed some people on the 600-foot-long Deepwater Quay, about three miles from Dog Nose buoy, apparently attempting to attract his attention. Waving and shouting, they appeared to be pointing at something in the water just out from the quay. He reached for his binoculars and at the same time had the ship's searchlight switched on, its beam swung in towards the shore. And then he saw it, something bulky and floating low in the water.

Barrett hurriedly mustered a crew and ordered one of the ship's boats lowered. They rowed frantically across towards the quay, the people shouting directions to them all the way.

Willie Duggan's body was floating face down about 15 yards out from the quayside. There was a lifebelt around the neck and another rising and falling on the waves close by.

Willie had managed to get his boots off, but not his overcoat. His forehead was marked by a small superficial wound, but it was the sea that killed Willie Duggan, not the propeller of the *Poplar*. Dr Hegarty ("Hay-ga") examined the cold body, tried artificial respiration, and subsequently estimated that death had taken place about three hours earlier.

Father Tim Murphy administered the last rites, Mrs Duggan was given the devastating news, and Willie's body was removed to the morgue at Cobh General Hospital.

Around midnight pieces of the pilot launch were found floating among the seaweed and trash at the sea steps across the road from the entrance to the railway station. It was close to where they had pulled Willie Duggan's body out of the water. Some more bits of wreckage were discovered on the following morning in the camber across the road from the Soldiers' Home and Sailors' Rest. They, too, were identified as having come from the pilot launch.

Pilot Lynch was still on board the *Poplar*, and James Horgan was still on Spike Island.

Cobh started to settle into deep melancholy, and it became a sad town in a broken world. Then rumours began to circulate through the bleak savagery of that winter.

Willie's Funeral

M
Y FATHER TOOK Norma, John and Margaret to half past ten mass and brought them home immediately afterwards instead of to O'Neill's sweets shop for bullseyes. Then he went down to Higgins & Walls, the newsagents and tobacconists on The Beach, for the Sunday papers and his beloved Woodbines. He was very quiet when he came home and stood inside the hall door for longer than was strictly necessary just to shake the rain off his neat, brown, felt soft-hat which he had bought recently in Danny ("If you Want To Get Ahead Get A Hat") Hobbs' shop near the Grand Parade end of Patrick Street in Cork.

His lips had taken on that straight-line, thin appearance, and his forehead wrinkles had deepened and looked permanent. He and my mother went into the sitting room together and closed the door behind them.

I went up to the top front bedroom and looked out the same window that I had stood at the night before. The *Poplar* was still down near the Spit at anchor.

That night in the cathedral, the rosary was offered up for the repose of the souls of the men who had died in the harbour, and for their families. It was announced that Bishop Roche would be saying a special requiem mass.

Of the pieces of wreckage found floating near the Cobh waterfront, one was reported as having seemingly "been cut off by some sharp metal object." ("Oh, My God, the propeller, what *else*?") The wood fragment was estimated to be about 18 inches square.

Two naval caps were found floating in the camber. One of them had a peak. It was believed to have belonged to Petty Officer Lloyd. The other was an ordinary sailor's hat, and was thought to have been Seaman Frank Powell's.

As is usual when only some of the facts of a case are known, speculation fed rumour, and very soon both were rife throughout the town. Some of what was said was outlandish, some of it scurrilous inasmuch as half-baked theories and wild exaggerations were paraded as facts. Words like "blame" and "guilt" began to be used with shameful irresponsibility. Almost everyone involved in the horrendous happening outside Spike Island (even those whose involvement was no more than peripheral) was adjudged by someone, somewhere in the town, to have been "responsible" or "the real culprit".

In the days ahead, Petty Officer Francis Lloyd's wife would become demented. Her eyes looked terrified. She was a very visible and audible figure as she made her way to the camber, to the slipway near where they found her husband's cap. She probed and pushed among the cans and swirling seaweed and pieces of cardboard and paper and old tree branches carried in by the tide and wind, looking for her Frank, and beseeching Sweet Jesus to send him to her.

At school, Pat Higgins would become the saddest-faced boy I had ever seen. For a long time, whenever we played soccer with a tennis ball in the schoolyard of St Joseph's, we'd always pass the ball to Pat Higgins, *give* it to him really, instead of trying to beat him on the outside. It was the only way we could let him know how sorry and sad we were about him not having a father anymore.

Mrs Duggan, white-faced and dressed in black all over, seemed permanently in shock and on the edge of tears, and would open her front door no more than a few inches so that less than half her face was seen by anyone who knocked at No. 10.

"Well at least *she* got her husband's body back, poor Mr Duggan, God rest him," Mrs Carty said to my mother. "She can bury him, have a proper funeral. The other poor creatures haven't even got a corpse to grieve over."

In Cobh, and on Haulbowline and Spike Island, preparations were being made for the removal of Willie Duggan's body from the hospital to the cathedral, where it would be received by Father Tim Murphy, the priest who had administered the last rites, and Father McCarthy, the curate on Haulbowline.

It seemed as if half the town's population turned out for the short procession down the hill to St Colman's. Petty Officer John Dolan was in charge of the escort party from the Marine Service. The officer commanding Haulbowline, Lieutenant Commander George Crosbie, wasn't there, but he was represented by Lieutenant M. Bannion. There was also a group of other naval lieutenants, as well as army officers, members of the LDF and LSF, the Garda Síochána, various town dignitaries and a huge crowd of ordinary townspeople.

Mrs O'Brien and the Cronins closed their shops on Roche's Row and went along to the cathedral to be there when the cortège came down the hill.

"Poor Mr Duggan – he was such a lovely *quiet* man," Mrs O'Brien said to my mother.

* * * * * * * *

I remember the day that Willie Duggan was buried. I remember it for all sorts of reasons, not the least of which is, because, at the age of ten, I experienced something it would take me years to recognise as grief. In those days, it probably wouldn't have entered into the adult consciousness that children, also, might experience grief. The adults were too busy trying to handle their own grief, and counselling hadn't yet arrived as a much-needed service. The general perception about grief and children was, "Kids? Ah, for God's sake, they don't know *what* grief is – they're only *children*, and besides, they're very resilient. They wouldn't understand."

I *didn't* understand what I was experiencing, didn't understand the swirling mass of emotions, the sense of loss and puzzlement, the questions – like: will I ever get over not being able ever again to see Mr Duggan coming up the terrace and saying, shyly and warmly, "Hello, Billy", and being so *nice*? And: isn't it terrible that he'll never again come out the door of No. 10, and never again walk down the hill in his uniform to go to work? And: why does "The Last Post" make you feel as if your heart is breaking, and why does the bugle sound so lonely, and *final*, and so much like an *ending*? And how is it that sometimes no matter what colours your eyes see in a harbour town, you can seem to be living in a grey world?

Willie Duggan's was the first military funeral I ever saw. I remember the leading seamen in their naval uniforms doing the slow march, the deliberateness of those arrested foot movements, the down-pointed toes of their highly polished boots, the strained faces of the sailors, the wide-spaced beating of the muffled drums, the cap on the tricolour on the lid of Willie's coffin, the long-drawn-out funeral procession up the hill from the cathedral, past Verling's and Milwood's and the convent school at the top of the town, and the field where John Duffy pitched his circus tent every year; and then down the steep bendy road to the Old Church cemetery.

I remember it because I looked at the faces of James Horgan and Chief Petty Officer Frank Barry, and because all the defence forces were represented, and I had never before seen them together at the one time. The Gardaí were there, and the Port Control, and even the Knights of Malta Ambulance Unit, harbour officials, politicians and representatives of Irish Shipping Ltd.

The chief mourners, apart from Willie's wife, included a sorrowing old man easily identified as Willie's father, Willie's Garda brother, Denis, and his sister, Mrs M. O'Callaghan.

Father Tim Murphy again officiated, this time assisted by the cathedral's administrator, Father O'Connor. Father McCarthy from Haulbowline was also at the graveside.

Then the lone bugler blew his tragic notes, and the firing party pointed their guns up at the dark clouds in the grey, failing light and fired three volleys, a last salute to Willie.

When it was all over, I walked, sobbing, up the hill and back to the town, not knowing anything, understanding nothing at all. I'll *never* forget the day Willie Duggan was buried.

The Damned-and-Blasted Cur

RIFF HOWLED AT eight o'clock in the night, and I wondered whose turn it was this time.

Una Bunworth, who lived in No. 7 and whose father was the postmaster, said, "It's awful the way people say these things about poor old Riffy. I thought Catholics weren't supposed to believe in superstition."

She was right of course.

The Bunworths were Church of Ireland. They lived next door to the Batsons, who were also Church of Ireland. The Batsons lived next to us. Like everyone else who lived on Bellevue, we were Catholics, so there was an irrefutable logic in Una's addressing her comments about Riff to me. The only thing was, I didn't know what answer to give her which would satisfy her and still allow our side to come out with some credibility.

I tried what I had seen Italians do in Hollywood movies – I shrugged, turned down the corners of my mouth and spread my upturned palms.

Una laughed and gave me a stiff push on the shoulder.

"You're an awful eejit, Billy Nolan, do you know that?" she said.

But the truth of the matter was that it only took Riff to

throw his head back and yowl at night for a knock to come on our front door soon afterwards, and a distraught or pleading voice say to my mother something like, "Oh, could you ever come quick, please, Missus Nolan? Me father is very bad."

The Bunworths' house was the only one on the hill where Riff wasn't shooed away. They never aimed a kick at him or threw water on him or cursed him and at him. There was always a crust or a bone there for him. I couldn't understand that.

Time after time I heard Mam saying to Dad, or Danny Dinan, or Mrs Wilson, "Did you hear old Riff last night? Did you hear him howling? As sure as God, someone on the terrace will be on his deathbed before the week is out."

Riff was the most dejected-looking dog I have ever seen. He looked rusty, and was rangy, dirty and full of fleas. Whenever he came down the hill from where it levelled out at the top and where his owners lived, he slunk along by the far wall and ran with his ginger head and misery-laden face close to the ground, his eyes looking sideways with all the appearance of cowardice. His tail was permanently between his legs, and a lively kitten or a playful pup could send him running away, yelping with fear. But as soon as he crossed the boundary formed by the iron gates leading into his owners' place, he would turn around, and bark with mock defiance – but ready to flee at the slightest threat.

He had another nasty trait, which he shared with two other dogs on the terrace – the Moloneys' treacherous Brandy and Ryans' bad-tempered, snarling, wire-haired terrier Sneezer – the mean habit of sneaking up behind you, if you were a child, and trying a furtive snap at your ankles or calfs.

The breadmen hated Riff, and the coalmen hated him, and the postmen detested him. Queenie Meade who lived close by the Buckleys, the owners of Riff, didn't trust him. He was the most damned-and-blasted cur in the whole of Cobh.

"Do you hear him?" my mother said to no one in particu-

74

lar. She made the sign of the cross and said, "God between us and all harm. I wonder who it is going to be?"

"Why do you say that, Mam?" I asked.

"I've never known that old thing to howl in the night but someone around here died soon after."

Mrs Wilson in No. 11 had said, "I wish to the Lord they'd do away with him. Put him in a bag and throw it in off the Deepwater Quay."

But would doing away with Riff stop all dying in the neighbourhood?

Daisy Sullivan came to the door on the evening following the latest howling episode and said, "Can you come down quick, Moll? Pappy's been taken bad."

Mam came into the dining room where I was doing my homework at the same table as Dad was writing up the minutes of the Cork County Board of the Irish Amateur Boxing Association.

"Daisy is at the front door," she said, shrugging into her street coat. "Mother Sullivan sent her up for me. I don't know what time I'll be back. Don't wait up for me."

When she banged the front door behind her, my father said, "I've said it to you before, and I say it again, your mammy is a wonderful woman."

I knew that. He didn't have to tell me.

"Whenever anyone around the place is in trouble, they come running for her."

I knew that, too.

"Whether there's someone coming into the world, or going out of it, they send for Mammy Nolan first, and then the doctor."

"I know," I said. "She's terrific."

"That's what she is – terrific."

I couldn't remember Mam ever being slim. She had a mother's shape, though her wedding photograph, the one done by Leopolds' of Cork and which stood on top of the piano, showed her as a lovely, demure, slip of a young woman.

But her motherly bulk meant, for us, comfort and love and, almost always, calmness.

"We're very lucky to have her," Dad said.

"I know."

He didn't often talk that way about Mam to me, and I suppose the rarity added power to his remarks. There was no mistaking the depth of the feelings they had for each other, but they felt no need to express anything of this to us. Not that they didn't have periodic rows, fallings out.

"Any husband and wife who say that they've never exchanged a cross word are either telling lies, or they don't know what worry and trouble are all about," my mother said to me once when I became upset over harsh words I had overheard between herself and my father.

Their rows were rare occurrences and hardly ever took place in the presence of us children. They were careful about that. But I *had* been present to hear and witness anger, and there was no doubt in my young mind but that the accusations flung between them were heartfelt at the time of their utterance. I had tried to make myself invisible, and I said some mental prayers.

A two-day silence on my father's part followed that particular bust-up, and then 24 hours of the uneasy tolerance that goes with the mending of bruised vanities. And then ... fierce remorse, a making up and the taking of action on desires to make amends.

My mother was called on to help children and adults to fight fevers, beat pneumonia, dress wounds, deal with convulsions. She laid out their dead, comforted the relatives and travelled to funerals in the chief mourners' cars: she attended more funerals in Cobh than anyone except the undertakers and the priests.

On top of all that, she made and iced wedding cakes and Christmas cakes, did great Christmas puddings and made the best trifles in the entire world. And she never had a spare shilling for herself.

"We're very lucky to have her," Dad said. That, and the "your mammy is a wonderful woman" remark made my eyes wet.

At five to eleven Mam arrived home.

"Are *you* still out of bed? You'll never get up for school in the morning!"

"Ah, I will."

Dad stood up and helped her off with her coat.

"How's poor Pappy Sullivan?"

"Ah, sure he's finished, Eddie. He's very far gone."

"Have they had the doctor?"

"Yes. He left just before I came away."

"And what did *he* say?"

"Much the same. Said there was nothing else he could do for him that I hadn't done."

"And who's down there now?"

"Sister Fidelis." (Yes, the same one.) "She was coming in the door as I was going out. I told Daisy and May Lou that if they wanted me during the night to send someone up. It's only a matter of time, I think."

In bed, I lay awake for a very long time in the dark thinking about Pappy Sullivan. He had been part of my childhood since the morning I was born at No. 15 Harbour Row on March 19, 1932 – "the year of the Eucharistic Congress," as Mam always identified it. "You were at it."

And now Pappy was dying.

Is he afraid? I wondered. Does dying hurt? . . . Is it awful to lie there *knowing* you are dying? Especially if you don't want to die . . .

Is it scaring to know that when you go, you could face hell (for all eternity), or purgatory (for a desperately long time), or heaven (if you're dosed with luck)? Isn't it impossible to understand that a *thousand years* wouldn't even amount to a *beginning* of eternity?

And suppose you remembered a sin you hadn't confessed, but now you *couldn't* talk, couldn't confess it, would that mean you'd be condemned for ever and ever to flames which would be sheer agony, but which would never entirely burn up your soul, and never go out?

That was a very long night.

They didn't come for Mam before morning, but just before we went off to school, Daisy was at the door again.

"He's taken a turn for the worse, Moll. Can you come down?"

My mother spent the whole day till half past four down in Sullivans', and only came home then to prepare my father's dinner. When he was finished, she went back down again.

It was very late when she finally came up the hill. She looked worn out. All the life was gone from her voice.

"Poor old Pappy," she said. "God rest his soul."

Dad went over and sat in silence beside her.

"Did he go hard?" he asked after a while.

"Ah, it was a blessed release for him, Eddie."

"Mam, were you with Pappy when he died?" I wanted to know.

"I was."

"Jay, I don't know how you do it."

"Sure if the living wouldn't do something for him, who else could?"

She relapsed into silence again, and sat looking down at the ground. My father glanced across at me and put his finger to his lips in a clear signal that I was to keep quiet, not ask any more questions just yet. He knew my mother needed a period of silence, a few minutes to compose herself, gather her thoughts. He put a reassuring hand on her shoulder. Several minutes passed before Mam started to speak again.

"When I saw he was going, I called them in. They were there when he died . . . Afterwards, I washed him, shaved his poor face, put on his habit which Daisy got from Buckleys', and combed his hair. I put some cotton wool in his mouth to take away that awful sunken look, put his false teeth back in, and put pennies on his eyes to keep them closed. Then I folded his hands across his breast and entwined his rosary beads through his fingers. If you saw him now, he looks as peaceful as a baby."

Then she started to cry.

* * * * * * *

They held a wake the next day, and Pappy's body was to be taken to the mortuary chapel in the cathedral in the evening.

From up where we lived, I watched the people arriving and going into that sad house whose blinds were drawn but whose front door, on which the black crape of death was hung, was open. I felt a familiar sort of emptiness, complicated by dread, because I knew what was facing me. I went down as far as the postbox from where I could see without being noticed. The people who arrived went in quietly to the hushed hallway, clasped the hands of weeping women, whispered things to them, and then went into the room where the corpse of Pappy Sullivan was on the bed where my mother had laid him out.

I couldn't stand looking at the scene for long, so went back up the hill, stole into our house and hid upstairs in the kitchenette.

In the end, I had to answer my mother's calls.

"Oh, there you are! You'll have to go down to Mother Sullivan's, you know, to pay your last respects to Pappy, and say a prayer for him."

"Aw, Mam, I *couldn't*. I just couldn't!"

"What are you talking about? You'll *have* to! Mother Sullivan has always been very good to you. Go on now, like a good boy. Hurry up."

"But what'll I *say*?"

"Just tell Mother you're very sorry. That's all you have to say."

Down at the bottom of the hill I hung around the lamp post for about 20 minutes, trying to pluck up courage. When I went to the door, the hall was very dark, and I was on the

79

point of leaving again when Mother came out to see some-one off. Her face was twisted and red around the eyes, nose and mouth. Her mouth was all collapsed.

She took my hands in both of hers and shook her head, her eyes brimming again, her lower lip clamped tight by her teeth.

"Billy," she said. "Poor Pappy."

"I'm very sorry, Mother," I said.

"I know you are, Billy son. I know you are . . . Go on in and see him. There's no one in the room."

She went downstairs towards the kitchen, and I stood by the door of Pappy's bedroom, scared to go in. The only light in there was from two flickering candles, and the red glow from the Sacred Heart lamp.

Eventually I went in, and there on my left was the bed with Pappy stretched out in his long brown habit. I knelt down, but not too near that bed. I couldn't keep my eyes off the shrunken pale face. I kept looking at the throat ("put yer oul finger down yer trote an' give yerself the gawk . . ." – why did *that* come back to me at *this* moment when I was almost pissin' meself? Sacred Heart!) to see if there was the tiniest, tiniest movement. Suppose they'd made a mistake!

Supposing he suddenly *sat up* – and me the only one there!

Or suppose he sat up very slowly, and his eyes opened, and he turned and *stared* at me!

I set a world record for the fastest sign of the cross and got out of that room, and out of that house, without saying good-bye to Mother Sullivan, or Daisy or May Lou or Tessie.

I couldn't. It had been too hard saying goodbye to Pappy.

* * * * * * * *

Boyish Billy Batson from next door went off to war, away to join the RAF. He came in to say goodbye to us, and hugged my mother, and said, "God bless, Moll. Pray for me, won't you?" And my mother, weeping, said that of course she would, and, "May God protect you, Billy, love."

Then he hugged each of us children – Me, Norma, Margaret and John – and asked us in turn to pray for him. And when he did that, I thought, so Protestants *do* believe in prayer!

We stood on the doorstep and watched him, tall, slim and with blond straight hair, walking bravely down the street, and not turning until he reached the lamp post opposite Mother Sullivan's, where Pappy had died just a few days before. He stood, put down his small case, and waved twice.

Ma and Pa Batson waved from their doorstep, No. 8, and while big Pa, with his large round face, didn't reveal much emotion, Ma's face was wet with tears. They both went in after those last waves from Billy, but Billy's sisters, Jane and Vi, waved until Billy was totally out of sight, down beyond Whelans' at the end of Rose Hill.

I tried to imagine how *I'd* be if I had to face the Germans. This was a recurring thing with me, and the agony of it got worse instead of diminishing. I'd think of the pain I felt when I crashed into Eddie Forrest's bike coming around the corner under the railway bridge at Carrigaloe, the searing, stabbing agonies when the doctor put iodine on the lacerations. Well, the worst of that must surely have been nothing compared with being struck by a bullet? Or being torched in a blazing plane spiralling one-winged out of the sky? Or being in a tank which received a direct hit?

None of the accounts I read in the papers of men at war mentioned anyone running away in fear, or moaning with fear. I knew I'd probably do both of those things. I beseeched God very often to keep me safe from war because otherwise my awful secret would be revealed.

On the Sunday after Billy Batson left, a sea storm blew in from the south-west soon after lunch, and by tea-time it was howling wildly. The tide was coming in. At half past six, Mam said, "It's too bad a night to go to compline. Nobody would expect you to go."

"I'll go all the same," I said.

81

"Well, be sure you wrap up well, and wear your welling-tons."

Normally at compline I took my place among the boys on the left-hand side of the centre aisle. The girls, as at the children's mass, occupied the seats across from us. It was all in Latin, and we were given slim booklets with scarlet covers from which to read and sing the words. "Three psalms and responsory," it said on the fly leaf, and that might just as well have been in Urdu; it meant nothing at all to us.

Some members of the choir looked to me to be old enough to have been singing compline since time began – particularly a small, bent-over elderly man known variously as "the Gas-Pipe Tenor" and "Mahogany Gas-Pipe", and nick-named because he worked for the local gas company clearing meters. In wintertime he was permanently pissed off, and he wore his misery like a badge as he trudged the hills of the town in the cold rain.

I looked at his face frequently and asked myself: does he *have* to be that way? Or does he *choose* to be that way – the same way that Paddy Finn, the postman, who passed or called to our house at the same time every morning (ten minutes to nine) chose to be sympathetic and serious?

The bunch of nuns who came down the hill from the con-vent to compline were different from the children's mass detail. They were older and had quavery voices and parch-ment faces.

But on this particular night, I didn't want to be up near the altar among the others. Pappy Sullivan's death and Billy Bat-son's going away were still affecting me. I slipped into a seat about a third of the way between the main door and the high altar. On the way to the cathedral, I'd seen the familiar sight of a dislodged slate coming off a roof on Roche's Row and slicing through the air to crash into the base of the wall across the road, where it smashed and scattered. A thing like that could take the head off you.

It was hard to concentrate, even if the background sounds

82

were familiar. Once or twice the half-heard sound of a ship's siren lingered for a moment and was then obliterated by the wind. Doors banged in the sacristy. It was only when the priest lifted the big golden monstrance after the *Oremus* and held it high towards us, and three times made the cruciform sign with it, that I concentrated. I said quick prayers for Pappy, Billy Batson, Uncle John and Granda. But the moment was over in a very short time.

The altar was barely cleared when the rush for the door began. It was lashing rain outside, and the first to arrive at the door held back, resisting the crush from behind. I squirmed through the hesitators and rushed out, tying my sou'wester tight under my chin. Then I turned and bent into the gale.

I stayed close to the sides of the houses going down King Street, and when I got to Twomey's furniture store down near the bottom, I stood in the shelter of the doorway to watch the people hurrying down the hill on their way to Frennet's, where Claudette Colbert and Henry Fonda in *Drums Along the Mohawk* was the Sunday night attraction. Well, they could have it. About the only good thing about it, as far as I was concerned, was that Barry Fitzgerald's brother, Arthur Shields, was in it, and John Carradine. "That John Carradine is *lethal*," Crab Walsh was always saying. Anyway, Sunday night films were forbidden to me.

A couple of men come up around the corner from the square and weaved towards the pub. Its windows were steamed up on the inside. When the door opened, I heard someone singing a snatch of song, "Goodbye! . . . Goodbye! . . . I bid you all a last good" – and the door slammed shut.

I ducked out when the last of the picture-goers passed and went down across the square, past the Rob Roy which was kept by Mr Kemp, who wore "gentlemen's tweeds" and had two lovely red setters. Eventually I reached the railway station and went out along the Deepwater Quay to the Water's Edge, the Five Foot Way.

Will I, or won't I? I wondered.

There were no lights out here, and it was very dark. The waves were smashing in against the wall, the spray pouring in over the walk itself, high and stinging.

Bugger it! I will!

Why am I doing this? What am I trying to prove? Who or what am I trying to get away from?

Go on! Keep going!

The wind was, if anything, rising, howling eerily as it blew the sheets of rain. Only five strands of wire separated me from the waves, and at times I clung to the rusted railings at the railway side of the walk. But I was determined to go out as far as the second bridge. Why? No clear idea.

At last I reached the spot where the red-brick supports marked where the steps up to, or down from, the bridge were, and I slipped in there out of the worst of the rain. A lone figure passed by, heading in towards the town.

"Fierce night," I called.

"Fierce, absolutely fierce," he said without stopping.

I stayed there for a long time.

On East Beach, on the way home, I stood in the doorway of the BMC shop for a while and watched the mean lights of two small trawlers tied up at Lynch's Quay, bobbing up and down on the bouncing tide. I couldn't see the hulls, but I knew they were rusty. All trawlers are rusty.

I got very depressed.

Climbing the Preaching House steps towards home, I thought, this world is a lousy place. You'd be lucky to get out of it alive.

Saddest Christmas

THE BODIES OF Patrick Wilshaw, Francis Lloyd, Frank Powell and John Higgins still hadn't been recovered when the postponed inquest on Willie Duggan opened in Cobh's Town Hall eight days before Christmas. Presiding was the Deputy Coroner J. S. St Clair Rice.

The jury inquest brought in a verdict of death from asphyxia due to drowning.

They added a rider which, when its contents were made public, created furtive, destructive resentment, rancour and accusations among pockets of people in the town: "The cause of the accident was, first of all, the Port Control boat going alongside and not giving the pilot launch a chance to get away, and we condemn the Port Control boat for going alongside the ship before the pilot boat had moved out."

That word "condemn" was explosive, especially in the highly emotional climate of the aftermath of the tragedy. It acted as a goad to some individuals and groupings who were searching for scapegoats. They now felt enabled to indulge in harsh criticisms of the dead, whose relatives had to put up with a searing ignominy.

The jury's rider concluded with a recommendation: "We consider that every boat coming into the harbour should have a lookout on the stern to give clearance to the pilot, and that boats going alongside in bad weather should always have a boat rope down to them from the ship to prevent their drifting astern."

* * * * * * * *

James Horgan, it seemed to all of us who recognised him, surrendered himself to private anguish and loneliness.

In the cold dark days of low and sodden skies, I sometimes came across him kneeling by himself in a gloomy shadowed part of the cathedral, head in hands, hunched over, withdrawn, locked into a shell of despairing prayer.

I wanted to go over and touch him, or just kneel beside him. But I never did. I didn't dare.

* * * * * * * *

That was my first sad Christmas. Santa Claus (or Santy as we called him) was pushed into the background and became, in some curious way, an embarrassment even to think about. How could you concentrate on sleighs and reindeer and rooftop arrivals by a big round man dressed in red, with a black belt around his middle, and a white beard as big as a spade on his face, and rosy cheeks, and a sack of toys – how could you think of things like that with a sense of expectation when, at the same time, you knew there were at least five houses in the town where Christmas would be a time for remembering and crying, sorrow and tears?

In the cathedral that Christmas, "O, Holy Night" and "Hark! The Herald Angels Sing" and "Adeste" and "Silent Night" were given an added poignancy by the purity and innocence of Jack Kelly's boy soprano voice. ("A boy soprano's is the most perfect of all human voices," my father used to say.) Whether sitting or kneeling in the church during mass, or joining in the Christmas hymns, I found my thoughts continually straying away from the crib and all that it represented, to ships' slashing propellers and panic, and

86

furious winds, and rain coming viciously out of the darkness, and the terrible helplessness of the bereaved, and silent Christmas-morning kitchens, and very quiet mothers, and puzzled children whose fathers would not spend this or any other Christmases with them.

I wondered what kind of Christmas this would be for James Horgan, what he'd pray about, how he'd say it, who he'd pray to? I wondered what kind of pictures he'd have in his mind.

My mother called us all together in the kitchen after mass on Christmas morning and said, "Now I want you all to be very good today when Mrs Duggan comes in. No rowdiness or bickering with each other, do you understand?"

"When is she coming in, Mam?" Norma asked.

"She's having her Christmas dinner with us," my mother said. "I've invited her in. She has no one now, and this will be a very sad Christmas for her without poor Mr Duggan. So I want ye all to be on your best behaviour, and don't stare at her if she cries. Remember that – *no staring at her.*"

My heart dropped at the prospect of having white-faced, tear-stained Mrs Duggan, dressed in black, sitting tragically at our Christmas dinner, on the day that should be the happiest day of the whole year. But in the same moment, I learned something about acts of kindness and of love. My mother truly did have the faculty of imagining as her own the sadness and suffering of others, which was what had prompted her invitation to Mrs Duggan. And my father's gentle solicitude all that awkward afternoon was the perfect complement to my mother's huge compassion.

When the wren boys came to the door on the morning of St Stephen's Day and sang, "The wren, the wren that you must see . . .", I couldn't care less.

And at midnight on New Year's Eve, there was none of the old exciting compulsion to stand outside the front door at midnight and shout "Happy New Year!" to the Batsons and the Bunworths and the Wilsons and anyone else who might emerge to listen to the cathedral bells and ships' sirens and car horns blowing out the old year, and welcoming in the new – because this year there would be no Mr and Mrs Duggan to join in. So, no one in our family, except my mother and my father (who every year did the "first-footing", coming in with a piece of coal and a silver coin, having first "beaten out the hunger" by three times throwing a stale crust against the inside of the door) did anything about the passing of 1942 and the arrival of 1943. And it was done with only half a heart.

The Finding of
Patrick and Francis

FOUR BODIES WERE still missing.

"The sea always gives up its dead," my mother said again two days into the New Year. We were sitting side by side on the settee in my parents' bedroom watching the Harbour Board tug *Owen A Liath* and the Marine Service's ancient (over 50 years old) 103-ton Grimsby iron fishing vessel *Shark,* with the circular lifebelts fixed to the sides of her wheelhouse just below the windows, moving with rattling, clanking slowness around the harbour, sweeping, searching, looking for bodies and looking for the launches.

Four days later, a couple of hours' handline fishing were occupying the thoughts of Walter Cragoe as he went down from Belmont Cottages on to East Hill, and then further down to sea level to meet Michael and Charles Russell in Connolly Street. They decided to go out towards Dog Nose buoy. Apart from the fish, with a war on and ships being sunk, you'd never know what you might be lucky enough to find floating in the tide.

What they found was an overcoated body.

They noticed it in the water not far from where the accident to the pilot launch and the Port Control launch had occurred, and thought at first that it was a large piece of timber floating among the seaweed.

From the uniform, they knew it was an Irish sailor, of able seaman rank. They reckoned it had to be Patrick Wilshaw, though they didn't know for certain. You couldn't tell from the condition of the face, which was submerged.

They'd known Patrick Wilshaw since he was a small boy. The Russells lived just a couple of hundred yards from the Wilshaw home. They'd spoken with and said goodbye to Patrick Wilshaw's father and brother the previous night – the Wilshaws had returned to England only that morning. They were part of the massive exodus of Irish people who had gone to England to do "war work".

When the three fishermen manoeuvred their boat close to the floating body, they noticed that its hands were in positions which indicated that the man, up to the moment he had died, had been trying to divest himself of his heavy overcoat.

Between them, they secured the body, and then started rowing, beginning the long slow tow to the same boat harbour at the eastern end of the town from which the pilot launch had set out on its last journey on the evening of the 12th of December. The spot where he was brought ashore was close to where he had lived with his parents, No. 21, the Mall.

Two Garda sergeants, O'Riordan and Butler, took charge when the men and their gruesome find landed. The body was eventually taken to the morgue at the Cobh General Hospital.

Patrick Wilshaw's sister, Mrs Blower, and his uncle identified the body by the 27-year-old man's cigarette case.

* * * * * * * *

Mrs Lloyd still searched the cambers and went down the steps of the Pier Head to look underneath it. She stared in between the piles of the North German Lloyd Pier, and the piles at Lynch's Quay where the red Harbour Office stood, and the old rotting black pier at the sea end of the Cunard White Star office.

She was seen going down the sea steps out beyond the bandstand on the Promenade, and poking around the Naval Pier and at the slip alongside the Yacht Club. Near the station she found a long stick and pushed aside the seaweed and the rubbish that came in on the flood tide. And if you met her on the Five Foot Way which took you out to Whitepoint, you wouldn't know which way to turn because, wind-bitten and miserable and wild-eyed, God love her, she looked mad.

Up on Plunkett Terrace the Powells tried to cope with what had happened to them, and in Connolly Street Mrs Higgins still had her children to look after no matter how devastated she herself had been by losing John.

* * * * * * * *

While the loss of the five men in the harbour turned the thoughts of the townspeople inwards on their own world and their own agonies, outside in the bigger world the war was raging. It went on remorselessly, cruelly, on land, in the air and at sea. Radio news bulletins and newspapers bristled with reports of U-Boat sinkings, bombing raid casualties, advances and retreats, claims and counter-claims – and statistics relating mainly to death. There was no getting away from death.

In the grim winter evenings, I took to sneaking out and going down the hill to the waterfront and, if it was raining and windy, slipping into the shelter of a shop doorway on East Beach, into a small refuge scooped out of the bleak savagery of the weather. I'd look out towards Spike Island and try to imagine what it must have been like in the water on *that* night, look at the sky and try to see the scud flying by on cold winds, look at the hulking shadows of the ships, mainly rusty old coasters, that passed up and down the river. I'd loiter in a corner, depressed, and not really knowing what depression was.

Winter was *always* grim, only this one was somehow worse: no birdsong; damp tangles of wet dead grass; naked beaten trees; deserted streets; biting winds; ageing crumbling houses streaming with rain; bad daylight dwindling early over the town and harbour; the few red-faced frowzy town drunks staggering out of pubs, getting drenched, surrendering to despair, and stumbling along to the next pub; and the poor of the town embittered by poverty and want.

And there was the sea, always the sea, the endless grey ocean, swishing past the piers, or pounding them.

And specifically, there was Mrs Lloyd ("Wouldn't your heart bleed for her and the little boy?") ceaselessly grieving, endlessly searching, searching, searching for Frank.

Those of us who hadn't lived long enough to know now learned painfully the true implications of words like "mourn" and "bereaved". We heard them often, from parents and teachers and adult neighbours, and from sad-faced priests like Father Egan and Father Coleman.

They talked to us of sorrowing families and consolation; they spoke of loved ones, and the slenderness of the thread that separates life from death. They intoned, countless times, and meant it, "Eternal rest grant unto them, O Lord, and let perpetual light shine upon them. May their souls, and the souls of all the faithful departed, through the mercy of God, rest in peace. Amen."

* * * * * * * *

On Thursday the 7th of January they buried Patrick Wilshaw, the second son of George and Bridget Wilshaw. Like Willie Duggan's, his coffin, too, was draped in the tricolour, and "full honours were accorded".

Patrick Wilshaw's funeral was to St Colman's Cemetery. Otherwise the ingredients were much the same as at Willie's: deeply-felt sorrow, and the tears that go with it; the escort party

92

under Petty Officer Dolan; the detachment of troops; the army and naval officers; the watch commander on the night Patrick died, Chief Petty Officer Barry; the Marine Service Pipe Band and the firing party; the bugler to sound "The Last Post"; the dignitaries – and the townspeople. The cathedral's adminis-trator, Father O'Connor, was assisted by Father Egan.

While Patrick Wilshaw was being buried, the search, by dragging, for the three missing bodies (those of Francis Lloyd, John Higgins and Frank Powell) and for the two sunken launches, continued without success.

* * * * * * *

Nux McCormack and I began going downtown to the Har-bour Office Pier after school, hanging about trying to find out if there had been any new developments regarding the finding of the two launches. The *Owen A Liath*, the pugna-cious little tug owned by the Harbour Commissioners, could often be seen, together with the *Flora*, a motor launch, mov-ing slowly backwards and forwards across Curlane Bank.

"I dunno will they ever find them," Nux said towards the end of the week midway through January. We were standing on Lynch's Quay looking out towards Dog Nose buoy, blow-ing on our hands to get them warm. The red Customs House was behind us.

"Sure they were probably cut to shreds by the *Poplar*'s pro-peller, and the pieces would have been swept out to sea by the tide," Nux said. "If the pieces ended up in Bantry Bay, or on the coast of France, or anywhere, nobody would know where they came from, there's so much wreckage about already with so many ships being sunk."

"Do you mean the bodies?" I asked.

"No, you eejit! – the *launches*." Pretending to be peevish was part of his act. "The bodies'll come ashore all right," he said. "The sea always gives up its dead."

"Well, it's taking a long time to give up Mr Lloyd and Mr Higgins and Frank Powell," I said.

He didn't answer that. We stood silently looking out towards the harbour mouth. Nothing was said for a minute or two. Then Nux turned and began walking away, saying, "I'm going along to Englishs' to see if Terry is there. They might have heard something in the shop. Are you coming?"

I followed him along past Casey's toy shop and Radley's pub, where old Bill Buckley's broken-down mongrel was curled up outside waiting for Bill to come out roaring drunk the way he did at the end of every week after collecting, and spending, most of his World War I Royal Navy pension.

I stood outside English's butcher shop while Nux went in to ask if Terry was there. He wasn't, but someone told Nux that the *Owen A Liath* had been out on Curlane Bank all morning with Pilot Lynch and the pilot master, Captain Murray (who was also the deputy harbour master), aboard. There was a diver with them in case the grapnels caught anything. The idea was that, if that happened they could send the diver down to investigate.

"And did they find anything?" I asked.

"Will you hold *on*?" Nux said exasperatedly. "I'm *tellin'* yeh! Pilot Lynch was there to guide them as close as possible to the exact place where the accident happened. Anyway, after a few hours today they found *something*, but the tide was too strong for the diver to go down."

"So what are they going to do now?" I asked.

"Janey, boy, you're so fekkin *impatient*!" Nux said.

"You shouldn't use that word."

"What word? 'Impatient'?"

"No, the soldier's word – the 'f' word."

"I *didn't* use the 'f' word." I said '*fekkin*'."

"Well, anyway, what are they going to do now?"

"They've marked the place with a red flag," Nux said, pouting. Then, "If you're so bloomin' smart, why didn't *you* go into the shop to find out? See? You were afraid – I had to do your dirty work for you."

He walked away and crossed over the road towards the

CYMS hall. I knew where he was going to then – to his father's office. Nux's father was manager of the local labour exchange. He was a small, square forceful man with a loud voice and a passion for swimming. I didn't bother following Nux. I went up East Beach past Pakie Neill's sweet shop and along Harbour Row and up the Preaching House steps to Harbour View, then up to the corner, where I turned right, past Balbirnies' and up the hill to home, all the time wondering what the grapnels had snagged on out on Curlane Bank.

Inside the house I searched until I found the *Examiner*. That thing that Nux had said about the tide being too strong for the diver to go down intrigued me. I looked up the tide tables. High tide at Cobh that day was due at 2.48 in the afternoon. They must have snagged the underwater "thing" during the strongest part of the flood. I supposed they'd go back to the marker flag around slack water some day soon.

But before they had a chance to, the sea gave up another of its dead. The body of Petty Officer Francis Lloyd was found face down on the strand at Whitepoint on Sunday morning, 17th January. It was near the high water mark. As with Willie Duggan and Patrick Wilshaw, the body of Francis Lloyd, too, was wearing its heavy naval greatcoat.

No one would ever know how far Francis' body had travelled, but the sand still clinging to the clothing gave rise to the theory that when Francis went into the water on the night the two launches went to the bottom, he, too, must have gone straight down, and been held there on the sandbank by the clutching kelp. The way the theory ran, it was the drags carried out by the *Owen A Liath* on the Friday that probably released Francis' body.

The Petty Officer's insignia on the uniform was what clinched it in convincing Gardaí that it *was* Francis Lloyd's body they were looking at because you'd never have been able to make an identification just from looking at what used to be his face. That was what confronted Sergeant Butler and

Garda John ("Skater") Cahill when they arrived at White-point in mid-morning from the Garda Barracks at West-bourne Place, having learned at around 10 o'clock from Michael Mulcahy of Lower Midleton Street that there was a body on the strand. Dr Hegarty had the hideous job of exam-ining it. When the clothing was searched, they found a pipe, a spectacles case and a key. The pipe and spectacles case were Francis Lloyd's. The key was identified by Chief Petty Officer Tom Alsop as also being Francis Lloyd's – it was a key to the Port Control Pier.

Chief Petty Officer Barry, who had been on the launch with Petty Officer Lloyd on the fateful night, made a positive identification at Cobh General Hospital.

Mrs Lloyd's long search for her Frank was over. She wouldn't have to poke around among the refuse in the cam-ber any more.

* * * * * * * *

The venerable old MPV (for Mine Planting Vessel) *Shark* was selected to take the coffin bearing the body of Francis up the river from Cobh to his native Cork city for burial, and she clanked and rattled her way upriver at eight knots until they reached the Customs House Quay where the sad cargo was unloaded.

A modest man in life, Francis Lloyd would never have expected that the lord mayor of Cork would attend his funer-al. But Alderman R.S. Anthony did go to St Finbarr's Ceme-tery, together with the by-now usual contingent of Defence Forces representatives, Cork Harbour Commissioners repre-sentatives, civic and political dignitaries, neighbours and friends, and others who wanted to pay their last respects. The pipe band attended, and the firing party, and the lone bugler.

And, of course, the next of kin, including the Lloyds' small son, not yet three years of age.

There were still two bodies missing – those of John Higgins

and Frank Powell, each of whom had been motorman on the launch on which he died.

* * * * * * * *

On Monday the 25th of January, the Port Control launch was raised from the seabed where she had been lying in 35 feet of water. The two vessels involved in her recovery were the hopper *Owen A Curra*, and the tug *Owen A Liath*. Once they had the launch on the surface, she was secured so that she wouldn't sink again.

They made a slow careful journey in the western channel to the Spit light, where they turned westwards, and then up past the town. Finally, with even greater care, they turned into the basin at Haulbowline and they tied up in the north east corner, close to the 10-ton crane.

There the launch was lifted out of the water. A few feet away from the bow of the launch on the starboard side were three telltale cuts. They were clean cuts, each a couple of inches wide and about 14 inches apart, and they extended from the boat's keel right up to the bulwarks. The *Poplar*'s propeller had gone through the wood of the boat like a warm knife through butter.

There was no sign of Frank Powell or John Higgins.

Now, apart from the two bodies, all that remained to be found and raised was the pilot launch.

* * * * * * * *

When they eventually found the *Carraig An Cuain*, she had been lying at the bottom of the harbour for 66 days. One side of her, the port side, was intact. The starboard side was completely wrecked, everything from the keelson and stringers to the planks and timbers, even the two supports for the cabin deck-house. The seating accommodation was destroyed and the steering gear partly wrecked. She was full of mud.

They lifted her very gingerly and suspended her from the crane of the hopper *Owen A Curra*, and brought her to Haulbowline. The Harbour Board, careful about such items of expense, calculated that the cost of salvaging the two launches came to £813.

The memories of the harbour tragedy were revived by the publishing of the details about the condition of the pilot launch, the deaths given a new lease of life. The everyday happenings in the town had, for a while, swamped consciousness of the 12th of December affair. Not that people deliberately disengaged themselves from the happening itself or from the sorrow it had brought, but life goes inexorably on, and when you are thrust into a valley of darkness, you learn that you cannot live the whole of your life at the bottom of that particular chasm.

Therefore when some members of the defence forces ran riot in the Soldiers' Home and Sailors' Rest, and wrenched washbasins off the wall and caused a lot of damage, and were prosecuted and appeared in court and were found guilty, people talked about that and said wasn't it a disgrace.

And when Staf Gebruers composed a special anthem for the town's "Step Together Week", some people said wasn't he marvellous, and others said that yerra it was OK, but they wouldn't smother their mother for it. One woman was heard to say, outside Hanlon's on The Beach, "What sickens me is that it's always the bleddy foreigners who get everything in this damned country."

My mother was coming back up Bellevue after a visit to Mother Sullivan when Mrs Bunworth, the postmaster's wife, opened her front door and came out on to the top step and said, "Hello, missus, isn't it dreadful weather?"

"It would get you down," my mother said. "Trying to get the childrens' clothes dry has my heart scalded."

"Have you seen Mrs Duggan at all?" Mrs Bunworth asked.

"She doesn't go outside the door," my mother said.

"She must be desperate," Mrs Bunworth said. "That was a terrible business altogether out there." She gestured with her head and eyes towards the harbour mouth. "It'll leave its mark on this town. The town will never forget it. It won't be able to. It'll be thought about and spoken about every day, for *ever*, I'd say. Five men to lose their lives like that. Desperate. . . Desperate . . . I don't know will the place ever get back to normal again."

Thomas Thurlby, 40 and from Bishop Street, never had a chance to find out, because his head was split open.

He was down in the Holy Ground, in Connolly Street, working as a labourer for the Town Council, demolishing a derelict house. A large stone fell from the top of the front wall and smashed his skull, tearing it open so that his blood poured out and seeped into the dusty debris where he collapsed on the ground.

A doctor was called, and when he looked at the condition of Thomas Thurlby's broken head, he knew straight away that it was touch and go as to whether Thomas would live. The comatose man was taken to the hospital as soon as possible where he was pronounced "unconscious and in serious danger".

"Is there a bleddy curse on the Holy Ground, or what?" Danny Dinan said when he came with the milk the following morning.

"I wonder will your man die?" I said to Nux McCormack halfway through a game of handball in the shed at the bottom of the playground after school.

"Who?" he said, practising dead butts, which was hitting the ball to just about an inch above where the wall met the ground, so that the ball came back straight along the floor, giving you no chance at all.

"The man who was injured down the Holy Ground," I said.

He hopped the ball the way you do for a serve, then whipped his cupped right palm at it so that it arrowed straight and hard for the bottom of the wall, came back without as much as a quarter of an inch bounce – perfect.

"What man in the Holy Ground?" he asked.

"The one from just along the road from the gate, from

Bishop Street," I said. "The one who was hit by the stone."

"Jakers, do you know what it is, boy, you're a terrible fekker for talking in riddles!"

"There, you've said it again," I said, inserting a note of accusation into my voice.

"I did *not* use the soldier's word, and you better not say that I did!"

Nux came straight at me, pushing me with his chest, his hands back.

"I said 'fekker'."

"Same thing," I said.

"Ah, shove off, will you! Now, are you going to tell me or not – *what* man was hit by a stone in the Holy Ground, and who threw it?"

"No one threw it," I said. "It fell."

"From where? The sky?"

"No, Mr Smarty, from a *wall*. He was knocking down a house for the Council and the stone fell on top of him from high up and burst his head open – *that's* the man I mean."

Nux looked shocked then. He sulked for a moment, stuck out his bottom lip, put the sole of his boot on the black hairless old tennis ball and rolled it backwards and forwards a few times.

"Cripes, that's terrible," he said. "I didn't know about it. I hope he doesn't die."

But Thomas Thurlby did die, the following day. The inquest found that death was due to laceration of the brain and haemorrhage. They didn't wear protective hats then.

Things like that pushed the townspeople's awareness of and sensitivity to the raw hurt caused by the harbour disaster slowly into the background. By the time the dark January days were coming to an end, I even began to wonder whether my memory of the weather on the night of the disaster was accurate. "Memory is unfaithful," I had heard my father say one Sunday morning in an argument with Ben Nagle about the Cobh Choral Union. Well, was *mine* unfaithful as far as

100

the 12th of December was concerned? Had an unfaithful memory exaggerated and distorted facts?

I got my answer when the crew of the Ballycotton lifeboat had awards of £45 made to them "for searching in Cork Harbour in a strong gale with a very heavy sea for the crews of the pilot launch and Port Control launch which foundered in December".

No, it had been a bitch of a night right enough, one on which we had been reminded of the savagery and remorselessness of the sea.

A Sunday Kind of Love

SUNDAY WAS THE quietest day in the week. And why wouldn't it be? Didn't all the shops, apart from the sweet shops, the newsagents and the tobacconists, stay closed from Saturday evening until Monday morning, together with most of the other places of work, and even the schools?

At the front door early one Monday morning I heard my mother saying to the relief milkman that she couldn't see why the tobacconists should open at all on a Sunday. After all, it was the Lord's Day, and didn't he remember the third commandment?

"Ah, look missus, I gev up religious exams when I got me confer and left school. I couldn't even tell yeh the *first* commandment, let alone the third. So, if you don't mind, an' beggin' yer pardon, we won't talk about the bleddy commandments now. Aw-*right?* Let's give it a rest like."

"*Oh!*" my mother said, shocked, making the sign of the cross and trying to push me away from the door and in the hall. "That's an *awful* word to use about the commandments of God!"

"Well, I'm sorry, missus, but –"

But my mother wasn't in any mood to listen to his buts.

"That's enough of that!" she said. "You're a brazen caffler to talk to me that way! You're a *heathen*, that's what you are –"

"Oh, *Jesus* –"

"If *your* mother –"

"Oh, for Christ's sake, missus, leave her outa this! She'd crucify me if she heard that I'd been –"

"Well, I have a damn good mind to go down to her right now! But I *won't*. I don't like sneaks" (I wondered where that left Sister Fidelis) "going behind other people's backs and making complaints. But you can count yourself lucky! Don't you *ever* again refer to the commandments as 'bleddy commandments' in my hearing. Is that clear?"

I almost shouted, "*Yes*, Mr O'Sullivan!" But I caught it just in time.

The milkman concentrated on appearing mollified, and was largely successful, though relief had a lot to do with his expression. His mother, a low-sized, all-in-black, white-faced widow with a severe, Sicilian, matriarchal look, was another elderly person of a female persuasion known to rule her son with a tyrant's severity. He was terrified of upsetting her.

"And incidentally," my mother went on, "the third commandment, for your information, is, 'Remember that thou keep holy the Sabbath day.' *That's* why I don't see any reason for the tobacconists to open on a Sunday. And apart from that, they're only catering for a dirty, filthy habit."

I'd never heard Mam using those words to Dad who, after my mother, God, and the family, loved Woodbines more than anything else in the world.

I could see the unfortunate man at the door struggling, trying to decide whether or not to answer my mother's tobacco attack. Eventually, with a last drag on his cigarette end, he took another deep breath and said, "Ah, be reasonable now, Mrs Nolan! I mean a man *hasta* have his oul smoke. And as far as I can remember, with *all* the 'Thou shalt nots' in the commandments, nowhere does it say 'Thou shalt not smoke!' Am I right or am I wrong?"

My mother folded her arms across her bosom and stared at him in disbelief.

"Are you deliberately mocking the Ten Commandments?" she asked icily.

"I'm not, missus, I'm not, ah, Jazus I'm not! I'm deadly serious. I mean the oul com . . . the commandments say, 'Thou shalt not *steal* . . . Thou shalt not *bear false witness against thy neighbour.*'"

"I thought you said you didn't *know* the commandments?"

"In a manner of speakin', yeh, that's true. But 'Thou shalt not *kill*' is there, and 'Thou shalt not *commit adultery*' – chance'd be a fine thing! – and 'Thou shalt not *covet thy neighbour's wife –*'"

"Mam! Mam!"

My mother whirled around.

"Are you still there?"

"Mam, what's 'adultery', and what does 'covet thy neighbour's wife' mean?"

The push nearly dislocated my shoulder.

"Get in there and get ready for school! You *shouldn't* be listening when adults are talking."

As she slammed the glass door shut behind me, she turned back to the milkman, and I just caught her saying, "See what you've started now!"

But the way you spent Sunday *was* different from any other day in the week. We knew it was the one day when we had to dress up in our best clothes and were expected to stay neat and clean and tidy all through the day.

My mother, like most mothers, went to the first mass in the cathedral. Getting out of bed in a cold house at half past six on a dark, maybe wet, winter's morning must have been penitential. Not that the kind of mothers we had should ever have had to do penance. That was Mrs Carty's view anyway.

"Look, any woman who raises a family is a saint," Mrs Carty said. "The priest, Father Coleman, told me that in confession."

So at about twenty minutes past seven on Sunday mornings, these "saints" could be seen hurrying along the deserted streets, black coats drawn tight around them, their Sunday hats getting their weekly airing or drenching, prayer books and rosary beads bulging the pockets out of shape, and down inside their woollen gloves, the clenched sixpences to put on the collection plate as they went into the church. They all, to a woman, disliked the men who stationed themselves behind the green-topped tables at the church door.

"I can't stomach the way that fella stands there every Sunday, eyes like a hawk on him, watching and noting what everyone puts into the plate. It's all wrong."

It seemed to me as a child that the obligation to hand over money at the door was like being *charged* to get in – the way *we* had to pay our fourpences (ninepences if we were flush) to get in to see Johnny Mac Brown or Gene Autry or James Cagney or Edward G. or the Bowery Boys, or Pat O'Brien or Abbot and Costello or the Three Stooges, or the Dead End Kids, at Frennet's picture house, or Paton's. And for God's sake, whoever heard of an admission price for *mass*? I didn't say that out loud, mind. I didn't want to end up with my ear in a sling.

But on the few occasions I went with Mam to first mass, I could see the beady, reptilian eyes of Mr Righteous (whoever he happened to be) watching the release of every coin from every hand that moved towards the plate, and carefully noting, too, I'd swear, those who walked in and ignored the plate completely.

Most of the early-mass-mothers would have spent an hour or so in the church on the previous evening going to confession, following that by completing a crowded schedule which entailed bathing the younger children, going down town to do the shopping, paying the bills, dashing home again to iron the clothes, darn the socks, soak the peas and fall into bed exhausted around midnight. Father John Coleman had got it right when he made his saints comment to Mrs Carty.

Some of the mothers took the small liberty of leaving the church at the last gospel, to rush home in time to get the rest of the family up and ready for mass, and maybe have a little gossip with another woman on the way, a woman they mightn't otherwise see from one end of the week to the next.

Into the house then, and coat off, scarf off, hat off, and up the stairs to the bedrooms.

"Come on now, up and out of bed! Ye have three quarters of an hour to get ready, and I *won't* call ye again!"

Five minutes later, "Aren't you up out of bed yet? Ah, for goodness sake get out of it and come down here – ye'll be dead late for mass!"

That would usually prompt an, "Awright, I'll be down now."

But Sunday after Sunday Mam's patience was tried beyond endurance so that finally she would have to drag her weary feet up the stairs again to the top of the house, where she would haul the clothes off the beds and say angrily, "Ye make me so *cross*! For the love and honour of God get up! *Now* look at the way ye have me, and me just back from the altar. Every other child on the terrace is dressed ready to go, and ye still lying there! I don't know where ye got yeer dirty lazy habits from, honest to God I don't."

Find their socks, wash their faces, brush and comb their hair, straighten their bows (the girls), tuck their shirts in properly (the boys), locate their prayer books – it was helter-skelter punctuated by pushings and shovings and pinchings, and all the time my mother imploring the Holy Family to get this lot out of the house before the mass bell stopped ringing in the cathedral.

This 9am mass was the children's mass, and everyone who was still attending school was expected to be at it – no excuses. The boys sat on the left-hand side of the main aisle, the girls across on the other side. The youngest sat up the front, and the older you were, the further back from the altar rails you sat.

106

The two girls schools were run by the nuns, the Sisters of Mercy, whose convent was across the road from the bishop's palace ("Why does the bishop have a *palace*, Mam?" "Because he's a *prince* of the church.") didn't have any lay teachers. Two or three nuns were rostered each week for children's mass duty. Their job was to control and cut out any giggling that might go on among the girls, and to lead them, and indeed all of us, in the hymns. So when Staf on the organ, straining to make his short legs stretch to reach the foot pedals, came to the end of his brief musical introduction to each hymn, it would be Sister Eucharia's or Sister Agnes' or Sister Paul's clear tuneful voice you'd hear first:

I'll sing a hymn to Mary,
the mother of my God . . .

or

Faith of our fathers, living still,
in spite of dungeon, fire and sword . . .

or

To Jesus' heart all burning
with fervent love for men . . .

or

Hail, Queen of heav'n, the ocean star,
guide of the wand'rer here below . . .

The first and last of that quartet were the most frequently sung, and it always seemed to me that the nuns sang the first one with great commitment. After all, weren't they *women* singing *to* a woman? And even though I didn't yet know what to be a virgin meant (or didn't mean), and had no intention of asking, I *did* know that nuns *had* to be virgins to be nuns. So they were singing to one of their own, weren't they, even if *they* weren't "of David's Royal Blood"?

And further, didn't each one of them have Mary as her first

107

name in religion – Sister Mary Eucharia, Sister Mary Gerard and so on right through the order? Sure 'twas no wonder their scrubbed faces, looking to a window above the high altar, were shining and their eyes transfixed with piety and longing and spotless holiness during "I'll Sing a Hymn to Mary".

When they finished that hymn, it was as if they had to come back down to earth again, back down to a Sunday morning in Cobh. And charming though Cobh could be, "Watching the wild waves' motion/Leaning her back up against the hills/And the tips of her toes in the ocean", it was still only Cobh, County Cork, and surely not a patch on heaven, or wherever the hell they'd been until they got to the end of the hymn's last lines: ". . . when wicked men blaspheme thee/I'll love and bless thy name."

All right, so it was back down to God's house they came, but it was still just a harbour town, with "Cuckoo" across there in the men's aisle, saying his private prayers out loud and finishing all the unison prayers well behind or very far in front of everyone else, and "Beds" over in the women's aisle, flirting outrageously with her eyes and sowing the seeds of her next mortal sin.

Whatever the truth of it, the nuns' chorus ended with them once again resuming their weekday looks.

The nuns wore long-to-the-floor black habits which divested them of human shape and personality. Their faces were enclosed by the hard sharp edges of their wimples, their rosary beads hung down from their broad leather belts, and they conversed in hushed whispers with their fingers clasped before them – except when in the classroom. There, for instance, flinty-faced Sister Agnes spoke in a hard, loud, high-pitched voice that could scare you enough to pee in your pants. But of course we were only 5 when we were in her Junior Infants class in the girls' school. The Presentation Brothers didn't teach infants. When we got a bit older, reached 7 or 8, and were out of Sister Agnes's jurisdiction, the most her whiplash voice could have made us do was cower and cringe, or maybe run away. The ageing process gave us strengths, developed our character and helped us control our sphincter muscles.

Sister Eucharia was something else, and at ten going on eleven I was in love with her and Deanna Durbin. For several years I was convinced she *was* Deanna Durbin, with the lovely smile, the white, white teeth, and the glistening eyes (Sister Eucharia had them all), Deanna Durbin with her shoulder-length shining hair and her glorious voice as she looked upwards and sang "The Lights of Home". I never saw Sister Eucharia's hair, but I knew that underneath that ridiculous enveloping white wimple, her hair *had* to be long and brown and shiny. And though I never heard her singing "The Lights of Home", I saw the same upward look and heard the same glorious voice, except that she sang "I'll Sing a Hymn to Mary" – sang it, though, in exactly the same way that I knew Deanna Durbin would sing it.

I couldn't understand how someone as beautiful as Sister Eucharia/Deanna Durbin could have gone into a convent and become a nun. And I didn't believe she would always remain one. When I got over my Deanna Durbin conviction, I replaced it with another: Eucharia would be "discovered" by a famous Hollywood producer and become a film star.

Along with so many other predictions throughout my life, it turned out to be totally wrong. As I write these lines, she is still alive and living in Cobh in the convent. Needless to say, she remained a nun and kept her name – she is still Sister Mary Eucharia.

* * * * * * * *

I can't remember my mother ever spending less than three hours cooking the Sunday dinner, and there has never been anyone whose meals have tasted as good as hers. I can still summon up the odours of her roast beef and Yorkshire pudding, and if I work on it I can get the distinctive taste of her gravy, poured in generous measure over those golden roast potatoes, done to perfection, as was her mashed mixture of carrots and parsnips. Her sherry trifle was almost sinful. And only once since those days have I tasted a butter icing coffee sandwich to come even close to Mam's.

And Dad never once failed to say thanks. "That was a marvellous meal, Mam, my old Moll-Doosh!" he'd say, and put his arm around her shoulder, and give her a squeeze and the most affectionate of kisses. It was all of a piece with that man, whether it was dressing up as Santy Claus or the Gulpin or Timber-Toes for us, and for all the other children on the terrace, at Christmas, or saving shillings for months on end from his meagre wages to buy surprise presents for Mam – just to see the expression on her face. Even as a child, I knew with certainty that one of the things most dear to him in life was the joy he got from giving.

He liked to be appreciated, but I don't think he craved it. And he never could hide (not that he'd want to) the appreciation he felt for things done for him. Saying thanks was a big thing for him, something he tried his mightiest, by example, and just the rare few words, to inculcate into all of us.

I sometimes wonder even now if he knew how much I personally appreciated him, what he was and what he did, and if he ever knew that, from the time I began to think of such things, I wanted to be like him when I grew up, wanted to be for my own family what he was to us and Mam. Of course I never succeeded. But I tried. And when I go to visit the grave where he and Uncle Willie are buried in Deansgrange cemetery in Dublin, before I leave I always put my hand on top of the low stepped stone, think of it as his shoulder, pat it, and say, "Love you, Dad. I'll be back again soon . . ."

The dinner over on a Sunday, and after drinking a cup of tea from the best bone china set, which was kept for Sundays and other formal occasions, Mam would have her first sit down of the day in one of the easy chairs in the drawing room. Ten minutes reading the paper and her head would begin to droop, and then drop forward, her chin coming down to rest on the top of her chest. That was a signal for all of us to leave the room as quietly as shadows so as not to disturb her.

"Your Mammy is a great woman," my father said to me on one of those Sundays. "Fancy a walk?" I was at the front door waiting for him when he came out smoking a Woodbine, the dog, Smut (because he was black), bouncing happily at his heels.

I loved those Sunday afternoon walks because it was then I learned about my dad's growing-up years in Dublin. He turned the Sunday afternoons into magical hours for me.

That day we went up to the top of Bellevue and turned left in through the gates of Tarrant's Avenue, and then up what struck me as being like a rough-floored, sloping church aisle. It was the way the tops of the trees, which grew out of steep banks on each side of the pathway, met high up to form an extended arch that gave that impression.

We went out the back road, Dad talking all the way, me endlessly asking questions, he answering patiently and fully and colourfully. Only five foot four and a half inches tall, he'd once said to me, "Your Uncle Willie says that I'm a 'typical Dublin jackeen'. It's not a term that I like, no more than I like certain other vulgar Dublinisms like 'gurrier' and 'bowzie', but Uncle Willie uses it to take a rise out of me."

"And what height is he?"

"Exactly the same, to within an eight of an inch!"

Dad was born in the Rotunda on the 1st of June 1901.

"Dublin, indeed Ireland, used to be very proud of that," he said, and took a drag on his cigarette. He left a pause of a few seconds, and of course the silence invited a question.

"Proud that you were born there?" I asked.

He knew what I was up to, and gave me an old-fashioned look through eyes that were twinkling.

"No!" he said. "Proud of the Rotunda, because it was the first maternity hospital in what they incorrectly call the

111

British Isles – Ireland, England, Scotland and Wales. The Rotunda goes back to midway through the 1700s."

He was baptised at the pro-cathedral, a fact which inevitably prompted another question.

"What's a *pro*-cathedral, Dad?"

"Let's see now . . . what do you think the word 'pro' means, eh? Well, I don't suppose you'd know yet; you won't be doing Latin until you go to the college. It means for, in place of, or a substitute for. You see, Dublin's two Catholic cathedrals, St Patrick's and Christ Church, were taken over by the Protestants after the Reformation" (What, I wondered, was *that*? But I'd wait until another time to find out) "and the city never got around to building its own Catholic cathedral in its place. Do you follow me?"

I said I did.

"Right. They decided they'd build a good impressive church, anyway, to take the place of the two cathedrals. At one stage they were thinking of putting it in O'Connell Street, but they were afraid of the official opposition that'd whip up. That was before Catholic Emancipation. The spot they were thinking of was later used for a building to a different god entirely – the god of commerce. They built the GPO there. I think, meself, they should have stuck to their guns. But, they didn't. They settled for a much less impressive site, away at the back of O'Connell Street. Are you still with me?"

"I am."

"Good man. Well, that's where I was baptised, in the pro-cathedral."

"And is it . . ." I couldn't think of the word I wanted.

"Is it what, son? Impressive? Grand? Is that what you were going to ask?"

"Yes."

"Aw, it's a lovely building, *very* impressive. In a different way from St Colman's Cathedral here in town, you understand. You have to stand back from it to appreciate it, and there's not a whole lot of room to do that. Not the way you can stand on one side of O'Connell Street and look over and see the GPO on the other side. But it is, it's a lovely impressive building with sort of a Greek temple look to the outside of it, and pillars, Doric columns, all up the full length of the church on the inside, on each side, from the main door up to and around the high altar, which is made out of marble. Massive. Ah, you'd be proud of it right enough. But we still haven't got a full Catholic cathedral in the capital city, and that's a fright to God. And maybe something the hierarchy should be ashamed of."

We made our first stop at the bottom of Cuskinny Hill where the road flattens out after a humpy-backed bridge over the water flowing out of the marsh.

Smut took off like a hound out of hell, chasing through the reedy grass, stopping to sniff and bark and chase imaginary rats and making little buck-leaps into the air at the sheer joy of being free in a wilderness. At one stage he misjudged his footing and was suddenly up to his belly in water. But he was a consummate actor and pretended it was all intentional, and hit off across the channel in a frantic dog's paddle. On the opposite shore he scrambled out, ran on three or four paces, stopped and shook himself ecstatically, sending showers of droplets off his body at every conceivable angle. Then off with him again, darting in ever-changing directions.

After watching him for a few minutes, we both turned and crossed over to the sea wall. The stony strand ran away from us to the water's edge, and we stood there for a while looking straight out the harbour.

"Used you go on walks with your dad?" I asked my father.

"No," he said. "I hardly got the chance. He died too young, when I was too young . . . Isn't that a great view altogether, a beautiful view?"

I thought he had changed the subject so abruptly because it was too painful or emotionally upsetting for him, and I was sorry I had asked the question.

"It's lovely," I said.

"O'Connell's heart must long for it."

I was lost, hadn't a clue what he was on about now.

"What do you mean?"

"Daniel O'Connell, the Liberator. You've heard of Catholic Emancipation, haven't you?"

I'd heard about it, but not much, and I'd heard of Daniel O'Connell, too, and his fight on behalf of the impoverished Irish Catholics. Sully – Mr O'Sullivan – was a big admirer of O'Connell and told us that some day he'd tell us the whole story.

"Amazing character, O'Connell was," my father said. "First Catholic to take a seat in the British House of Parliament. Great speaker, great orator. We hear about Adolf Hitler's ability to whip up frenzies during his speeches to huge crowds. I don't think Adolf could hold a candle to Daniel O'Connell. And do you know why I say that? Go on, try. Have a guess."

"Well, I don't know *how* you could say that, Dad."

"Say what?"

"That Hitler couldn't hold a candle to Daniel O'Connell. I mean, Hitler is now, he's still alive, Daniel O'Connell is dead for ages, isn't he?"

"True. He died nearly a hundred years ago."

"So how can you compare someone who's alive with someone who's dead and lived in a different century?"

"Good point. You're *thinking*, Bill!"

He had a way of pursing his lips when arranging his thoughts. He did it now.

"You can do it if you have criteria to work on, some elements in each that you can measure against each other. You see, Mr Schicklgruber – Hitler's real name, by the way – has had the use of microphones and loudspeakers. Daniel O'Connell had only the strength of his own voice. And yet, this amazing man spoke to crowds of *400,000*" (he spoke the figure slowly and with great emphasis) "in Lismore and Mallow, and a crowd as big as maybe a *million* at Tara! It was said

114

he had them in the palm of his hand. He was what they call nowadays a mob orator – and that's what Hitler came to power on, his ability to sway the mobs who were mobilised to attend his rallies. Janey, can you imagine what it would've been like for Daniel if he'd had a Mickey Glavin around with his microphones and tannoys?"

The vision of bustling little Mickey in his grey stained suit and his cigarettes which he chain-smoked from lighting to the time he spat out the soggy ends, without ever once having removed the fags during their smoking lives, making his short-legged hurrying way around Daniel O'Connell, caused me to sputter with laughter. My father just smiled and licked his lower lip, removing a scrap of tobacco from the self-same Woodbine brand that Mickey smoked.

"Now, what made me say Daniel's heart must long for that?" and he nodded towards the panorama that lay before us. This time he didn't wait for me to admit that I didn't know. "Well, O'Connell would have seen that view many times on his way back from London after a visit to the parliament. The town'd have been much smaller then, and there was no cathedral. But it wasn't so much the town that would have lifted his heart, though he went to school here. No, it was the fact that it was beautiful Ireland he was coming home to. He loved Ireland. Loved Kerry. But he died in Italy, and though his *body* is buried in Glasnevin cemetery in Dublin, his *heart* is buried in Rome. And I'm sentimental enough to think that at times it must long to see that view once more. There you have had it. And I don't expect you to think I'm right.

"Different perspective altogether from the one we get up in Bellvue Terrace, isn't it. Spike seems much further away when you're down here. And the expanse of water looks much larger . . . Has Mr O'Sullivan talked to ye yet about perspective?"

"No, not yet."

"I'm sure he will. He'll probably tell you something that

115

Samuel Johnson said: 'Distance has the same effect on the mind as on the eye.' Will you remember that?"

I said I'd try. I didn't know who Samuel Johnson was, but I repeated silently a few times what my father told me he had said, and hoped I wouldn't forget it.

"You like being in his class, don't you?"

"Sully's? Yeah, he's great."

"His name is Mr *O'Sullivan* – not 'Sully'. Give him his full name. People are entitled to their names, and you should always respect that."

I took a deep breath before I said, "But what about me? My full name is William Joseph, but Mam and you and everyone else calls me Billy, or Bill."

He laughed and pulled me close.

"That's different, son. 'Billy' is an affectionate shortening of your first name – the same as 'Eddie' is with *my* name, Edward Joseph. No, what I'm talking about is the use of *nicknames*. Sure, this town is a holy terror for nicknames, much more so than Dublin is. In fact I bet *you* could mention more Cobh nicknames, and *it* a town of only about 5,000 people, than I could rattle off nicknames from the country's *capital*. Would you believe that?"

I couldn't disbelieve it, but it surprised me.

"Tell you what," he said, "see how many you can remember. Just say them as they come to you."

That was easy, except that in some cases I didn't know the person's real name, because it was never mentioned.

" 'Sharky' Griffin . . . 'Shoot the Moon' . . . 'Dunks' and 'Gobik' Hegarty . . . 'Shiner' Martin . . . 'Awright-upta-de-house' . . . 'Gummer' Flynn . . . 'Brodduck' Walsh."

I paused for a breath, and noticed that Dad had turned away.

"Go on," he said, "any more?"

I thought his voice sounded slightly strangled.

" 'Crab' and 'Harmer' Walsh . . . 'Henry Yot' . . . 'Suds' Sullivan . . . 'Chops' Donovan . . . 'Stinger' Nash . . . 'Flower'

116

Devlin . . . 'Galloper' Hogan . . . 'Skim-the-Ditch'."

Dad, his back fully to me now, was waving his hand. I thought his shoulders were shaking. I kept on talking.

" 'Dirty Bitch' . . . 'Simon Diddle' . . . 'Goggsy' Mayer . . . 'Gorgeous' O'Neill . . . 'Sabu' Moynihan . . . 'Rosie Apples' . . . 'Miss Tut-Tut' . . . 'Trotsky' . . . 'German Sausage' . . . 'Moll Doll' . . . 'Houdini' . . . 'Vesty' Nicholson . . . 'Flop' O'Neill . . . 'Infant of Prague' . . . 'Moll the Hopper' . . ."

"Stop! Stop! *Enough*!" my father said, turning back to face in my general direction, but, I'm certain, unable to see me because his face was scarlet, and there were tears of laughter pouring from his eyes. "My God Almighty!"

He took a fit of coughing then, and ended up wiping his eyes and blowing his nose.

"Oh, my *God*!" he said.

That was a vintage Sunday. I was learning more about my father all the time. Some of the things he mentioned went over my head when he first said them, but whenever I asked him to explain or describe, he did it without hesitation and without impatience.

I hadn't a clue what the Forty Foot was, or the Bull Wall, or the Ha'penny Bridge, or Traitor's Gate, but he made them real places for me, and put real Dubliners in them. I'd never heard of Zozimus or Matt Talbot, but he made them come alive, and by the time he had finished telling me about them, I felt I almost knew them.

What strange characters they were, and what a contrasting pair! Matt Talbot was on his way to becoming a very holy man when my father was a boy. He's now on his way to becoming a saint, this Dubliner who was an alcoholic, who was brought into my father's home by Granda Nolan for whom he worked as a labourer, and was given food by Nan Nolan because he was collapsing with weakness. When he died, they found on various parts of his body the cutting chains of self-mortification.

Zozimus, though, was something else. He was born in the Liberties in a place named Faddle Alley.

Knowing how hot my father was on the business of real names, I asked, "Was Zozimus his real name?"

"No, it wasn't at all. His real name was Michael Moran. Some people used to say that the name Zozimus was a 'maki-er-upper' as they called it. But it wasn't. *I* don't think so, any-way. There was a *pope* named Zosimus, who spelled his name with an 's' in it instead of a 'z', and a Greek writer, a histori-an, who spelled his name the same way."

"And are you saying that this Michael Moran fella read about that pope and the other man, and called himself after them?"

"No, no, I'm not saying that at all. For a start he couldn't read – he was blind. From birth. So I don't know *how* he came by the name. But of course he had a phenomenal memory, he was known for that, and maybe someone who *could* read read him something, some time, about one or the other, or *both* of the Zosimuses as far as I know."

"And was the blind Dublin Zozimus able to work?"

"Oh, be the hokey yes! Sure, it was his work that made him such a famous character."

"Well, what did he do?"

"He wrote what we, as kids, used to call 'pomes'. But they weren't really poems, not in the true sense. He wrote rhymes and ballads and sang them along the quays by the Liffey bridges. And he had his own way of attracting the attention of the passers-by. Never varied it. What God deprived him of in the way of sight, he made up for in other ways, like his memory and his voice. It was as loud as a fog-horn. If he shouted up by Christ Church, you'd hear him as far away as Clontarf.

"So when Zozimus decided to perform some of his ballads, he'd stand at his chosen spot, and you just couldn't ignore this great fog-horn of a voice bellowing out:

Ye sons and daughters of Erin, attend
Gather round poor Zozimus, your friend

Listen, boys, until yez hear
My charming songs so dear.

"And, Dad, did you ever see him or hear him?"

My father laughed again, and took a fit of coughing, banging his chest to try to clear it. "Coughing well today!" he said. "No, I never saw or heard Zozimus – he died nearly a century ago."

When we got to the small country church in Ballymore, we decided to slip in and say a few prayers. I wasn't sure what we should do about Smut. I didn't like the idea of tying him up outside, because the poor little divil might think we were abandoning him or punishing him for something he didn't do. At the same time I was hesitant about bringing a dog into the house of God.

"He'll be no trouble," my father said. "I never yet heard a dog bark in a church. On the outside, yes, but inside, never. God loves animals, too, you know, and in their own way they probably sense that. Maybe they respect it. We don't know. We don't know what they think or even if they *can* think. He'll be fine, mark my words."

"But what if he, you know . . ."

"Lifts his leg? He won't. I'll make a bet with you. How much?"

"Tuppence," I said.

"You're on. But if I win, I'll take it, mind. Are you sure you want to go ahead with it?"

"I'm sure."

I gave Dad the tuppence as soon as we got outside again. He took it. Smut had behaved perfectly, didn't even pant the way dogs do when they've been running, just sat there, looking around, and then spread-eagled himself, with his head on his paws, his heartbreakingly beautiful brown eyes facing the altar.

St Francis of Assisi would have been proud of him, would have called him "Brother Dog".

119

* * * * * * * *

We were toiling our way up Cuskinny Hill on the way home when, just before we turned the first corner, Dad stopped and looked back down the hill.

"We've had many a happy summer picnic back down there on the strand, haven't we?"

"Yes," I said, "lots. And at the Valley."

"That's right, at the Valley."

"And down at French's, and the Batteries, oh, and over on Paddy's Block."

"Ah, yes, Paddy's Block. And we'll have *more* . . . Do you really love the picnics?"

"I love them."

"As much as going to the pictures?"

"Well . . ."

"Hard to answer that one?"

"Yeah."

"Well, it was a damned stupid question. But you really *enjoy* the picnics, even now that you're not a small boy any more."

"I don't think small or big has anything to do with it, Dad."

"You're right! *I* enjoy them, and it's many a long day since *I* was a small boy . . . You didn't mind me asking, did you?"

"Of course not!"

"I just wanted to know."

I stole a look at him. He was facing down the hill. There were stone walls on each side of the road, inside them venerable old trees with grey wrinkled bark. Somehow I knew that at that moment my father wasn't seeing any of this, wasn't actually looking at the scene spread out below us. His eyes were facing in that direction, all right, but in reality they were seeing something different.

The clues came a minute or so later when, following a long sigh from him, we turned and resumed our walk up the hill.

"You were asking me earlier if I used to go on walks with my own father, and I didn't give you much of an answer. I didn't

120

get much of a chance to get to know him. He was dead before he was forty.

"Living and being brought up in a city is much different from living in a town of this size, where the sea is almost on your doorstep and you're out in the country among green fields within a few minutes if you go in the opposite direction.

"Remember I was asking you if you enjoyed the picnics? Well, we never had seaside picnics when I was young. We went out to Killiney a few times on the train, and paid a few visits to the swimming baths on Merrion Strand. But it wasn't the same. Half of Dublin was doing the same thing, and there's an awful lot more people in a capital city than there is in a place the size of Cobh.

"I was never in a boat until I came here, and the first one I was on was a *tender*, the second one was a Cunard liner, the *Franconia*. Would you credit that? In fact that was the day I first laid eyes on your mother – herself and her sister, your Auntie Rita. I still have the pass I was issued with. It's dated 'Queenstown, 10/10/26'. I didn't speak to them then, but I met them the following day in the States Hotel on Westbourne. But all that's by the by. I was telling you about my father."

His father, William Nolan, was employed as a sawyer at the time Dad was born. A cabinet-maker by trade, he was a foreman cabinet maker at the time of his death. It was while he was in that job that Matt Talbot was his assigned labourer.

"My father had a wonderful bass voice, and the year that John McCormack won the Feis Ceoil gold medal for tenor singing, 1903, my mother, your Nana Nolan, was there for the finals, and she heard the adjudicator, Maestro Luigi Denza, saying to my father after the presentation, that while McCormack, as a professional singer, would undoubtedly go on to carve an international career for himself, there was an international career there for him, too, waiting to be taken up. I believe that he begged him to consider it very seriously. And

121

McCormack, too, tried to persuade him to go to Italy with him and study under Maestro Sabatini in Milan.

"But my father, an intensely religious man, said that his voice had been given to him as a gift by God, and that from then on, the only times he would sing in public would be to sing sacred music, or in church, or in choirs. And he stuck to that to the day he died.

"He felt that as his voice was a gift, the only proper way for him to thank God for it was to use it in His service. So, instead of singing under Sabatini in Milan, he chose to sing under Dr Vincent O'Brien in Dublin. Wasn't it an amazing decision?

"And he had no big ideas about wanting to be a soloist, which his Feis Ceoil success and the things that Denza had said to him would have given him every right to.

"I think the last time he sang in public was with the Vincent O'Brien Choir when they did Handel's *Messiah* in the Round Room of the Rotunda in January of 1905. There was a chorus and orchestra of over 170 altogether, 134 of them singers. And there, listed among the basses, was 'Mr W. Nolan', bearing out what I was saying about him not having any big ideas about his status. As far as I know, the proceeds went to the St Vincent de Paul Society.

"There you are," he said. "You never heard all that before, did you?"

"No."

"So when you asked me about going for walks with my father, and then I asked you about the picnics and whether you still enjoyed them, a lot of that stuff was going through my head. I'd love to have had the kind of relationship with my father that you and I have. I'm very, very lucky."

I could see his eyes glistening behind his glasses when he looked down and smiled at me.

Trying to Figure God

T HINGS WERE HAPPENING everywhere, not just in Cobh. Hearing them talked about replaced thoughts of the tragedy.

Cobhman Jack Doyle, who came from the Holy Ground and had become famous first as a professional boxer of questionable merit, dubious ethics and flawed pedigree, and then for going to Hollywood, and also for barely-spoken-about carryings-on with certain English and American socialite women, was said to have married a small dark attractive actress named Movita, and married her again – this time in Dublin.

It was discussed in heads-close-together whispered conversations following exhortations to "run along now like a good boy and see if the baby is all right". But if you were skilful enough you could catch snippets of conversation.

"I remember him with the arse out of his pants, little snotty-nosed kid."

"I thought yer wan was supposed to be a Mexican film star."

"Film star, me eye! She was a *bit* player."

"Mexican, me eye, too. Sure wasn't she born in Arizona?"

"Where's that?"

"Oh, somewhere away out west. But it isn't in Mexico, that's for *sure.*"

"God, but ye're awful bitchy all the same. Her *parents* were Mexican."

"Ah, it's not the same, missus."

"An' do you know what – Movita isn't her real name at all."

"What is it, so?"

"Let me see if I can get this right – Maria Luisa Castanide." (It was said as if it rhymed with tide.)

"God knows, she's *welcome* to him. I wouldn't let him darken me door."

"Oh, I don't know now all the same . . ."

"May God forgive you, you dirty thing!"

"Here, come to think about it, Jack isn't *his* right name either."

"What is it then?"

"Joseph Alphonsus."

"*Alphonsus?* Jesus, Mary and Joseph!"

"There's Jack now for yeh."

"Mm-mm. I bet *you* couldn't get a priest to marry yeh to the same man a second time."

"No, nor the first time, either! You seem to forget I'm a Protestant."

And so it went. They were right, though, about it being the second time around for Jack and Movita. That's if you were to believe Jack's story. Not everyone did. He said they'd been married already by a Catholic priest in Mexico. It's just that they wanted a public marriage in church. So, Very Reverend G. Turley, Adm., obliged them in St Andrew's Church, Westland Row, Dublin.

"Wouldn't you think they'd do it in *style?*" Miss Ryan, in her white coat, said in Darcy's Grocery and Provision Store at the bottom of King Street.

"What do you mean?" Ethna Rogers' mother asked her.

"What do you mean what do I mean?" Miss Ryan shot back. "If he's so high an' mighty, and she's a fillum star, wouldn't

124

you think that at least she'd have a long dress, even if it wasn't white, instead of 'a smart grey costume'? Some people have no class."

And Miss Ryan sniffed as only Miss Ryan could, and that was the end of that conversation.

Well, until Mrs Rogers told Mrs Murphy, and Mrs Murphy spoke about it out loud to anyone who cared to listen during the interval of the whist drive in the parochial hall.

Another famous man, famous for different reasons, was married around the same time, and almost *nobody* in Cobh talked about it – except "Dicky Dan". He told us he had made up a joke. "Why did Sir Thomas Beecham marry the pianist Betty Humby? Because she was good at the runs – get it? Beecham – Beecham's Pills – pianist – runs? Aw, forget it, ye're thick!"

Danny Murphy wasn't thick. He was very clever as well as very studious, but he didn't hear Dicky Dan telling his "joke" because Danny Murphy usually went straight home after school to do his homework and read and listen to the wireless. Danny had been born with only one full arm, and half an arm.

Something he told me one day got me into a mild frenzy – trying to visualise 12 million.

"A million is what again?" I asked him.

"A thousand thousands."

"A thousand thousands. Now, let me think about that – a thousand *thousands*. . . And a thousand is ten *hundreds*, right?"

"Right."

"So, if you were to count to a hundred, a million would be –"

"Ten thousand times that," Danny said. "You'd have to count to a hundred ten thousand times to count to a million."

"And how many dead and wounded Russians are the Germans claiming?" I asked him.

"Twelve million, eight hundred thousand," he answered.

"So, twelve *million* would be a hundred-and-twenty thousand *hundreds?*"

"Yep."

At times there were great depths of silence in and around Danny. I used to think there was a melancholy there, too, but maybe it was something else.

His father was tall, bespectacled, remote, grave, always wore a hat, and was relatively elderly. Manager of one of the town's bakeries, he was a widower when he married Danny's mother. By the time that Danny came along, Mr Murphy's first family was almost reared, and Danny grew up a lone child among adults. It made him a very serious boy. His parents and grandmother, Mrs Knight, were very conscious of Danny's partial disability and so were extremely protective of him. Not that they needed to be – no one, not even the school bullies, would dream of hurting Danny. No one would even allude to that half-arm in the half-empty sleeve, let alone ask him what happened and whether it ever hurt.

Danny was born with a lively acquisitive brain which was able to retain everything he read, or heard on the wireless, which was why he was able to come up with all sorts of amazing facts and figures. He wasn't too serious to read comics. He read *The Wizard*, and loved the Great Wilson; and *The Champion*, in which Rockfist Rogan, RAF was his favourite; and he'd regale all of us with descriptions of what the funny characters in the *The Dandy* and *The Beano* and *Radio Fun* were up to. He particularly liked Pansy Potter and Desperate Dan.

But war statistics were serious stuff, and he loved figures.

"And how many times the population of Ireland would 12,800,000 be?" I asked him.

"About three-and-a-half times," he said. "Not only that, but the Germans are also claiming to have taken nearly *five-and-a-half million* Russians as prisoners."

"My God!" I said. "I can't take it in."

"And they're saying they destroyed 34,000 Russian tanks," he added, "but I don't believe that."

126

"Why?" I asked.

"Because I don't believe the Russians ever *had* 34,000 tanks. That's just propaganda," he said, "and propaganda is usually lies dressed up as truth."

"All right," I said, "can we have a look at these long division sums now?"

* * * * * * * *

Thinking and wondering about the harbour tragedy became an obsession with me. Would the bodies of Pat Higgins' father and Frank Powell ever be found now after such a long time? They could have floated out to sea, I thought, and come ashore unidentified and unidentifiable in another country.

Or they could have been washed out into the deep Atlantic and then burned in the kind of sea-on-fire that occurred when tankers were torpedoed and exploded. ("Jesus, please look after Uncle John.") Or maybe their bodies were eaten by sharks, and only white bones left to sink? Or perhaps they were still trapped, held down by tangling seaweed on the floor of the harbour out on Curlane Bank?

I kept these thoughts to myself, and gradually the tragedy ceased being a topic of conversation or speculation.

Pat Higgins still looked sad, and his face seemed to lengthen. Con Lynch's father for a while took on a spectrelike appearance and where, before, he'd recognise you if you said, "Hello, Mr Lynch," now he'd turn his preoccupied gaze absentmindedly in your direction and say, "Oh, hello . . . ah . . ." and never manage to get your name out.

Mrs Duggan, in her black widow's weeds, had a flinty, disapproving, dark-eyed look, below the surface of which lurked a resentful sorrow. You felt that she would find it impossible ever to smile or laugh again.

I used to wonder, God forgive me, what would happen to the beautiful square-rigged ship-in-a-bottle that I used to look at in their front room when Willie was alive. All my life, since

127

I first saw it, I had wanted one of my own. (It wasn't until 1994 that I got my first one. I bought a tiny and exquisite bottled model of the German bark *Rickmer Rickmers* of Hamburg in the fishing port of Gloucester in Massachusetts. I rarely look at it without thinking of Willie Duggan.)

As the weeks lengthened into months, the tragedy disappeared off the pages of the papers and out of the minds and mouths of most of the townspeople. For the relatives of those who died, it became the grief that did not speak, and yes, it probably bade their hearts to break.

For a ten year old beginning to think seriously about life (and death) and to ask questions, it was all hugely and disturbingly puzzling. You'd get to a point of what you thought was understanding, only for the whole picture to fragment suddenly again. "Understanding" was ephemeral. It slipped away from you and left you convinced you knew *nothing*.

But you couldn't escape news of the war. It came into that harbour town as it came into every city, town and village in the land. The things it told of invariably entailed death. There was no getting away from death.

The deaths of the five men in the harbour had been a terrible shock, but if you read the papers, or listened to the wireless, or heard the gossip, you learned of other things in other places, and you came to the inevitable realisation that death on a massive scale, caused by war, was continuous and inescapable. Although I couldn't readily assimilate all the statistics I was bombarded with, I nevertheless found them curiously fascinating. And the more fascinating they became, and the more of them that came accompanied by descriptions of people and places and things, all of which humanised the figures, then the more the horror and the facts of the harbour tragedy were pushed into the background of my mind.

Not that only statistics of a gargantuan nature occupied my thinking and seriously affected my emotions. For example, by comparison with the number of people wiped out in individual bombing raids, what happened in New Zealand in a

Japanese prisoner-of-war camp would be reckoned relatively minor. Nevertheless, learning that 48 POWs were slaughtered by their armed guards was horrifying – made all the more so by the official "explanation". The prisoners, it was said, attacked the guards. The weapons in the possession of the prisoners were listed as stones, tools and improvised clubs.

So, the armed guards opened fire on them. They killed 48 and injured 60. One New Zealander died. Japanese authorities in Tokyo spoke about the threat of reprisals.

The pictures left in my mind of the mowing down of the prisoners were profoundly disturbing.

When I read of a German field marshal and 15 generals surrendering to a Russian army lieutenant, bringing the battle of Stalingrad to a close, it wasn't the fact that 100,000 Germans were said to have been killed, or starved to death, that stayed in my mind; it was that the Germans had *eaten* all that remained of the Rumanian cavalry's horses.

And when I read that a middle-aged woman, carrying a baby and a bundle, tripped and fell on her way into a London Underground tube station which was being used as an air raid shelter, I felt very puzzled at God. An elderly man tripped over the woman where she lay on the ground, and that caused hundreds of others to fall, building up a wall of bodies which blocked the passageway. Result: death on a massive scale from suffocation . . . 178.

The ironies didn't stop there. The woman who fell first survived. The baby died. Not a single bomb was dropped on the area that day.

Why did God allow that to happen?

I was puzzled, too, when nine people were killed in Waterford city when the northern wall of Ballybicken Gaol collapsed on top of eight one-storey houses in King's Street between midnight and 1am on the 4th of March.

These, I thought, were terrible, pointless deaths. As were the ones that occurred when St Joseph's Orphanage, run by the Poor Clares in Cavan's Pearse Street, became an inferno at 2 o'clock one morning, and 35 young people, ages 4 to 18, were turned into cinders as fire swept through the dormitories. Miss Smith, the cook, aged 87, was also burned to death. They had to bury the lot of them in a single grave.

How did God allow *that* to happen? No one could give me answers.

Mary Ellen Barry was 20 and lived in County Kilkenny. Taking her sheep dog for a walk, she wrapped its leash around her arm for safety. The route she took passed close to a quarry pond. Spotting something, the dog leaped forward towards the water. He pulled Mary Ellen Barry after him and, unable to stop herself in time, she fell into the pond. They found her body later. The dog was beside her. Dead. The leash was still wound round Mary Ellen's arm.

Why did God allow *that* to happen? I couldn't figure it out. But then I was only 10, and the older people said they couldn't figure it out either.

Death of a Sporting Hero

WHEN THE GENERAL manager/secretary of the Cork Harbour Commissioners, Eugene Gayer, submitted to the Pilotage Committee his financial statement for the half year to 31 December 1942, the document showed that there was an amount of £114-7s-3d "available for distribution among the pilots".

Each of the 17 pilots got £6-14s-0d.

You read about something like that and, if you were a child, it meant little or nothing to you. But if you were an adult like, say, Danny Dinan, you had a reaction.

"Six pounds fourteen, missus? The miserable buggers, that's all I can say," Danny said. "They'd have done better not to give them anything – sure six pounds fourteen's a bleddy insult."

But Mrs Moloney in No. 5, said, "It's a nice little windfall now all the same, Danny."

" 'Tis in my arse," Danny said, waiting until she had gone in and closed the door behind her. Danny wasn't daft. He didn't want to lose a customer, and Mrs Moloney was, if not a daily, then a frequent communicant, and had great belief in the Legion of Mary.

"Those bleddy buggers in the Harbour Commissioners are

so stingy they wouldn't pay a ha'penny to see the Blessed Virgin driving along The Beach in a Baby Ford," he said to me at the front door.

The use of God's name in other than prayer situations was seriously frowned on – unless dramatic circumstances, or tragedies, seemed to warrant the "taking of the Holy Name in vain".

"Jesus, Mary and Joseph, missus, wasn't that terrible about poor John Coveney?" Danny said to my mother one Monday morning halfway through March.

We had heard the news of the Haulbowline accident on the Saturday and had been shocked. John Coveney was a huge man, something of a mythic hero to those of us who were already interested in sport, particularly soccer and athletics. He played in goal for Cobh Ramblers, his enormous body seeming to fill half the space between the posts where he stood, or jumped about, or prowled.

He was the strongest man around our town. Each year we gasped as we saw him hefting the 56 pound weight at the Ballymore Sports, which were held in the same sloping field at Carrignafoy in which Cobh Ramblers played their home games. John would grab the ring on the top of the massive weight ("Janey Mack boy! that's half a *hundredweight!*") and heave the chunk of iron up into the air, the veins standing out on his neck and on the sides of his temples. He won the 56-pounds-over-the-bar event time after time. More often than not he'd also win the 56-pounds-without-follow. Height or distance, John Coveney was your man.

As a powerfully built boy, he had won several field events at the All Ireland Athletics Championships in faraway Dublin. And as a 33-year-old unmarried man, he was a member of the LDF (Local Defence Force) and was, as my father said, "a fine representative of the best type of young Irish manhood".

He was the first person I'd heard described (by my father, wouldn't you know?) as a "gentle giant". Everyone in the town, and on Haulbowline and Spike Island, loved big John Coveney.

The Coveneys, like my mother's people the Sextons, were Haulbowline residents, and John had grown up with the Sexton children. When the news broke that John had been crushed by a travelling crane on a high-up gantry, disbelief mingled with shock.

"How badly injured is he, Dad?" I asked my father when he had finished giving my mother the briefest account of the accident.

"I don't think there's much hope for him, I'm sorry to say," my father answered. "The crane driver didn't see John where he was working, and he never had a chance. The poor chap was pinned against something. I was told that his screaming and moaning could be heard all over the island. When they got him down eventually and off Haulbowline, he was taken right away to the Bon Secours Hospital in Cork, but he's not expected to live. He's in a terrible condition."

There was no football match on the Sunday, but I called up for Nux, and we walked together up to Villa Park where a hurling match and a camogie match were to be held to raise money for the Cork Harbour Disaster Fund.

The games were very terrible. Utterly devoid of skill. Just a lot of axeman swings and misses, some burst heads among the hurlers, and beefy, thick-legged, red-faced girls in jet black woollen stockings and passion-killer bloomers whose elastic-tightened knicker legs came halfway down their white thighs. The whole affair was about as interesting as a pound of Tom Hanlon's suet.

But before the first game started, we all stood still and silent around the ground in memory of John Coveney.

Here was someone else I'd never see again. Never again stand close to the netting of his goal and watch him in his green polo-necked gansey diving at the feet of an inrushing forward. Never again see him turning to us and smiling, and saying, "How are ye?" Never again see him heaving that brutally heavy iron weight high into the air at the Ballymore Sports of a summer Sunday.

"Died in the Bons on Saturday," Danny Dinan said at the front door on Monday morning as he ladled out the milk. "It's in the paper today – internal injuries and a fractured hip. Honest to Jesus, missus – God forgive me! – but there's some bleddy hoodoo on this cursed country. Hardly a week goes by but some new terrible thing happens."

He looked around to see if there was anyone who might hear him. The hill was deserted clear to the top where the rusted-through black gates led into Buckleys' place, and Batemans'. Joe Buckley's dog Riff was barking somewhere, probably down on the slope of the cliff. In the other direction, the road was also clear, away down beyond the lamp post to where Church Street began at Whelans'. There wasn't a soul about.

But Danny kept his voice down nevertheless, and looked over his shoulder a few times, just in case. "Do you know what I heard a Protestant woman sayin' down outside Dowling's? She said it's all the fault of that old bastard De Valera."

My mother motioned me to go inside. But I dawdled long enough to hear Danny say, "Mind you, she didn't use that exact expression about the old shite, but I know she *meant* it. She said he have the country ruined, an' that by stayin' neutral and gettin' others to do our fightin' for us against Hitler – and gettin' killed – he's bringin' bad luck on the country. Bad cess to him! What do *you* think of that now, missus?"

"Who said it?" my mother asked.

"Ah, now, that'd be telling," Danny said. "And I don't want to be the one carryin' gossip or givin' scandal." He turned to me and said, "Go on inside now, you!"

My mother pushed me into the inner hall and pulled the glass door shut so that she and Danny could continue their chat with a modicum of privacy.

I sat on the stairs and started going over in my mind all the Protestants I could think of in the town. There were the Bat-

134

sons and the Bunworths next door to us; the Balbirnies down at the bottom; the Batemans and Tarrants at the top of the hill; there were the Caseys in King Street, East Beach and out beyond Velvet House cross; there were the Birds at the back of the island; the Wilcoxes, Henry Myles and his wife, the Phippses, the Vickerys, Canon Titchburn, the Glassons, Harry Deane, Ruby Robinson, Dr Ledlie . . . I couldn't think of any more. And, oh, yes, Commander Hume. *He* must be the one Danny heard, I reckoned. But he wasn't a *woman*. No, but Danny was probably being clever, just *saying* it was a woman he heard.

Commander Hume was a crusty old retired Royal Navy officer with an English accent, a face like his own Pekinese and a loud, sometimes patronising, sometimes abrasive manner. I decided that if Danny had heard anyone at all (you'd never know with Danny, he was a great one for hopping the ball) it had to have been Commander Hume. Hume was sure to feel that way about Dev. The neutrality thing stuck in his craw, as had the denial of the country's ports to Britain. Yes, it *had* to have been Commander Hume.

"Who did Danny hear saying that about De Valera, Mam?" I asked when my mother eventually came back into the kitchen.

"Never you mind," she said. "He didn't tell me. And even if he had done, I wouldn't tell you."

"Why not?"

"Because it's political talk, and you're far too young to be getting involved in politics. Politics have been the ruination of this country, and if I have anything to do with it, you'll steer well clear of them. Now get your coat on and go off to school or you'll be dead late, and I'm not writing any notes for you."

The thing she said about politics having been the ruination of the country puzzled me because I didn't fully understand what she was getting at. Politics were never discussed by herself and my father in front of us. Certainly there were infrequent mentions of the 1916 Easter Rising, and the Civil War, and the Black and Tans. And names like Pearse, and Connolly and Thomas Clarke, as well as Michael Collins and Michael O'Higgins and De Valera were heard in vague (to me) references which had hints of underlying bitterness.

It would be at least another 25 years before I'd come across Mao Tse Tung's observation that political power grows out of the barrel of a gun, and even longer than that before I would realise that politicians were among the least-loved people in society because, for most of them, politics became the studied disregard for the people they purportedly set out to serve; instead they concentrated on the naked pursuit of power.

But even as a child you were confronted with the evidence. Wasn't Hitler a politician? And Churchill? And Roosevelt? Wasn't the dropping of 900 tons of bombs on a German city on one night by the Stirlings and Halifaxes and Lancasters of Bomber Command an act brought about by politicians?

Wasn't the pursuit and killing of Jews in the sewers of the Warsaw ghetto a political act? And the killing of thousands of Polish officers whose bodies were found in a mass grave at Katyn near Smolensk?

These were the kind of things we were hearing about and reading about every day, because they were what was known as "news". But no one had the willingness or desire, or the time, to explain about politics to children. So you tried to figure it out as best you could. Not that you spent *all* your time at it.

"Jaze, that Rachmaninoff must've been kicking himself all the same," Nux announced the day we heard that the great Russian pianist and composer had died at his home in Beverly Hills, the suburb of Los Angeles famous as the area where Hollywood film stars lived.

"You mean just because he died?" I said.

"No – *before* he died!" Nux said with a touch of his put-on exasperation. "How could he kick himself *after* he died?"

"Why don't you say what you mean, or mean what you say?" Danny Murphy said in his quiet, ultra reasonable, non-aggressive way.

"Ye're all *thick*!" Nux said, and quickened his speed and walked away from us out the Low Road on the railway station side. We let him go. In fact we slowed down. By the time we reached the place where the road did an S-turn near the station master's house and you could look across the tracks towards Haulbowline, Nux was 50 yards ahead of us, pretending we weren't there, or that anyway he wasn't with us.

Out close to the edge of the river a lone seagull was perched on the top of the old cog-wheeled crane. It looked around, screeched in that ugly way that gulls have, then spread its wings and lifted off lazily into the wind. It flew in and screeched again when it was over us.

"There you are, that's what *he* thinks of you!" I called out to Nux, who had been tracking the flight of the gull.

Suddenly he got a fit of the giggles and bent over, helpless, holding on to the rounded top of the low wall to steady himself. We strolled up to him, and tears of laughter were running down his cheeks.

"What's so funny?" someone asked.

"That bleddy gull," Nux said. "When he circled and went right over the top of ye, I suddenly had an image of him spillin' his load, or dive bombin' ye like a Stuka and leavin' his mark. God, it would have been hilarious!"

"Yeah, well, I'm sorry you were disappointed," I said, "but at least you got a laugh out of *imagining* it. Now – what was all that about Rachmaninoff kicking himself?"

Nux was the only one of us who was learning the piano.

"Ah, it's just that I was thinkin' that there he was, a pianist, composer, conductor, and he sold his most famous piece of music for only four quid, four lousy pounds! I mean if it was you, if *you'd* written something, and then heard it played all over the world on wireless programmes and at concerts and everythin', and you never got a penny more out of it because you'd sold it for four lousy quid, wouldn't *you* be kicking yer-self? That's all I meant."

"Wasn't that his Prelude in C-sharp Minor?" Danny Murphy asked quietly.

"It was, yeah," Nux said. "I'm tryin' to learn it at the moment, *tryin'* – it's brutal."

"Well, *I* read that he said he'd become so tired of it that he was very pleased when he heard it turned into a dance band number," Danny said. "So maybe he wasn't kicking himself after all."

He let that little gem hang unanswered in the air for a few seconds. A discomfited Nux kicked a non-existent stone off the footpath.

Then Danny said, "He was only 20 when he wrote it. He was a student at the time, at the Moscow conservatory."

Another small hiatus, and then Nux looked up at Danny and said, "Murph, you're a dinger!"

And Danny smiled his small chin-on-the-chest smile.

Singing the Shanties

ALTHOUGH I WAS born in Cobh, my earliest memories relate to Haulbowline – standing next to Danny Bowen, the breadman, in Dan Fitz's ferryboat, with the gorgeous smell of hot, freshly baked loaves from O'Reilly's bakery wafting out of the enormous lidded wicker basket resting on the floorboards of the boat. He would deliver the bread up to Mrs Murphy's shop on the "Ordnance side" and at my grandmother's house, and to the houses of Guard Walsh and the Coveneys and the Dobbs' and Mrs Codd and the Brierleys.

To a small child Nan and Granda's house on Haulbowline was magical and extraordinary. It was yellow and had high-peaked gables and steep stairs and a stone-floored scullery as well as a big kitchen. It had a drawing room into which the sun seemed always to shine and in which there were polished brass shell casings in the fireplace, and gleaming walnut furniture, and an upright piano which was always kept in tune.

Living in the house with Nan and Granda were my aunts Winnie, Kitty, Lillian, Doreen, Tracy and, when he was home from sea, Uncle John. There were photographs which showed the two sons who had died – Pat as an RAF officer in India in the 20s, and Jim, who hadn't made it beyond childhood. Auntie Rita, who had married a gentle Scottish marine engineer named Bob Houston, and my mother, Mary Winifred (Molly), completed the family.

Granda Jim came originally from County Waterford where his father was a wealthy merchant. It was always hinted and sometimes said in that house on Haulbowline that there had been something fishy about the way Granda Jim's father's will had virtually excluded Granda Jim. But Nan would leave papers showing that Granda Jim brought it on himself.

He hadn't wanted to go into the family business of hides and leathers, just wanted to become an engineer. After leaving the Christian Brothers School, he spent a short time at Cork University studying engineering, but it was a marine engineer he wanted to be. He was commissioned in the Royal Navy in World War I, was with Jellicoe at the Battle of Jutland, served on the *Prince of Wales,* and "came ashore" to take a job with the new oil refinery at Haulbowline.

A powerfully built, squat man with pure white hair ("He went white almost overnight at sea when he was a young man," my mother told me), a brilliant talent for story-telling, and a mischievous sense of humour, he was given to using the occasional colourful expletive with surprising force and effect. The tip of one of his fingers was missing. My mother also said that he was seasick at the beginning of every voyage, and like many professional seamen (including some lifeboat men) he couldn't swim.

Granda always shaved in cold water, even in the depths of winter, and when he sluiced the cold water over his face to rinse off the shaving soap, he would shake his chin and cheeks, and blubber out his lips before the towel went near his face.

The household revolved around him, though it was Nan who ran it like a tight ship. When he sat at the head of the great kitchen table with his back to the range, he was like a presiding monarch.

I was their first grandchild, but I can't remember being singled out for preferential treatment. The family was too big, the goings and comings too many, the noise of living too loud and the attitudes too sane to allow any "spoiling".

Though we lived in Cobh, I spent many idyllic summer days on that harbour island, many hours pushing seagull feathers into salvaged lumps of cork (bits of floats from fishing nets) to form a primitive sail and throwing the "corkoodies" into the tide to race off the slip behind the mast house where Dan Fitz carried on his business of boat repairing. The blue Ballycotton Lifeboat came there every year for her annual overhaul.

"Mine sailed the farthest," Auntie Tracy (who was only five years older than me) would taunt. I could never best her. Few could. If under threat, she could whip up an instant emotional scene. If that yielded no results, she would cry, and if crying didn't work, she would scream. And if that didn't work, she would go into a foot-stamping, kicking, hand-flailing, red-in-the-face tantrum that was truly awesome. She was the least likely candidate you could imagine ever becoming (as she did) a major in the Queen Alexanders Royal Army Nursing Corps, because she was a surly, frowning, bad-tempered child with, as a young girl, one of the most dislikeable personalities that I have ever encountered. She grew up much the same. Even her own sisters gave her a wide berth.

The one place that was off limits for us as children was the disused basin of the decaying naval dockyard where some big old tankers were moored to the jetty, awaiting disposal, and where Uncle Bob was the engineer in charge of maintenance. The fact that we were strictly forbidden to go near the basin was only a partial impediment to Tracy. I used to follow her there, and we'd pick our way among the rusting pipes and boilers and iron plates which lay among the summer weeds and scutch grass.

When Nan asked us where we'd been, Tracy would lie barefacedly, her sulking brazenness the perfect giveaway to her guilt. The threat that Granda would be told would impose its own braking effect on going to the basin again too soon.

Nan was a pale-skinned, attractive woman with a slightly aristocratic air about her. She had titian hair which, when she let it down for brushing, fell in a shining cascade to her waist. Possessed of a quiet musical speaking voice, she had strong tinges of a Scottish burr in her accent. I never heard her raise her voice, but in matters relating to the running of the household and her family, what she said went.

There always seemed to be musical soirees going on in that island home. All the older girls could sing, and all had been "put to the piano".

Granda sang unaccompanied, and for some reason which I never fully understood, all he sang (in my hearing anyway) were sea shantys – or, to give them their proper name, chanteys. As far as I knew, he had never served his time before the mast on sailing vessels. He was a marine *engineer*, and that meant that his sea time was spent on steamships. But it hadn't stopped him from learning and knowing the words and rhythms of the songs that were originally sung to help with the capstan work, raising the anchors on windjammers, or hoisting the topmasts or yards of a square-rigger.

"Blow the Man Down" was the first one I ever heard him sing, followed (and he made me think it was about me) by "Billy Boy". Then, scarcely pausing for breath he launched into:

> *We're all bound for Liverpool, I heard the captain say;*
> *Heave away, my Johnnies, heave away.*
> *Oh, there we'll have a bully time, with Nell and Julie May,*
> *Heave away, my Johnny boy, we're all bound to go.*

He had only just finished the verse when a quietly admonitory voice (my grandmother's) said: "Jim, the *children!*" It stopped him in his tracks. I had no idea why, because I thought that song was about Uncle John. Nan, obviously, knew better.

Granda gave her a sideways look, said nothing, but started into another shanty straight away.

What'll we do with the drunken sailor?
What'll we do with the drunken sailor?
What'll we do with the drunken sailor
Earl-eye in the morning?

'Way, hey, and up she rises.
'Way, hey, and up she rises.
'Way, hey, and up she rises.
Earl-eye in the morning.

We all clapped, except Nan, who pursed her lips prettily and shook her head.

"Daddy, sing 'Whiskey Johnny'," Auntie Doreen said. She was a couple of years older than Tracy, and the only one who wore glasses.

"'Whiskey Johnny'?" he said. "I will if your mother will give me of her largesse and pass me a drop of Mr Power's finest. Will you, Kate?"

Nan made a little glance-to-heaven gesture and reached for a whiskey glass from the scrolled silver tray on the drinks table. She held it in her lap while Granda cleared his throat and began:

Oh, whiskey is the life of man,
Oh, Whiskey Johnny.
It always was since life began,
Oh, whiskey for my Johnny.

When he came to the end he turned to Nan with his hand out. She poured him a drink and gave it to him saying, "Ye men, ye're all the same!"

The drink was down his throat and gone in a couple of seconds. He handed the empty glass back, pulled me up on his lap and started on another shanty.

The only other person, apart from Nan, who could divert him from whichever shanty he wanted to sing was Mrs Denver, who had an impressive operatic bosom, a commanding manner, and owned the European Hotel. I was occasionally taken by Granda to the bar where he bought drinks for his cronies and, in true sailor fashion, spun fantastic yarns. I was a little older then, and Granda was back at sea as a Chief Engineer.

"Are yeh going to give us a song, Jim," one of the men said one day when I was with him.

"No better man," the little character with the Joxer Daly face and the greasy cap said. "Go on, Mr Sexton, give us 'St Patrick was an Irishman'."

"Well, I don't know if I can remember all the words," Granda said, playing hard to get, wanting to be persuaded.

"Sure if yeh forget 'em yeh can always 'dowdle'."

Granda made a pretence of trying to remember, then cleared his throat, fixed his eye on something on the wall, and started:

St Patrick was an Irishman
He came from Dublin City.
Away, haul away, haul away Joe.

He drove the snakes from Ireland
And then drank all the whiskey.
Away, haul away, haul away Joe.

He built a church in Limerick
And on it put a steeple.
He held high mass for 40 days
But couldn't fool the people.

Mrs Denver sailed down the narrow channel between the bar counter and the wall, stood right in front of my grandfather, took the sort of breath which raised her frontage several inches, and in a voice that would have cut through tempered steel said just two words: "*Mister* Sexton!"

Granda halted in mid breath, seemed about to say something confrontational, thought better of it, changed his mind and instead said, "Right, madam, we'll have 'Leave her, John-

ny, leave her'. Would that have the approval of your censori-
ous mind?"

"It depends on the words, Mr Sexton. I'm not familiar with
them, though no doubt I am about to become so."

"You are indeed, ma'am. How perceptive of you!" Turning
to his little captive audience, he flashed an enormous wink
and said, "Now, lads, this is what's known as a pumping song,
used on the windjammers whenever the pumps had to be
manned and a tough job of work done."

Before starting, he turned to his pint of stout which was
standing on the counter. He eyed it longingly for maybe half
a minute, then wiped his mouth and chin with his right
hand, and finally lifted the glass and drank deeply from it.
Wiping the creamy froth from around his lips with the back
of his hand, he launched into song:

Oh, pump her out from down below,
Leave her, Johnny, leave her.
Oh, pump her out and away we'll go,
For it's time for us to leave her.

He sang all eight verses, ending with:

The rats have gone, and we the crew,
Oh, leave her, Johnny, leave her.
It's time, by God, that we went, too;
It's time for us to leave her.

He turned to Mrs Denver, and making a courtly bow, said
to her, "And it's time for us, too, madam, to leave your establishment. Good day to you."

So saying, he lifted me down off the high stool on which I
was perched, pulled down my coat, and said, "Come along,
Sunny Jim. If we don't go home the womenfolk'll have the
gendarmes" (he gave it its correct French pronunciation)
"out looking for us."

Hand in hand, elderly man and small boy, we walked along
East Beach past Dowlings' and Caseys' and Walter Barry's, up

145

past Moynihans' and Pakie Neill's, up the steps, across the road to O'Keeffe's grocery and provisions store where the smell of smoked bacon came out on to the pavement, then up past O'Connell's pawn shop, past Cassidy's boot and shoe repair shop, where Mr Cassidy and one of the Rasmussens sat in verbal isolation from each other, past Maisie Ryan's house where Charles Lynch was practising Chopin, and on to No. 3, Harbour Hill where Nan had the dinner waiting for us – crubeens for Granda, mashed potatoes, bacon and cabbage for the rest of us.

"Did you have that boy in a pub?" she asked Granda, and before he had a chance to answer she said: "You ought to be ashamed of yourself! What kind of an example is that for an innocent child? And I'll bet your so-called friends drank all you'd buy for them and never put their hands in their pockets once."

She was dead right about the last bit. When she turned away to get down the Yorkshire Relish, Granda gave me a big conspiratorial wink, and started cutting into his crubeens.

He was some Granda.

Ruby and the Daunt Rock

O N SUMMER SATURDAYS, if you were a boy and were down around the town pier at the camber where the big black old *Kathleen* was moored close in against the steps, there was a chance, a slim chance, of getting a trip out to the Daunt Rock lightship. It depended on how help-ful you were in lugging sturdy little kegs of fresh water and twine-tied parcels and bags of coal and baskets of foodstuff across the top of the pier, man-handling (boy-handling?) them down the steps until they were level with the deck of the *Kathleen*, pushing and pulling them over her gunwale and then helping to stow them on board.

It also depended on how early you caught the eye of Ruby Robinson and established yourself in his consciousness, how respectful and subservient you were prepared to be towards him, how successful you were in making yourself mute and keeping out of his way and being invisible at appropriate moments, and on whether or not Ruby had a head on him that morning. Ruby owned the *Kathleen*.

She was an ancient, sturdy, single-masted, black-painted timber tub, not totally unlike a Galway hooker in appearance. Gaff-rigged, with an old, patched, brown canvas sail, she had a lot of freeboard, a perpendicular bow line and an overhanging stern. Her mast was short and fat, and her bowsprit had long ago been unshipped. The black paint on her hull was always blistering or blistered. With a permanent berth in the east camber where she was tied up for nine out of every ten days, she was a part of the town. And though there was nothing of grace about her, to us she represented the chance of adventure through a trip out to sea.

Her sometimes dysfunctional diesel engine was housed below deck in a cramped cockpit at the stern, just forward of the tiller, which came inboard and upwards from the head of the rudder. Ruby was known to attack the engine frequently with a heavy ball hammer and a torrent of vile language.

He had the contract for taking fresh water, fuel, mail and food and other supplies, together with the crewmen returning from shore leave, out to the Daunt Rock lightship, and bringing back into Cobh the empty kegs, the letters for posting and the men whose turn it was to spend time ashore.

While none of us would dare call Ruby anything but Mr Robinson, we felt free to call his sole employee, deckhand and odd-job man Charlie Jones, by his first name. Charlie, who had an equally well-known brother Fergie, came from the eastern extremity of the town and was a hard-working, friendly man with bad teeth. He never raised his voice, even though he often unwarrantedly caught hell when Ruby's head was giving him gyp.

"Rube", as my mother called him, was nominally a Protestant, but it was widely believed that he had absolutely no beliefs at all in any form of god or religion of any kind.

"You'd need to be careful of that class of fella," Dick Nash told my father. "Atheism is contagious you know."

None of us ever caught it. Not from Ruby anyway.

Brown-faced and bald-headed, Ruby had those deep wrinkles around the eyes that seamen get from squinting up at white sails reflecting the westering sun. As a local sailing expert, reputed to know every current and eddy of the Cork Harbour waters and able to pin-point where wind-gusts off the land would hit those waters, Ruby had done, and still did, a lot of squinting. Everyone connected with sailing, except possibly Skipper Regan who owned the *Cygnet* and thought he knew more about sailboat handling than Uffa Fox and Captain Bligh combined, said that as a helmsman Ruby had no peer.

The funny thing was, he rarely took the helm of the *Kathleen*. Other than when they were warping her around from her berth to the iron ladder at the eastern end of the pier or coming in alongside the lightship, he left the steering to Charlie. Charlie was required to run backwards and forwards and up and down steps and vertical iron ladders to tie up and let go the ropes on the pier's bollards. Ruby reckoned he himself was too old and too well-off to be doing that kind of caper. Anyway, he was the boss, and what the hell else was he paying Charlie for if not to do the running around?

Once they were clear of the Pier Head, Ruby, having decided the route ("We'll go across the bank"), let Charlie have the helm. Not that Charlie had to deal with any problems relating to the *Kathleen's* speed through the water. The venerable old lady's under-powered propulsion unit worked her up to a maximum of about 4 knots. And that was with a following wind.

But it was more than the Daunt Rock lightship would ever do under her own power – because she had no power to propel herself. The only way she would ever move through the water, apart from being towed, would be if torn loose from her mooring and driven by the force of a gale, which is what happened in 1936, as we all knew from our parents and people like Sean Scanlon's father.

Sean's dad was a lightship master, and his version of the 1936 story, when he could be enticed to talk about it, would stand the hair up on the back of your neck. It involved southeast gales which lashed the coast and ripped the lightship away from where she was secured to the Daunt Rock. For three whole days she drifted, buffeted, battered, pitching and rolling in the terrible seas whipped up by the unrelenting wind, the crew aboard her in desperate danger.

Cobh people, and others with haunting knowledge, prayed and sweated out those long days and nights, hoping against hope that it wasn't going to be a repeat of the *Puffin* disaster. Also a lightship stationed on Daunt Rock, she foundered in a storm in 1896. Not one of her crew survived. But the 1936 prayers were heard. Our Lady Star of the Sea must have done some strong interceding. No lives were lost, which was something of a miracle.

The day I made my first trip out with Ruby was one of those days when Sean Scanlon, who lived on Roche's Row just a few doors up from Mrs O'Brien's shop, was going out with his father, who was returning to duty after a spell ashore.

Mr Scanlon was acknowledged to be "a lovely man". On the stout side, he walked with the traditional seaman's roll, and if you passed him coming up King Street, Church Street or Rose Hill in his impressive navy blue, brass-buttoned, serge uniform, you got a thrill out of the fact that he always said hello and always knew your name.

"Hello, Billy! How's your mammy?"

"Fine thanks, Mr Scanlon."

"There's a good lad now," he'd say.

That would be all, but it was enough.

One Saturday morning after Mr Scanlon had kissed and then waved goodbye to his wife, his daughter May and his two sons Sean and Tomas, he touched the peak of his cap in token salute to Mrs O'Kane and my mother, who were chatting outside Mrs O'Brien's shop.

"Good morning, ladies!"

"Morning, Mr Scanlon," my mother said. "Safe journey, God bless."

He touched the peak of his cap a second time and said, "Thank you very much, Mrs Nolan, and God bless you, too," and strode off with his rolling gait to the corner where he disappeared down the steps to Rose Hill.

"A lovely man," my mother said. "I don't know how that poor woman sticks it, though, him away so much. It's no joke bringing up children at the best of times, but when there's not a man in the house to control them, it must be very, very hard. I think she's marvellous."

Mrs O'Kane agreed.

On the day I decided to try my luck with Ruby Robinson, I thought the best thing might be to tag along with Sean to maybe gain acceptance through association. I was up and washed and in the kitchen when my father came down to catch the half-eight launch to Haulbowline, where he was working at a clerk at Cork Harbour Oil Wharves.

"What are you doing up so early, son?" he asked, surprised to see me at this hour on the day that those of us who went to school had a lie in.

"I'm going to try to get off to the lightship with Ruby Robinson. Can I?"

"Oh that's up to your mammy. Have you asked her?"

"Naw – not yet."

"It's not 'naw'. The word is 'no'."

"I haven't asked her," I said, "but would *you* mind?"

"No, I wouldn't mind."

"Thanks, Dad."

"That's all right, but don't forget now, get your mammy's permission."

I had no trouble with my mother once my father had given the go ahead.

"But be careful. Remember you can't swim. And be sure you're back here in time to get to confession between three and four."

When Sean Scanlon came out of their house on Roche's Row carrying one of his father's bag, I just "happened" to be hanging around the lamp post at the bottom of Bellevue. It was in the middle of the junction where Harbour View, Mervue, Bellevue Terrace, Roche's Row and Rose Hill all came together. Dinny Twomey's and Alex Hansen's houses

151

and Cronin's pub were on one side, Mother Sullivan's, the Purcells' and the Chandlers' houses were across on the other side of the junction. Mr Chandler was a pilot.

"Are you going off this morning, Sean?"

"I am. The old man is going back."

"D'yeh think I might be able to get a trip?"

"Sure, you could come down anyway an' try. Ruby can only say no. He can't *eat* yeh!"

When Ruby came out of his shed at the end of the pier carrying his seaboots and oilskins, I sidled up to him and walked beside him, asking beseechingly, "Would you ever take us off with you today, Mr Robinson, *please?*"

He looked down at me and said, "Ah, don't bother me at the moment, youngfella, will yeh? I'm busy, and besides, me head is splittin'."

The bottom seemed to be about to fall out of my morning.

"Aw, *please*, Mr Robinson – I'll be very quiet, honest I will."

He kept on walking and talking.

"I'm fed up of fellas askin' to come out with me and then gettin' sick all over the boat and wantin' to go home to their mammies. That gives me a pain in the hole . . . I dunno . . . Ask me again later."

Deflated and more than a little hopeless, I said, "All right, Mr Robinson, thank you very much indeed."

A few of the lads arrived after a while, hoping the same hopes as myself. Charlie was already filling the water kegs from the tap at the shore end of the pier.

We busied ourselves fetching and carrying. When Sean Scanlon's father eventually came out the pier and joined the few other men going back after shore leave, I moved close to them in order to be seen when Ruby said, "Good morning, Captain Scanlon!"

"Morning, Ruby! Lovely morning."

Ruby looked at the sky and it seemed to me that he sniffed. "It's nice now," he said, "but I wouldn't be surprised if we had rain before the day is out."

"You could be right, you could be right . . . Well, are we all set to go?"

"All set."

Mr Scanlon stepped aboard, followed by Sean and then the other men from the lightship's crew. Nux McCormack, Ronnie Lincoln and his brother Cyril (down from Dublin on holidays and staying with the Conways at *Teresina*), Con Lynch, John Driscoll and I stood uncertainly in a little group on the top step.

"Well, come *on*! What the hell are ye waitin' for?" Ruby shouted. "D'ye expect me to go up and *carry* ye down?"

How one of us didn't go headlong into the tide in the rush I never knew.

"Stay quiet there now, let ye, and no actin' the maggot!" Ruby said, and then ducked down into the cockpit to wrestle one of Mr Kelvin's diesels into reluctant, protesting, smoky life. The first burst of swear-words wasn't long in coming from down that open hatchway. They were directed at all engines in general, and at the parents of Mr Kelvin in particular.

Mr Scanlon took no part at all in the proceedings, but Charlie ran and hopped about like someone with St Vitus's dance, and Ruby started calling the *Kathleen* for all the hoor's ghosts and sonsa bitches that ever lived, and then began to use words with biblical connotations in such profane profusion and with such vehemence that I wondered whether I'd have to confess to listening to them without blocking my ears when I went to confession in the afternoon.

It was low tide, and the mud-bottomed camber stank in the early morning sun. The mud smell was compounded by the stench of rotting fish guts and fish heads and the decomposing bodies of skate and starfish which had been thrown there from fishing boats at the far slip and Clayton Love's fish shop across the road on The Beach near Thomson's cake shop. Gulls were swooping, screaming, scrabbling and scrapping, in ferocious counterpoint to Ruby's chorus of vile swearing.

153

The cathedral clock struck 11 as Charlie cast off the bow rope and scrambled down the iron ladder to jump aboard. After coiling the rope, he passed us on his way back aft to take the tiller, muttering out of the side of his mouth, "Let ye stay quiet now and keep outa his way and ye'll be awright!"

He eased the high black bow of the *Kathleen* away from the edge of the Pier Head, and we chugged out slowly past the North German Lloyd Pier to begin a slanting run down across the harbour towards the Spit Bank lighthouse. There Charlie would push the tiller across towards his left and bring the *Kathleen* around to point due south towards the mouth of the harbour and Roche's Point. Spike Island would be on our right, or starboard side, as we aimed for the centre of the wide gap between Forts Camden and Carlisle.

I loved the view of our town you got from the water – the multi-coloured terraces that looked as though they were stuck on to the sides of the hill; the huge, grey, granite cathedral with its 300 foot spire tapering to a needle point; the little square-towered, brown church where the town's few Protestants ("Proddy-woddy greenguts/Never said his prayers/Along came a Cat'lic/And threw him down the stairs" – whenever I heard the cornerboys singing that out, I used to shrivel and feel deeply ashamed) went on a Sunday; the black skeleton of a pier outside the Cunard White Star office; the Bishop's Palace, imposing and many-windowed, on Spy Hill, and below it the descending roofs of Barrack Hill's identical houses, looking for all the world like a riffled pack of cards . . . I picked out Bellevue Terrace, and though I couldn't be certain, it looked to me as if someone was waving a white cloth to us from one of the top floor windows of number nine.

I thought the town looked so beautiful, and I felt a profound private pride to be from and of that town.

"Sure we have the finest bleddy natural harbour in the wurruld – why wouldn't we be proud of it?" Mick Long, with all the quivery jowls and the porter belly and the gruff voice and the I-know-everything attitude, was forever saying, if he had

you for an audience for even ten seconds. "Not another harbour in the entire god-damn wurruld to touch it. I can *tell* you
now: it's . . . very . . . bleddy . . . *unique*! No two ways aboud-it!
An' I don't care *what* the fekkin bleddy British say, or the Aus-
tralians either for that matter, with all their oul claims about
Sydney. Know what I say? *Bullshit*! They only come *trottin'* after
Cork Harbour, an' you can take my word for that!"

Looking back at the town and the sweep of the bay from
the *Kathleen,* Nux said, "It's supposed to look like Naples."

"I said that to Mick Long once."

"And what'd he say?"

"He said we had all the Naples here anyone could want,
and that anyone who said they'd like to 'see Naples an' die'
needed their . . .'" I hesitated because I didn't want to repeat
the word. "Needed their so-and-so heads examined.' And
that it was a case of *bíonn adhairce fada ar na buaibh thar lear.*"

"Well, he's *thick*," Nux said. "Probably never been further
than Belgooly in his life. Sure what the hell would *he* know?"

We lapsed into silence, but kept sweeping the harbour with
our eyes, looking in towards Cuskinny Bay and then further
right from that towards where the harbour narrowed into a
channel at East Ferry; then back to the town again, along the
Holy Ground, the Baths Quay with its huge brick chimney,
the red-brick Customs House, the clock tower of the Harbour
Office at Lynch's Quay, English's butcher shop on East
Beach, the CYMS hall, Murray's ship chandlery, the Soldiers'
Home, the GPO, the Promenade on Westbourne with its
bandstand and big old Russian cannon captured in the
Crimean War and presented to the town by the captain of a
troopship, the Yacht Club (the first in the world), the Tech,
Scott's Church, the Crescent, the railway station and Deepwater Quay, and the Water's Edge, or Five-Foot Way, which
runs all the way from the Deepwater Quay to Whitepoint.

Didn't Thackeray the novelist and Father Matthew, the
man who founded the Pioneer Total Abstinence Association,
frequently walk together along that same Water's Edge, and

hadn't Sully told us that Thackeray said it was one of the pleasantest walks in the whole of Europe?

"Do you think Mick Long knew that?" I asked Nux.

"Mick Long wouldn't even know that Thackeray was a *writer*!"

"Did *you*?"

"No," he said, "but that's beside the point."

"Well, there you go so!" I said.

"Yerra, up me gansey!" Nux said and turned away with a pout. "What're yeh tryin' to start an argument for?"

He slid on his bum across the deck to the other side of the boat and hung his head over the gunwale, looking down at the small bow-wave going away from the hull in one arm of a spreading vee. Presently he raised his head and said over his shoulder to me, "Hey, look, langer! There's Spike! Come on over an' take a look at it."

As I began to walk over in a crouch to join him, Ruby bellowed from the stern, "Don't ye be messin' about up there now, d'ye hear? I don't want any a ye fellas fallin' overboard. I have enough to do!"

None of us had been beyond the pier at Spike Island. Its green, humped mass with the line of houses down close to the shore, the fort walls higher up, and the facts that there was a huge moated prison there and heavy guns trained out to sea were about as much as we knew about that strange, green, alien island.

We had been told – again by Sully, who else? – that John Mitchell, an Irishman sentenced to deportation to Van Diemen's Land, spent some time in the prison "and wrote part of his famous *Jail Journal* there". None of us had ever heard of *Jail Journal*, so we reckoned it couldn't have been all *that* famous. But Sully didn't even have to look at a book in order to tell us that Mitchell had written, about his time on Spike: "Gazing on grey stone, my eyes will grow stony."

Well, there it was now off the starboard bow, looking as strange and mysterious as ever.

Within a few minutes the *Kathleen* was beginning to dip her bow into the swell, and I leaned over the gunwale and looked down to watch the red-painted underside of the hull below the water line, coming out and glistening wetly before plunging down deep again.

Up . . . glisten . . . pause . . . down . . . pause . . . up . . . glisten . . . pause . . . down . . .

And then it happened: first the queasiness, then the retching, and finally the whole terrible, bitter jet of sick thrusting up my throat and barrelling round my mouth and . . . out; and the vomit coming in great gouts, and bits of carrot and cabbage and God knows what else from last night's dinner and this morning's breakfast spewing over the side, and my stomach heaving and contracting, and me wanting to let go my grip of the gunwale and just topple into the tide and go down into blackness and relief, to get away from it, to die . . . But it kept on coming, and coming, and coming, and I never felt so sick in the whole of my life. I really did want to die . . .

"Poor oul Nolan! Don't worry boy, the first ten years are the worst!"

It was John Driscoll trying to be funny.

I felt a hand on my shoulder and turned halfway around, water streaming out of my eyes. Charlie was kneeling beside me on the deck. He had asked Mr Scanlon to take the tiller.

"Don't try to stop!" he said. "Get it all up outa yeh an' you'll be grand. Put your oul finger on your tongue or down your trote and give yerself the gawk good an' proper . . . There you are! Just the job. You'll be awright now in a few minutes."

I didn't think I'd ever be all right again as long as I lived. I'd done just what Ruby said gave him a pain in the hole, got sick all over the boat. And yes, at that moment I *did* want to go home to me mammy!

When I eventually sat back and wiped my sour mouth with my hanky, and then lay down with my cheek against the warm planking of the deck with the smell of caulking going straight

157

up my nose and making me feel queasy all over again, Nux leaned across and said, "Are you OK, knackers?"

I didn't feel like answering, or even nodding.

"A good oul feed of boiled fat bacon now and you'll be fair to Midleton!" he said.

Before he had even finished, I was back at the side, dry-retching, and shuddering from the bitter taste of the bile which eventually came up. After a while I inched my way back until I was where the *Kathleen*'s thick mast went down through the deck to the hull below. I clung hard to the mast, pressing my belly against it in an attempt to stop the heaving in my strained stomach whose muscles were screaming.

The first words I uttered when finally I was able to talk at all were to Nux.

"You're a dirty louser, boy! And you were the one who told me I should have laughed at Gerald Taaffe when he fell off his bike!"

"Ah, you can't take a joke, Nolan, that's the trouble with you," he said, and the pout was already on his mouth even before he turned away.

It was only then it dawned on me that we were lifting and rising slowly with the motion of the ocean, not moving under our own power. There was a disturbing silence apart from the sounds of the waves lapping against the sides, and the creaking of the hull.

"What's up?" I whispered to John Driscoll who was nearest to me.

"What're yeh whisperin' for? We're broke down, driftin'. Ruby is tryin' to fix it."

It was bad enough to have emptied my innards into the sea, but now we were going to go on the rocks and . . .

"Come on, yeh bleddy bastardin' thing!" Ruby roared as he straightened up in the engine well and swung viciously at the flywheel with the hammer.

Whether by sheer coincidence or not I have no idea, but the engine immediately sputtered, died, coughed, sputtered again and caught, and within seconds, sending up a small cloud of black smoke, settled into its normally abnormal rhythm again. I thought the smell was going to make me vomit some more, but the sick subsided.

* * * * * * * *

As we eventually circled the lightship, I began wondering how high those white letters on her side were, the ones spelling out the word DAUNT.

We were still about thirty yards from the lightship when her crew, leaning over the side watching our approach, began to call out.

"How-ya, Charlie – is it yerself?"

"Hello, Rube! How's she cuttin'?"

"Begod we thought ye'd never get here at all! What were ye doin'? Havin' a picnic?"

"Ye might well joke," Ruby said sourly. It didn't stop the flow from the men on the lightship.

"Jazus, Paddy, 'tis fat yer after gettin'!"

"Mick, sure 'tis yerself!"

"Did one of the young lads throw up? Ah, sure Janey, we'll make men a them yet!"

Their accents were the biggest surprise. Living and going to school in the town, mixing with townspeople, occasionally going to Cork, or maybe Youghal or Kinsale, the only Irish accents we were accustomed to were Cobh ("We haven't got a Cork accent, boy – we're *cosmo*-politans," Mick Long asserted), Cork city and County Cork. Sully had managed to submerge his west Cork/Kerry accent into something resembling our own with an occasional insertion of posh.

To me, the men on the deck of the lightship sounded like country farmers, and what were farmers doing spending their lives on a ship that never went anywhere? Did that mean that the men never *did* anything? And didn't they get fed up never *seeing* anything except the coastline and the sea and sea birds, and passing ships homeward or outward bound? Did

159

they get browned off of not *going* anywhere? With every minute of their lives spent with the rolling, up-and-down, sideways-and-back motion of the ship, how come they weren't gawking their guts up day and night? Was it lonely out here in all God's hours and kinds of weather?

"I don't know how that poor woman sticks it," my mother had said about Mrs Scanlon. But how did Mr Scanlon and all the other men stick it? I supposed that they filled their time writing letters, reading, listening to the radio, maybe making ships-in-bottles. And of course keeping watches, maintaining the equipment, keeping the ship itself clean.

But were they ever afraid? When storms came and waves pounded them and the securing chains were put under terrible strain and there were no ships in the vicinity, they must have known how dangerous their position was. Did they pray much then? But in a heaving ship, pitching and rolling violently, how could you kneel down and pray, or keep a candle or a Sacred Heart lamp alight?

My mouth must have been open because just before we bumped in alongside the lightship and squashed the tires that Charlie hung over the side to act as bumpers and made them screech and squeal, one of the men looking down said, "You hafta be the lad who spewed up, are yeh? Did yeh get the pukes? Montezuma's revenge, hah?"

I nodded miserably.

No one on the *Kathleen* was talking at this stage, except Charlie and Ruby. Ruby was bobbing up and down in the hatch like a jack-in-the-box. One moment he'd be bent over the engine, fiddling with it, cursing, the sweat rolling off his never-ending forehead into his eyes. The next second he'd be up on his tiptoes to see how Charlie was doing guiding the heaving *Kathleen* in alongside the rolling, anchored lightship, and giving him advice. Charlie ignored him, grunting, and leaned far out, ducking low to see under the boom, watching, gauging, trying his level best to avoid a collision, and eventually getting us alongside. While Ruby held the tiller,

Charlie threw lines from bow and aft to the lightship, and the ship's crew gradually hauled us in alongside where we tied up.

Climbing aboard the lightship was going to be an experience fraught with anxiety as far as I was concerned. I watched how Mr Scanlon and Sean and Ruby and the men going back on duty managed it. They made nothing at all of it, but I didn't fancy it one bit. I couldn't swim. In fact I was afraid of the deep water, and there was an awful lot of deep water out here where we were off the coast, south-eastwards of Robert Head.

It was a case of trying to judge the precise moment that the *Kathleen* reached the exact apex of her upward surge on a wave and paused for a millisecond before dropping away quickly down into the trough of the next one. Even though the sun was shining and there was a nice sky, a fairly heavy swell was running.

Nux, as always, was to the forefront of everything. No sooner had Mr Scanlon put his head over the side and called down to us, "Right, lads, ye can come aboard," than Nux was stepping off the *Kathleen* with perfect timing and confidence on to the rope ladder, up the few wooden rungs, and swinging his leg inboard with a helping hand from a crewman.

"There y'are!" the man said. "*That's* the way to do it. Nothin' to it at all. Next!"

"Come on, it's easy," Nux added.

Ronnie Lincoln and John Driscoll took him at his word and made it *look* easy, but they were swimmers. Cyril Lincoln was next in line. A shy nervous boy with straight, floppy, blond hair, he skipped behind me and said, "Go on; you go next."

I could have stabbed him.

The *Kathleen* had no dinghy with her that day, and the lightship's lifeboat was slung inboard on the davits. If I fell in, they'd never get the boat into the water in time to rescue me. A non-swimmer could be drowned very easily away out here. Or I could fall between the lightship's and the *Kathleen*'s sides and be squashed to death, or get trapped out of

161

sight under the big iron hull of the lightship, down there in the surging green water which gets darker the deeper you go . . . *O Sacred Heart of Jesus, help and protect me!*

Nux was still waiting for me.

"Are you goin'ta be all day, boy? It'll be time to go ashore soon. Get a move on and stop bein' an oul cowardy custard!"

That did it! With pounding heart and sheer desperation, the next time the *Kathleen* rose up on a wave, I leaned out, grabbed the ladder's ropes and stepped off. In fact I stepped off a second or two too soon, before she was at the top of her rising motion. I was lucky to escape having one of my feet crushed, but the strong hands and arms of the seaman waiting there to help swung me up and in, and suddenly I was standing on the deck of the lightship.

"Jeekers, Nolan, I though you were never comin' up!" Nux said. "Come on, we can go down below."

I followed him carefully backward's down the ladder into the darkness of the crew's cabin, where a coal stove glowed redly in the centre of the floor and the hammocks swayed with the rolling of the ship. Only the master, and maybe the mate, had single cabins of their own.

When all of the supplies – the food, coal and water – had been brought aboard and stowed, the crew came down the ladder, chattering away in their "country" accents. They all wore the same type of navy blue gansey, and they all had ruddy faces and loud voices. They questioned and cross-questioned Charlie and the men returning to duty. How were things "inside"? Had Ford's laid off anyone recently? Did yer woman win that case and was oul so-and-so out of hospital yet? And when they had got all the information they wanted, they went away into corners to read their letters from home.

One of them, who was going back in with us and who had only one letter to read, came to where we were seated at the scrubbed mess table and answered our questions. After a while he said he'd make some tea, and he asked me, "Would yeh care for a drop of condentist milk?"

He didn't wait for an answer but took a tin out of the cupboard and a complex-looking knife out of his pocket. He opened out what looked like a marlin spike on the penknife, gave it a quick wipe on his sleeve and stabbed two holes in one end of the tin.

"There y'are, ye can suck it out." And we did. It was delicious – sweet and thick – and I made up my mind I'd save up for a can of it when we got home, and I'd drink every single sup of it myself.

We were told we could have a look around the ship if we wanted to, but were warned to keep our hands off things and not to be interfering with anything that didn't concern us.

We ran shouting and yelling from bow to stern of the ship, trying all the brass-handled doors we came across. Most of them were locked, but one opened inwards to reveal a mass of machinery with polished copper piping bending like an endless snake through it and around it. It was from this place that the humming sound you heard all over the ship came.

"The machinery room," I said.

"Janey, Nolan, we're not flippin' blind!" John Driscoll said. "We can see, yeh know? Any eejit could tell it's the machinery room."

"My granda is a chief engineer, and so is my Uncle John," I said by way of explanation.

"So what?" Nux said. "My old man is manager of the Labour Exchange."

"Mine is a pilot," Con Lynch said.

Before anyone else had a chance to say anything, Ronnie Lincoln said, "My father is a superintendent in the Garda Síochána."

"Your old man is a *cop*?" John Driscoll said.

"He's not a cop – he's a Garda Síochána superintendent."

"Same thing," Con Lynch said.

"A rozzer!"

"A bleddy peeler!"

"A flatfoot!"

163

"You know what it is," Nux said. "You oughta be *ashamed* of yerself, Lincoln, boy! . . . Who's game to go up the lantern?"

I had been dreading this. I didn't want to go up the ladder. It was so high that if you fell, you'd be killed stone dead. But the push came from behind, and we continued along the passageway towards the exit on to the open deck. There was one last door on our right. Sure that it would be locked like the others, I twisted the handle and suddenly found myself halfway into a small luxurious cabin, two men looking up at me. One of them looked surprised: that was Mr Scanlon. The other looked furious: that was Ruby Robinson. They had glasses of whiskey in their hands.

Ruby started to stand up, shouting, "Get to hell outa. . ." but Mr Scanlon cut him short. He put his drink down on the small table and stood up.

"Now, lads, ye can't come in here – it's private. Take a look around the ship. Ye can look anywhere ye like, but keep away from the wireless cabin and the machinery-room. And ye'd want to hurry, because Ruby will be leaving soon."

I tried to follow Nux and the others up to the lantern, but when I was halfway up that swaying, nearly vertical ladder, I made the mistake of looking down, saw the deck and the full shape of the ship away below me, felt the motion as the ship rolled, and the ladder, with me clinging to it, seemed to go away out over the water before coming back again and swinging to the other side. Suddenly I froze, terrified, and couldn't move; couldn't unlock my grip on the iron ladder, or move my feet, or even breathe properly; could neither go up nor down, but just cling there, rigid, convinced I was going to go crashing to the deck and end up with broken legs and a fractured skull . . .

When I eventually did manage to get my feet and hands to move, I went down rung by agonising rung, my eyes squeezed tightly shut, and the Sacred Heart of Jesus supplication being whispered over and over again. Why, I wondered, do I have to suffer from so many fears?

One of the crew came out of the companionway from the main cabin and, looking up, saw the lads at the top on the lantern platform.

"Get the hell down here outa that!" he shouted. "Do ye want to be killed?"

As they were climbing down the ladder, I got back aboard the *Kathleen*. Charlie was already making things shipshape for the return trip. The fellows came up to the bow where I was sitting and talked pointedly about the view from the lantern, and the amazing mirrors they saw inside the glass of the lantern, and how small the *Kathleen* looked from away up there.

After the last of the men going ashore boarded, Ruby and Mr Scanlon came out on deck and stood apart from the other men: the two bosses, exchanging jokes, laughing, pushing each other on the shoulder. Then they shook hands, and Ruby came aboard and immediately went down the hatch to the hated Kelvin.

* * * * * * * *

"Awright, let'er go forrad there, Charlie!" Ruby shouted.

The bow of the *Kathleen* swung out from the lightship's side. As we pulled away from her, all her crew came to wave us off.

"So long, Rube! See you again in ten days time!"

"Tell Mrs Denvir in the European hello for me, Rube, will ya?"

"Hey, Charlie! Don't forget to post that now, hah?"

"I won't." Charlie never said much.

"Goodbye, Sean. Goodbye, Ruby!" That was Mr Scanlon just before he turned and went into his cabin. I looked at Sean. He had tears in his eyes which he quickly knuckled away. The rest of the crew stayed at the ship's side and were still there ten minutes later, still waving, still watching us heading in towards the harbour. I felt sad for them, because I was sure they were lonely to see us leaving.

After a while I turned away from the lightship and looked in towards Roche's Point. We were going in on a flood tide, and the old *Kathleen* underneath us was zipping along as though pleased to be getting away from the deep sea in which she had aged and grown graceless.

"The Cow and Calf rocks," John Driscoll said as we came abreast of them. "Ever hearda the *Celtic*?"

I said that of course I had. We had a leather settee off her which my grandmother had bought at an auction in 1928 and which was now in my mother and father's house on Bellevue Terrace.

"Well it's around here she was wrecked," John said.

We gazed in silence, watching the tide swishing in and out, over and back across the rocks. All I remembered about what my mother had told me when we sat by the bedroom window one day watching the *Morsecock* away out at the point doing some salvage work was that "almost every house in the town has something off the *Celtic*" and that a number of men had lost their lives in an accident on the liner during the first salvage operation.

"They were gassed," she said, "but don't ask me how. I've forgotten; it was a long time ago."

Ruby, seeming to be in a more benign mood now (was it because the job was done, or was it, maybe, the whiskey in Mr Scanlon's cabin?), I went aft and said, "Mr Robinson?"

"What is it? What d'yeh want?"

"Do you know about the *Celtic*?"

"Of course I do. Everyone knows about the *Celtic*. Why wouldn't I? What do yeh want to know about her?"

And he told me how the 20,000 ton liner had been blown in on a lee shore during a gale in December of 1928.

"It's still a bit of a bleddy mystery why it happened at all. She had an experienced skipper, Captain Barry, or Berry, I don't know which, but he knew the coast and the harbour well. She was a White Star liner, yeh see, and herself and her sister ships, the *Adriatic*, the *Baltic* and the . . . eh . . . the . . .

Jazus, what was the name of her? . . . Charlie, what was the name of the *Celtic's* other sister ship?"

"The *Cedric*," Charlie said.

The *Cedric*, of course! Me head is goin'! But the four of 'em called here at Cobh all the time. There was a lot of oul talk that the *Celtic* struck the Pollock rock. I dunno if that was true or not, but anyway the gale blew her on to the rocks there, broadside, and that was it as far as she went. She was there for a long time, nearly a year, became part of the scenery I suppose you might say.

"I always felt sorry for her captain, poor oul bastard, because he was due to retire as soon as they reached Liverpool. A sad end to a distinguished career for him – his last voyage, and he wrecks his ship! There's no justice in this life."

"My mother –"

"What's yer name?"

"Billy Nolan."

"Molly Nolan – Molly Sexton that was – are you Molly Nolan's son?"

"I am."

"Sure, I've known Molly for years! And yer father, too – Eddie, 'E.J.', isn't it? What'd yer mother tell yeh?"

"She said some men died when they were tryin' to salvage the liner."

"She was right. See, the *Celtic* was carrying quite a big cargo of grain, along with a lot of equipment for Ford's in Cork. The foreign salvage experts who were brought in in the hope of saving her cut away part of the top portion of the hull, the idea being to try to refloat her and tow her into the inner harbour, but that didn't work. Then in terrible weather almost a year after she went aground, the grain cargo got soaked and started to putrefy, and then a pipe burst down in the number four hold, where there were men working. Poison gas came off the wet grain – hydrogen sulphide if the oul memory isn't gone entirely. Sixteen of the men were gassed, and four died tryin' to rescue 'em . . ."

He stopped talking and looked back towards Roche's Point which was dropping astern of us.

"That put a gloom on the town which lasted a long time," he said eventually. "Twenty people wiped out all in one go like that. I hope nothing as bad ever happens again, not in my lifetime anyway."

* * * * * * * *

I wandered back up towards the bow of the *Kathleen* and sat by myself with my back against the mast looking straight in the harbour. At about the same time as the top of the spire of the cathedral came into view, I thought, this is what the emigrants must dream about, whether they are in Dagenham or Detroit or Durban or Darjeeling – seeing the green fields of Ireland once more and feeling the huge feeling everyone experiences when they are coming home.

"Keepin' to yerself? Have we got leprosy or somethin'?"

Nux planked his backside on the deck alongside me.

"No," I said. "I was just thinkin'."

"You're always thinkin'. It must give yeh a pain in the napper. Listen, langer, there's a great gaff on in the Arch tonight – *The Sea Wolf*, with Edward G. He's dynamite. I saw the trailer, and I'd say it's great."

For a moment I could have throttled him for breaking in on my private thoughts, but that only lasted a second. Edward G. Robinson ("Emanuel Goldenberg's his real-life name," my father, who rarely went to the cinema, told me) *was* dynamite. Those slitted Japanese-looking eyes, the huge gash of a mouth, the strutting Little Caesar walk, the compact body and the menacing rasp of his voice – "Mother of Mercy, is this the end of Rico?"

"Are yeh goin' to come?"

"Definitely! I'm almost certain. Mam owes me four dee for doing some messages for her yesterday. Keep a seat for me."

"Deadly!"

When we arrived back in the camber, Nux, John Driscoll,

Con Lynch, Sean Scanlon and I helped Charlie to unload the *Kathleen*. We all said, "Thanks very much indeed, Mr Robinson," to Ruby, and it was agreed that the Lincolns were lousers to run off without lifting a finger, giving the excuse that Auntie Bridie would kill them if they were late for tea.

Finished, we tore in the pier in a wild gallop home and then to the cathedral for confession. I was just about to cross The Beach when I remembered something.

"I'll see yeh, later, Nux. You go ahead."

Another of those incredulous looks and a muttered, "D'yeh know what it is? You beat Banagher!" And then he was gone, across past the Rob Roy and up towards Power's shoe repair shop and then off up the muscle-knotting steepness of Old Street.

I trotted back out the pier to Ruby's shed. Ruby was nowhere to be seen, and I was glad of that because it was Charlie I was looking for. I couldn't see him on the boat and when I went to the shed door and looked in, I thought I saw a dim figure bending over, coiling ropes or something.

"Charlie!" I called.

"Yep. What is it? Did yeh leave somethin' behind?" He came out towards the door wiping his hands with a piece of cotton-waste.

"No. I just wanted to say thanks, Charlie – for helping me when I was . . . for helping me out there this morning."

Charlie looked away. Then he shook his head and said, "Not at all. Seasickness is one of the lousiest feelin's in the world. Always remember, though, you'll be awright if you put yer finger down your trote an' bring up the last of it . . . Go on, you'll be late for Edward G."

The film, *The Sea Wolf*, was fabulous, but it scared the hell out of me. It had Barry Fitzgerald, John Garfield and Ida Lupino in it, and Edward G. *was* dynamite. He was the baddie, a sea captain, rotten through and through.

There was a line in the film which stuck with me for the rest of my life, the motto the captain lived by: *Better to reign in*

Granda and the U-Boats

GRANDA HAD LOST part of a finger in some incident that was never fully explained to us. It wasn't the sort of thing you felt you could ask about, but at meals you couldn't help noticing the little stump of bone protruding from the middle of the top of the lopped-off finger. It looked like the blackened thick wick of a fat altar candle whose flame has been extinguished. But the circumstances of its happening remained a mystery, part of the overall, enduring complex mystery of Granda himself.

At one stage I let my imagination roam freely, thinking up scenarios, posing unasked questions such as, was it chopped off by a Fu Manchu figure in Hong Kong or San Francisco? Was it the residue of some unspeakable torture Granda had been subjected to in World War I? Had he fought a duel for Nan's honour, and suffered a mini-amputation from an insulter's sword? Or had he just got his hand caught in a machine?

I also went through a period of constantly worrying about how badly it hurt when it happened, and whether it still pained. And when I asked my mother about it, she said she didn't know and not to keep on bothering her about things like that, hadn't she enough to worry about?

On Haulbowline Island I had often stood in my grandparents' home looking at the framed group photograph of Granda and Nana and the surviving members of their family. I was in the picture, too, a baby in Mam's arms. Granda, broad-bodied in a dark suit, was seated in the front row and looked chirpy and proud, while Nan looked self-conscious and a little aloof. Auntie Tracy looked, as ever, pouting and surly and generally cross-grained. Auntie Winnie and Auntie Kitty and Auntie Lillian all looked plump and had the features with which they would mature and eventually grow old. Auntie Doreen, wearing the spectacles she hated so much, looked vulnerable and serious. Auntie Rita, trying for sophistication, looked formal. Uncle John looked slim and handsome and glad to be there. My father, smart in a light-coloured suit, had his chin in and looked as if he wished he were somewhere else. My mother looked pretty, a little shy, but proud to be a mother.

Missing were Jim, who had died as a child, and Pat who had been killed in India when serving as a flying officer in the RAF.

When the family moved off Haulbowline to live on Harbour Hill in Cobh, the photograph moved with them, and I still continued to look at it, searching the faces, trying to project myself backwards in time to a day I'd never be able to remember. And when Granda, in his sixties, went back to sea with Irish Shipping, and Uncle John, a chief engineer with British Tankers, was torpedoed in 1942 on a convoy to Murmansk (he survived after being picked up from the icy seas by a rescue ship), I once again took to staring at that photograph.

I tried to reconcile the squat smiling man in civvies, surrounded by his brood, with the elegant, serious-faced young naval officer of World War I. I also tried to reconcile the picture of the monstrous, lethal-looking dreadnought battleship on which he served as chief engineering officer in that war with the pathetic-looking tramp steamer he went to sea in in this war. And when he came back to Harbour Hill for his few days leave between Atlantic crossings, I sat hanging on his every word. Wasn't he (elderly in my eyes) making those frightful voyages in worn-out ships that sailed alone, out of convoy, with no destroyer or corvette escorts, no protection at all save the green-white-and-orange tricolour painted on the side and all the lights switched on at night?

The ships were barely seaworthy, yet they continuously crossed a vicious ocean that was teeming with U-Boats hunting in wolf packs which were sending hundreds of thousands of tons of shipping to the bottom of the Atlantic, killing the tens of thousands who went down with them. Hadn't they almost got my Uncle John? Sometimes at night, when looking out towards Roche's Point, we would see the huge flashes and red glows on the horizon when ships were blown to smithereens.

There were nights when I wished we *lived* at Roche's Point, because then I'd be nearer to the explosions out at sea and would be able (God forgive me) to get a closer look at what took place, instead of having to imagine. The U-Boats, which sailed originally from Germany and later from such Biscay bases as the French ports of Lorient, La Rochelle and Brest, lay in wait off the south and west coast of Ireland and picked off ships as they arrived from the USA, or headed out across the Atlantic, or were in passage from or to Australia.

Winston Churchill was enraged by this and nursed his resentment right through the war. His fury was at its height during the Battle of the Atlantic. Ireland's neutrality, and the stance taken to preserve that neutrality, were matters that still occupied his mind when preparing, and then delivering his Victory Broadcast on 13 May 1945.

Owing to the action of the Dublin Government, so much at variance with the temper and instinct of thousands of southern Irishmen who hastened to the battlefront to prove their ancient valour, the approaches which the southern Irish ports could so easily have guarded were closed by hostile aircraft and U-Boats. This was indeed a *deadly moment in our life, and if it had not been for the loyalty and friendship of Northern Ireland we should have been forced to come to close quarters or perish from the earth. However, with a restraint and poise to which, I say, history will find few parallels, His Majesty's Government never laid a hand upon them, though at times it would have been quite easy and quite natural, and we left the Dublin Government to frolic with the Germans and later the Japanese representatives, to their heart's content.**

But that was still in the future. Meanwhile I listened to Granda.

A natural spinner of yarns, he wasn't above the occasional colourful embellishment for effect. Talking to a group of his cronies one day in the bar of the European Hotel, he said that the ship he was on, the *Irish Rose,* was so old, and so heavy with cement that had been poured over thin rusted-through plates below the water line to seal leaks, and sat so deeply in the water that the Plimsoll mark was out of sight. "She was more of a bloody submarine than a cargo ship. We hit a huge wave off the Ambrose light when steaming eastwards one Monday, took it green over the bows, then went straight into it, and by Christ we didn't surface until the Wednesday!"

Of course they recognised it for the wild exaggeration that it was, but they didn't let on, didn't react with any form of audible or visible disbelief. He was buying the drinks. They were on to a good thing.

It was different when he was talking in his own home with my father. Then the more serious and reserved side of him came out. When he wasn't playing to an audience, his voice and manner were altogether more restrained. Up to the time that Uncle John was killed, Granda often talked of "the comradeship of the sea", and he referred to the Germans as Germans, not as the Hun, or the Bosch or the Krauts.

*Cited in *The Imperial War Museum Book of The War at Sea* Julian Thompson MacMillan London 1996.

About U-Boat captains, more than once I heard him say, "They have a job to do, which is sinking Allied ships. But not all of them are the ruthless, vicious bastards they're painted."

One Sunday morning after 10.30 mass, he and my father sat in the drawing room of No. 3, Harbour Hill talking quietly of how the war was going. My father asked him if it was true that *some* U-Boat captains had been known actually to *help* crews of ships which they had torpedoed.

"Sure didn't Prien do it?" Granda said.

"I'm sorry," my father said. "Prien? I'm not familiar with the name."

"You never heard of Prien? Gunther Prien? The fellow who took his submarine into the Flow in '39 and sank the *Royal Oak*? You never heard of *him*?" Granda sounded incredulous.

"I remember the sinking of the *Royal Oak* all right," my father said. "Of course I do, who wouldn't? All those men killed, over 800 wasn't it? It's just that I don't recall coming across the name of the U-Boat *captain*."

"Oh, that was Prien," my grandfather said. "U-47. Took her right into the heart of Scapa Flow. On the surface. At night. God knows how he did it, although I think meself that there was a bit of penny-pinching by the politicians between the wars, and the defences at Scapa flow were neglected. But still, Prien had to pass the blockships on his way in, and it was a very narrow gap. That took extraordinary courage and great ship handling. Banged four torpedoes into the *Royal Oak*, and then got out again and back to Germany. The Germans loved that."

Granda was familiar with Scapa Flow, the huge (50 square miles) stretch of sea among the Orkney Islands up off the northern tip of Scotland. It had been used as a fleet anchorage and main base during the 1914-1918 war and was now being used again as a naval base. The battleship he had served on in World War I had been one of the British Grand Fleet, and it had been from Scapa Flow that they had sailed to the battle of Jutland in 1916. So, names like Hoy, Burray,

South Ronaldsay and Flotta, the islands which formed the boundaries of Scapa Flow, were well known to him.

Prien and his entire crew were awarded Iron Crosses for their brilliant exploit and were flown to Berlin to meet Hitler. The very assured, very accomplished, very brave 31-year-old Gunther Prien became known in Germany as "The Bull of Scapa Flow". Scapa Flow made him a national hero in his own country and a favourite of Karl Dönitz, the German naval officer in charge of U-Boats. The American correspondent William Shirer described Prien as "clean cut, cocky, a fanatical Nazi and obviously capable".*

His sinking of the *Royal Oak* caused him to be viewed in Britain as a vile and dangerous enemy. His subsequent success as a hunter-killer in the north Atlantic (his ultimate statistics: 28 merchant ships sunk, totalling 164,953 tons) would turn him into what objective describers would term a feared and loathed adversary, while others settled for such sobriquets as "murdering bastard".

"But he sent brandy across to a wounded man in a lifeboat from a Cunard ship he had shelled," Granda said. "Then he stuck a torpedo into the ship and sank her. That was only a few days after war had been declared. He even asked the skipper of a neutral ship that was in the vicinity to take the crew of the Cunarder aboard . . . The comradeship of the sea can often prompt men to turn a blind eye towards official orders, Eddie. And Prien wasn't the only one who did it."

When the U-41 (captain Korvettenkapitan Adolf Mugler) sank the British ship *Darino* off the Spanish coast in November 1939, the submarine took a dozen of the ship's crew aboard, and later transferred them to another merchantman.

Information like this was passed around among seamen whenever they met ashore, in the bars of the ports at which

*W. Shirer, *Berlin Diary*, Hamish Hamilton, 1941, p. 190.

their ships called. They read the newspapers, listened to the wireless, took in and assessed the propaganda claims made by each side in the war.

"You develop a bullshit-detector," Granda said when my father asked him how much of what you read or heard you could believe. "Sure that's what propaganda is all about – lies and exaggerations and stirring up fear in your opponents, and making your own people feel good. You have to be able to *recognise* bullshit."

Granda enjoyed telling of the giving to other survivors, at another time and place, by another German ace, Kapitan-leutnant Otto Kretschmer (known to his colleagues as "Silent Otto"), of advice relating to the nearest land and the course that should be steered in order to reach it.

"What's more," Granda said, "he gave it in perfect English."

"How come?" my father asked.

"He was at Exeter University before the war," Granda said.

"And is he still out there?" my father asked, gesturing towards the mouth of the harbour and the ocean beyond.

"*No*, he's not." Granda said. "He's a prisoner of war. Got inside the escort screen of a convoy one night off Iceland and sank five ships within a couple of hours. That brought his total of ships sunk to well over 40 – 43 or 44 I think, and he was heading towards the 300,000 tons mark. He was actually on his way *away* from the convoy when a couple of destroyers depth charged him, forced him to the surface and started to shell the bejasus out of him. Different sort of character altogether from Prien, who was an arrogant bugger, a white horse of a different colour.

"'Silent Otto' knew his number was up and gave the order to abandon ship. The crew, apart from himself and his engineer officer, went into the sea, and Kretschmer then signalled to the captain of one of the destroyers, the *Walker*, saying he was sinking and asking that his crew be picked up."

My father asked him why the engineer officer hadn't jumped into the sea with the other men.

"Because he went below to open the sea valves to scuttle the boat," Granda said. "Poor bugger went down with her. Never seen again."

"And Kretschmer? What happened to *him*?"

"Rescued by the same destroyer as pulled the crew out of the water and brought back to England as a POW," Granda said. "At the rate at which fellows like Prien and Kretschmer, and another laddie named Schepke, sank ships, faster than they could be replaced, you'd have to wonder how much longer this war can go on. Old Dönitz's theories of wolf packs are paying dividends. I don't know where it'll all end at all."

Granda's own qualified admiration of some of the U-Boat commanders' skill and bravery, and sometimes honourable behaviour, was shattered beyond redemption even before the death of Uncle John. He knew, of course, that Dönitz had issued orders to his U-Boat captains to the effect that they were to rescue no one, and to have no care for the ships' boats, but he was able to set against that the facts that there were U-Boat captains prepared to ignore those instructions.

The turning point in his attitude towards the U-Boat captains came in the wake of the sinking of the 20,000-ton former Cunard liner *Laconia* in September of 1942. Following the attempted rescue of hundreds of Italian prisoners of war by U-Boat captain Korvettenkapitan Warner Hartenstein, Admiral Dönitz issued the chilling order(s) that all attempts to rescue members of ships sunk had to cease, adding, "Rescue contradicts the most fundamental demands of war for the annihilation of enemy ships and crew."

"'Annihilation'," Granda said. "So that's what we're down to? Now, *he's* a murdering, murderous . . . *bastard*!" He actually spat when he said the word. "By Jesus, hah? And he's trying to turn them *all* into murdering bastards. That's what we're up against."

Later in the same month as that in which he had issued his order that all rescue attempts had to cease, Dönitz went even further along the road of seeming savagery when he defined what he called "the so-called rescue ship" which sailed with most convoys (many of them ocean-going tugs or trawlers, their function being to pick survivors out of the sea) as "a valuable target . . . in view of the desired destruction of the steamers' crews".

The news of the torpedoing of the *Irish Pine*, and her loss with all hands, followed shortly afterwards. The *Irish Pine* was torpedoed in the Atlantic by the German U-Boat, U-608, in filthy weather at 14 minutes after midnight on the morning of the 16th of November. The ship had three huge tricolours painted on each of her sides, one amidships (flanked by the words ÉIRE in giant white letters), one near the bow, and one near the stern – the internationally recognised badges of her neutrality. But the captain of U-608, Kapitanleutnant Rolf Struckmeier, operating out of Lorient in France (it's on an inlet of the Bay of Biscay) and under the overall command of Admiral Dönitz, torpedoed her anyway, after stalking her for 8 hours. The *Irish Pine* sank, stern first, within three minutes. The sea was rough, with large waves forming, some of the crests breaking in the force 6 north-west wind. The temperature was 12 degrees Centigrade.

From about half a mile away, Struckmeier saw, and *recorded* that he had seen, a lifeboat being lowered. Obeying Dönitz's orders, he did nothing about picking up survivors from the 33-man crew.

When we got the news of the sinking of Uncle John's tanker, something in my grandfather changed, withered, died. He was no longer the Granda I had known. He became a strained stranger, an old man in a chief engineer's uniform with its four gold bands above the cuffs on each of the sleeves, who came home from the sea every six or eight weeks and who never smiled.

Mister Puccini

ON THE EVENING of the day the *Cork Examiner* carried the announcement that *La Bohème* was to be put on in the Cork Opera House by the Dublin Operatic Society, my father arrived home from work with an announcement of his own to make.

"Moll, we're going to the Opera House next week to hear Frank Ryan singing 'Your tiny hand is frozen'."

My mother stopped in her tracks (she was about to clear my father's soup plate off the table and bring in his dinner) and looked at my father, who had walked to the fireplace where he stood with his back to it, hands in his trousers pockets.

"*Really?*" she said, her eyes wide.

"Yep," he said. "*Really.*"

"Oh, Eddie, that's lovely! What night?"

"Thursday," he said smiling, delighted at my mother's delight.

"I must book Lillian or Doreen straight away," my mother said as she left the room, humming happily to herself. Lillian and Doreen Sexton, two of her younger unmarried sisters, lived with my Nan and Granda down at No. 3, Harbour Hill.

When my father was halfway through his dinner and my

mother was in the kitchen putting the final touches to dessert, I went across to where he was sitting at the table which faced the window that looked out on to the back yard.

"Dad," I said, "can I ask you something?"

"Certainly," he said. "Go ahead."

"That opera you're taking Mammy to see next week, what's it about?"

"Well," he said, finishing chewing a piece of meat, and at the same time buying himself some time to think of what he was going to say, "it's about love. It's a story about four people, two women and two men, and about life and love in a garret in Paris."

"Dad?"

"Yes."

"What's a garret?"

"A garret – let me see now, what's the best way to describe it? Penniless painters and penniless writers always seemed to be starving in garrets, usually in Paris. A garret is – it's an attic room away up directly under the roof of a house. It's an *attic*, all right?"

"Yeah, thanks, Dad."

"Mr Puccini based his opera on a novel by a writer named Murger – I forget his first name. As I was saying, it's basically about these four people, Rodolfo, who is a poet, his painter friend Marcello, and the two girls they love, Mimi, who's what was called a seamstress, and her friend Musetta who was . . . I can't remember what she was, but it doesn't matter."

"And do they own the garret?"

"Does who own the garret?" my father asked, looking surprised at the question.

"The painter and the poet fellow and the two girls?"

"No, *none* of them owns it! It belongs to a fellow named Benoit. You see, the four main characters in this story are very poor; they haven't a penny, they're broke, stony broke. They *have* to live in a garret."

"Why?"

"Because garrets were the cheapest rooms you could rent. They were cold and dusty and unfurnished, and often had rats and mice in them, and the stairs creaked, and there were draughts everywhere. Shocking places they were, terrible places to live in, unless you were a Bohemian."

"What's a Bohemian?"

"Well, it's a bit hard to explain. It means kind of unconventional, artistic. The bohemian life was what was aspiring artists went in for, and it's from that the opera got its name: *La Bohème*. And that, by the way, is the correct pronunciation – as if it were spelled 'La Bo-*em*', and not 'La Bo-*hame*' which you'll hear most people calling it. Now then, you were asking me what the opera is about.

"Well, I read somewhere once that it's about a woman who loved too much. I don't know under God what that's supposed to mean, but whoever wrote it is entitled to his opinion, no matter how wrong he might be. No, it's really about a *lot* of things – it's about happiness, and sadness, and sorrow, and misunderstandings. It's about jealousy and sickness. It's about Rodolfo falling in love with Mimi, and *her* falling in love with *him*. It's about Mimi getting TB, consumption, and being brought back to Rodolfo's attic for a reconciliation. But too late, and she dies, and it's very, very sad."

I thought about all of that for a few minutes, giving my father a chance to finish his dinner before it went cold.

"Dad," I said after a while, "where does that song –"

"*Aria*," he cut in. "You don't call them songs in opera. They're arias."

"Where does that aria about her hand being freezing cold come into it?"

" '*Che gelida manina*'," he said. " 'Your tiny hand is frozen.' Rodolfo sings it in the first act. He's a tenor, by the way, and Mimi is a soprano. He sings it when they're both kneeling on the floor in the dark searching for her key which she has dropped. His hand touches hers, and he feels how cold she is, and it's then he sings, 'Your tiny hand is frozen.' "

"And is the Frank Ryan who is going to sing it in the Opera House the same Frank Ryan that Auntie Winnie sang with here in Cobh?"

"The same one," he said. "Your Auntie Winnie sang a duet with him."

"And will she be singing with him in the opera you're taking Mammy to next week?"

"No," he said. "Not this time. *Some* time, perhaps, but not this time. No, they're bringing over a well-known continental soprano – at least they *say* she's a well-known soprano, but you can't believe a bloody word you read in the papers these days. Her name is Madame Elena Danieli. She'll be singing the part of Mimi."

"Thanks, Dad."

"It's a pleasure, son."

Later, when my parents went down to Harbour Hill to arrange for the babysitting aunt to come up on the Thursday, I went upstairs to the kitchenette where the wind-up black gramophone and the big, brittle black 78rpm records were kept on a high shelf. I took all of them down, together with the gramophone and the tiny tin box of gramophone needles.

The classical records, I found, were all together. There were so many of them, and so many exotic and difficult names: Rosa Ponselle singing "*Visi d'arte*" from *Tosca* by the same Mr Puccini as had written *La Bohème*; Enrico Caruso singing "*Celeste Aida*" by Verdi; Amelita Galli Curci ("She's a coloratura, remember," my mother had told me once. "Not like Auntie Winnie, who is more of a Wagnerian soprano") singing "*Una Voce Poco Fa*" from *The Barber of Seville* by Rossini.

I couldn't pronounce half the names. How could you get your tongue around Luisa Tetrazzini? Or Giuseppe de Luca? Or Beniamino Gigli? Or Feodor Chaliapin? Or Jussi Björling? . . . John McCormack, Nellie Melba, Lawrence Tibbett – they were no trouble at all.

Anyway, I pulled out a few that showed the composer's name as Puccini, took the old needle out of the gramophone player, inserted a new one from the little tin box, screwed it tight, wound up the machine, and listened over and over again to Gigli singing "*Che gelida manina*".

I didn't understand the words, but I knew that what I was listening to was profoundly beautiful and moving, and I got a tightening sensation in my chest. That Mr Puccini, I thought, was *amazing* to be able to do that to me with music.

I waited up till my parents came in, and when my mother went to make some cocoa, I asked my father to tell me what he knew about Mr Puccini.

"Giacomo Puccini," he said, a faraway look in his eyes. "A genius, a genuine Italian genius. Sit down there and I'll tell you what I know about him."

We sat side by side looking at the embers of the dying fire, saying nothing. Then my father gave a sort of sigh and started talking.

"Giacomo Puccini," he said again. "He was born in a town named Lucca, near Pisa, the place where the famous leaning tower is, and he died in Belgium, in Brussels, when he was 65. Some so-called classical music fans, musical snobs really, try to make out that he wasn't one of the *great* composers. If you come across any of that stuff, don't take any heed of it, it's just bullflop."

"What kind of a man was he, Dad?"

"A bit flamboyant. Loved big fast cars. Was nearly killed by one once when his driver took a bend too fast and the car went off the road, rolled over, and Mr Puccini was pinned underneath. He was fortunate to escape. He loved to dress in the height of fashion. There was a bit of the dandy about him, a bit of the Beau Brummel." I made a mental note to ask him sometime who Beau Brummel was. "He loved to buy beautiful things and surround himself with them. He loved beautiful women, and was always falling in and out of love. He made an awful lot of money from his music, and yet, you know, he was an insecure class of a man."

"What do you mean by that?"

184

"Well, he used to frequently get down in the dumps, get really very depressed and start saying things like 'I'm old and unhappy and discouraged.' He was always comparing his musical compositions with the work of other composers, and it made him unsure of himself. Like when he said, 'Beside Wagner, we're all mandolin players.'"

"Do you like Wagner's music, Dad?"

"Not much. It's an acquired taste, but it's a bit too heavy for me. I like bits and pieces of it – some of the music from *Tannhauser*; "The Ride of the Valkyries"; some of *Tristan and Isolde*. But in the main, no, I'm not a fan of Wagner. I much prefer Mr Puccini's lovely melodies. He used to say he wanted most of all to touch the heart. No one ever did it better, son. In fact I'd go so far as to say no one ever even *approached* him . . . Go on now, off to bed with you. You'll never get up for school in the morning."

"All right. Thanks, Dad. Just one last thing: when Mr Puccini died, what did he die of?"

"He died in 1924," my father said. "He got cancer of the throat, had a big operation on it, but then had a heart attack and died. And you know, he was working on his last opera, *Turandot*, almost right up to the end. But he never managed to finish it."

"So, who finished it?"

"Another Italian, Alfano – Franco Alfano, one of Mr Puccini's students. And all *he* got for his trouble was criticism and derision. You see, the world is full of begrudgers . . ."

He stopped talking for a moment, and the faraway look came into his eyes again. Then he put the palm of his hand gently to the back of my neck and said, "Run along now and go upstairs to *bed*."

On the night they went to see *La Bohème* I was allowed to stay up until they came up the hill off the last train from Cork, the 11.20, which got into Cobh station at midnight. My mother said she had cried all the way through the opera.

"And was Frank Ryan any good?" I asked my father.

185

"Ah, yes, he was, *very* good – but he's no Gigli."

"What do you mean?"

"Well, Frank has a fine voice, but it's a bit rough. He hasn't much finesse. There's no delicacy to his singing. Now, if you were to listen to Beniamino Gigli –"

"I *did*," I interrupted, "I listened to him piles of times the other night in the kitchenette when you and Mammy went down to Nan's."

"I hope you were careful with the records," he said, a small look of concern flitting across his eyes.

"I was – very careful," I assured him.

"Good man, I knew you'd be. As I was saying, when you listen to Gigli, even though the words are in Italian . . . well, let me ask you something: did you *feel* anything?"

"I did," I said, "but I couldn't describe it."

"There you are. Tell me, was it a *good* feeling?"

"It was sort of sad, or beautiful, or something like that," I said, embarrassed.

He put out his hand and ruffled my hair, and said nothing for about a minute.

"Yes, you see that's the combination of Mr Puccini's music and the way Beniamino sings it. Frank can't do it like that. He tends to shout a bit. But Beniamino – he sings from here" (he touched his heart) "as well as here" (touching his throat), "and he has more technical expertise than Frank has. They're the big differences. That's what I meant when I said Frank was very good, but he's no Gigli."

In the silence that followed, I could hear in my head what I had heard the night I had played "*Che gelida manina*" over and over again.

After a while I said, "Dad, what about Elena Danieli? Was she any good?"

He looked up from the programme he was reading. "Elena Danieli? Yes, she was fine, but I'd say now that her real name is Eily Daniels."

My mother came into the room at that moment with two

186

cups of steaming cocoa and heard my father's reply. "Oh, *Eddie!*" she said.

My father just laughed. "Well," he said, "why not? Rosa Ponselle's name wasn't Ponselle at all. It was Ponsillo, and she was born in Connecticut. So how do we know that Elena Danieli isn't Eily Daniels from Bohola or somewhere?"

My mother shook her head and said, "Oh, you're *terrible!*"

"Was she as good as Auntie Winnie?" I asked him.

It was my mother who answered. "Not a patch on your Auntie Winnie," she said.

"Not a patch on what your Auntie Winnie *will be*," my father gently corrected. "Staf says your Auntie Winnie has one of the finest natural voices he has ever heard, but she has years of training ahead of her. Frank Ryan has a great natural voice, too, but it'd probably be too late now for him to get the training he should have got years ago. And anyway why should he bother? He has enough money. He's a farmer, and he gets plenty of singing engagements . . . Come over here to me."

I went across the room to him and he put his hands on my shoulders. "Some day," he said, "some day when you get a little older, and if God spares me, I'll take you to see Mr Puccini's *La Bohème.*"

God did spare him, and he *did* take me to see *La Bohème* – but first there was *Faust* with Owen Brannigan playing Mephistopheles, and before that there was *Die Fledermaus* in Cobh.

* * * * * * * *

The idea of putting on an opera in Cobh in those wartime days was greeted by sneers and declarations that the Cobh Choral Union was getting above itself. Who the hell did they think they were? And did they really think it could be done? And even if it *was* put on, who'd go to see it? And where would they get the singers, and all the string and woodwind and brass players to form an orchestra? Who'd be the musi-

187

cal director – who would the instrumentalists and singers *listen* to, take advice from, be instructed by? Who'd produce it, and where? And what about the scenery?

"The world is full of begrudgers," my father said. "We'll *do* it, and to hell with them."

"Which opera will ye put on, Dad?" I asked him.

"*Die Fledermaus* by Johann Strauss," he said. "It means 'The Bat'."

"And is it a famous opera?"

"Very famous. Strictly speaking, it's what is known as an operetta."

"What's an operetta?"

"That's another thing that annoys me," he said. "There's a lot of old snobbery in music, as I was telling you when you asked me about Mr Puccini. Well the same snobs turn up their noses at operetta, as if it's somehow inferior, as if it's a *lower* form. Well, it's *not*; it's *different*. It's a light opera, or a short opera, that's what it is."

"And is this operetta *Die Fledermaus* a great one, like *La Bohème* is a great opera?"

"Probably the best one ever," he said. "A masterpiece. Just you wait till you hear the music."

Before that, though, I wanted to know about Johann Strauss. I'd been intrigued by the picture my father had painted for me of Mr Puccini, so this time I thought I'd try to find out for myself.

Daisy Sullivan was the answer. Long the town librarian and a close friend of my parents, she it was who pointed me in the right direction, which meant, first of all, climbing those narrow, slippery, railinged steps to the huge room of books.

Johann jnr (or the younger as some books called him) was one of six children his father had with his wife Anna Streim. He wasn't yet 20 when he decided to launch his own career, which would bring him into sharp competition with his father, who was also a composer and orchestra leader, something that drove a deep rift of angry jealousy between them, all of it stemming from the elder Strauss. It was only just before the elder Strauss died that a reconciliation took place. The son took over the father's orchestra and combined it with his own. Within a short time, Johann the younger had six orchestras on the go, playing nightly all over Vienna, and he made a point of putting in an appearance with each one, for however short a time. He employed a small army of musicians, copyists, assistant conductors, publicists, and agents. As with his father before him, he, too, toured Europe with his main orchestra and became a sensational success.

But composing attracted him more and more, and he began to work at it with great gusto and huge talent. Brahms was to say of him, "*There* is a master of the orchestra, so great a master that one never fails to hear a single note of any instrument."

"The laughing genius" of Vienna he was called, this man who became a millionaire, who once in Boston conducted 1,087 instrumentalists and 20,000 singers in front of an audience of 100,000. He found it hilarious! He said he was grateful that they all finished together!

He composed nearly 500 works, ranging from "On The Beautiful Blue Danube" to "Tales from the Vienna Woods", from "Voices of Spring" to "Vienna Blood". Among his operettas were *Der Zigeunerbaron* and *Die Fledermaus*, the latter, by general consent, a work of genius. It had been given its first performance in Vienna in April 1874.

And to think that now the Cobh Choral Union was going to put it on in Cobh at Easter with my father and Auntie Winnie, and maybe another aunt or two as well in it!

Auntie Winnie was to sing the part of Rosalinda.

Bustling Belgian and the Bat

"STAF MAY BE a bit odd, but he's a genius," my father said emphatically to my mother when he came in one night after a rehearsal.

"Oh, an interesting night then, was it?" my mother said, beautifully setting my father up with the cue for what he loved doing – explaining and describing.

"Oh, be the holy!" my father said, warming instantly to the invitation to talk. "That man gets so impatient with everyone, particularly the chorus. He gets so *angry*. And so *insulting*. He seems to forget that for the most part they can't read music, that by day they're either holding down jobs and trying to scrape a living, or at home minding children, cooking, washing clothes. And then they come out at night transformed into tenors and baritones and basses and sopranos and mezzo-sopranos, and have to try to get to grips with Strauss's music and Staf Gebruers's accent."

Staf was the bustling little Belgian who had come to Cobh before the war to become carillonneur, organist and choirmaster of St Colman's Cathedral. He also taught Gregorian Chant to the monks at Melleray in County Waterford, which he drove to and from in his black Ford Prefect to which was

190

bolted a fuel contraption that made the car look like a designer's nightmare.

He was a commited, intense man who played the carillon bells like an angel, massacred the English language and made the hair on the back of my young neck stand up whenever he played Bach's Toccata and Fugue on the organ in the cathedral. He was also the musical director of what was then known as the Cobh Choral Union, where he exposed all his impatience as well as his extravagant (Continental?) gestures.

"Did he give out to someone tonight?" my mother asked.

"Give out? He was like Mount Etna, Vesuvius and Krakatoa all rolled into one. He threw down the pencil he was using as a baton, picked it up, smashed it in two and threw the pieces across the room. He said we were a crowd of 'ith-yots'. He hit his forehead with the palm of his hand and said, 'It is im-*poss*-ible to make opera with peoples what does not listen to me, or watch me, or understand anythings.' Honestly, I thought either he was going to have a seizure, or that someone would walk up to him, tell him where to get off, to get to hell back to Belgium, and then walk out."

"So why do you say he's a genius?" my mother asked.

"Because he *must* be," my father said. "Before the end of the night we sounded like the chorus of La Scala, Milan."

"And how about the soloists?"

"Well, Winnie wasn't there tonight. She had the doctor today, I understand."

"That's right," my mother said. "When she woke up this morning, she could only croak, and her throat was very sore. Mammy sent for Ledlie, who came about 11 and examined her, told her she wasn't even to *talk* for at least 24 hours."

"Did she give her anything for it?"

"Not a prescription, no. She told Mammy to send one of the girls down to Jasper, or Mr Kavanagh, for a good bottle of glycerine, lemon and honey, and said that Winnie was to take plenty of it, and that she should be all right by tomorrow night."

"I hope she's correct," my father said. "Time's running out, and there's no one lined up to replace Winnie."

"Were *all* the other soloists there?"

"Yes, Paddy Sutton, Nodlag O'Brien, Louis O'Leary – they were all there except Winnie."

"And how are they getting along?"

"Not bad, but I think Paddy is struggling a bit. That part of Gabriel von Eisenstein is a big one, and I think Staf is wondering if Paddy is really up to it."

"He's not a patch on Frank Ryan," my mother said.

"Moll, we haven't *got* Frank Ryan, and we have no chance of *getting* Frank Ryan, and anyway, you should compare like with like."

My mother shrugged and said, "They're both *tenors*, aren't they?"

"Yes," my father said, "but there's tenors and tenors."

"*Exactly!*"

"Hold on a second now!" my father said, raising an index finger. "One man is a professional singer, the other is an amateur who holds down a job in the ESB. Fair is fair."

"I just hope Paddy Sutton doesn't make a hames of it," my mother said.

"*I* hope Paddy Sutton doesn't make a hames of it. We *all* hope Paddy Sutton doesn't make a hames of it. Indeed I daresay Paddy *himself* hopes he doesn't make a hames of it. Now be *reasonable!*"

"Ah, reasonable my eye. Why didn't ye go for Frank Ryan in the first place? I don't know what got into ye."

"*Nothing* 'got into us'. Frank Ryan wasn't *available!* And even if he was, what he's charging now we couldn't afford anyway. And thirdly, and maybe most important of all, Staf convinced us that we should prove to everyone, ourselves included, that this town could put on *Die Fledermaus* with its own talent, without having to hire anyone from outside. And if you want to know, I think that's a damn fine idea."

"I hope you're right," my mother said, and then, for good

measure, added, "I hope ye won't live to regret your decision. And there's no point in getting in a huff with me now because I said what I feel."

As the production date drew closer, my father brought home more and more tales of tempers and tantrums and traumas. More than once you got the impression that the whole project was in direst danger of folding up.

"Went half crazy tonight, he did. Singled out Mary Ann Collins and Marjorie Desmond in the string section and said that all they were doing was *scraping* the violins, and that if Guarnieri or Amati or Stradivarius were alive, they'd give up instrument-making for ever."

"And were Georgie and Archie listening to all this?"

"They were."

"And did they say anything?"

"Not a syllable."

"What kind of men are they at all?" my mother said with deep disgust.

"Maybe privately they agreed with him."

"I know they're no Fritz Kreislers," my mother said, "but Staf had no right to be *that* rude to them. And I think it's awful their husbands didn't stand up for them. They're not men at all – they're *mice*!"

My father made an elaborate, concentration-demanding task of stirring his tea, and said nothing, though I noticed that once or twice he flicked his eyes up from the cup and glanced over the top of his glasses at my mother.

"I'd expect *you* to stand up for me," she said.

"Of course I would, Moll," he said. You could tell by the eye twinkle that something mischievous was coming. "But sure you don't play the violin," he added.

She looked as if she was going to erupt into anger, but suddenly laughed instead. She knew what he was up to. After a while she said: "It's the *principle* I'm talking about . . . And that reminds me, Brother Eugenius stopped me down town this afternoon."

"Oh?" my father said, looking puzzled. "I don't see the connection between Staf, Archie and Mary Ann Collins, Georgie and Marjorie Desmond, playing, or not playing the violin, and Brother Eugenius."

"God, you're very slow. He's the headmaster – principle – principal?"

"Very droll," my father said. "Oh, very droll . . . What did Eugenius want?"

"He didn't want anything. He said they were very impressed with Billy's marks in the Christmas exam, and that by getting either first or second for the last three or four years, he was showing that he's a good scholar. Eugenius thinks that if he keeps it up, he'll definitely get a scholarship to the college in two years time."

This, said in my presence, was intensely embarrassing for me, but my father grinned, put his hand on my shoulder, and said, "Well, that's *marvellous*! Here –" He dug in his trouser pocket, pulled out a handful of change, selected a sixpenny piece and said, "Buy yourself a Studebaker!"

I said: "Thanks very much, Dad."

"I suppose you'll go to the pictures?"

"Yeah, there's a great Errol Flynn film coming to Frennet's – *The Sea Hawk*."

That tanner from my Dad was a godsend, because I thought Errol Flynn, as a sailing ship captain fighting the Spanish was, well, fantastic, and I'd love to have been able to fence like him and fight like him and jump around the place like him.

Thank God for Eugenius, too, I thought.

* * * * * * * *

The advertisement on the front page of the *Cork Examiner* caught the attention immediately, placed, as it was, in the most prominent position and carrying, as it did, a splendid and unmistakable illustration of St Colman's Cathedral.

Corkonian attitudes towards Cobh, its people and its doings were very similar to the attitudes of Dubliners towards

Cork itself, or Londoners towards Manchester or Birmingham. So, to have something recognisably Cobh on the front page of "de paper" (or even "*de* paper") was a cause for rejoicing among people of the town.

Easter Week Attraction In Cobh

That's what the top line of the advertisement said, brandishing a fine disregard for the paper's house style regarding capital letters. It then went on:

St Coleman's Choral Union

in

'*Die Fledermaus*'

by

Johann Strauss

Chorus 60 voices

Symphonic Orchestra

Conductor – Staf Gebruers

Monday to Saturday

Thompsons open for teas

Tuesday to Saturday

The "Thompsons open for teas" was out of place, we felt, but we all loved the "Symphonic Orchestra" line, and "Chorus 60 voices" was very impressive, too.

"The Corkies can put that in their pipe and smoke it," I said.

"They can shove it up their jacksies!" Dingle said. "*They* have the bloody Opera House, but it's *we're* putting on the opera."

"Operetta," Nux corrected.

"It's all the same," I said.

"Who said so?"

"My dad did, and he knows."

"Yerra, 'tis all the one difference," Tony Nash said. "Com 'ere, Nolan, isn't your aunt or somethin' singin' in this *Fledermaus* yoke?"

"She is," I said; "my Auntie Winnie."

"Will it be any good?"

Before I had a chance to answer, they all pitched in.

"What's it about?"

"Any gangsters in it?"

"Of *course* there's gangsters in it! – Al Capone and Bugsy Siegel an' the lot of 'em. An' George Raft, too, for good measure."

"Oh, yeah? How about Johnny Mac Brown and Gabby Hayes?"

"They're not gangsters, yeh eejit – they're *cowboys*."

"Well, you could have *singin'* cowboys – Gene Autrey and Roy Rogers?"

"Yeah, an' you might as well have Trigger, too."

"Hey! Hold it! *Shurrup*!" It was Nux. They became quiet very suddenly. He turned to me. "What does *Die Fledermaus* mean?"

"It means The Bat," I said.

"An operetta about *bats*?" he said incredulously.

"No, no, it's about *people*. From what I can remember my dad telling me, one of them goes to a carnival *dressed* as a bat, and he's let go home in broad daylight in his fancy dress, and he decides to get his revenge – somethin' like that anyway."

"And there's some good music in it?"

"The parts of it that I've heard are terrific."

"Is it heavy stuff?"

"No, not really." I was getting into deep water now. "Look, I've never seen it, or heard it right through."

"Could you whistle any of it – would *we* be able to whistle any of it?"

The only thing that came to my mind was the waltz, and I started to whistle that. It was on one of the records at home, and I'd heard it on the wireless many times.

I had hardly got into the tune when Nux said, "Oh, yeah, I know that," and he started to whistle along with me. Most of the others joined in then, some of them whistling, others going, "da-da- da-da- da-da-, da-da- da-da- da-da-, da-da-, *boom, bum-bum, boom.*"

"Who else is in it apart from yer aunt?" Nux said when we got to the end and tailed off.

"The Gaspipe Tenor"

"Jasus!"

"Louis Leary."

"The *breadman?*"

"Yeah . . . Nodlag O'Brien – Mosso's sister . . . Mick Fitzgerald."

"From the electrical shop on East Beach?"

"Ah-hah . . . Ben Nagle."

"The auctioneer Ben Nagle? Looks like one of the Western Brothers?"

I nodded.

"One of the Kidneys . . . I can't remember who else."

"And it's going on in the Atlantic Theatre, right?"

"Right."

"That'll be a change anyway from the Young Mens'."

"It's going to be relayed by Radio Éireann," Danny Murphy said.

"Ah-hah-yeh-boy-yeh!" Dingle said triumphantly. "That's another thing'll drive 'em spare in Cork. Not just Cobh puttin' *on* an opera, but havin' the bloody thing broadcasted as well." He gave a little triumphalist "yahoo!" and sang, "'Here's up 'em all, said the boys of Fair Hill.'"

* * * * * * * *

A week or so before opening night my father brought home some carefully rolled sheets of unlined white paper which he spread on the dining room table. Then he went upstairs to his wardrobe and selected half a dozen pencils from the box he kept there. With fastidious care, as well as great neatness and sense of symmetry, he sharpened them, laid them down in a precise line and asked me for the loan of the compass and protractor from my geometry set. He then got down to designing

197

the prison scene which opens the third act of *Die Fledermaus.*

"I have no experience of this kind of thing at all," he said. "I could make a pig's ear or a horse's ass of it, but somebody *must* do it. There's been a mix-up."

I never knew him to make either a pig's ear or a horse's ass of anything he undertook, basically because he was such a painstaking man who never skimped on effort and had a craftsman's philosophy about work.

After several hours, when he reached the stage of not being able to improve on what he had done and had got as close as he could to the effect he was searching for, he finalised the drawings and asked me to lend him the box of water colours which had been one of my Christmas presents. Again, with the same patient precision he devoted to anything he did, he coloured the drawing. To me it looked like a work of art, and I told him.

"Ah, it isn't, it isn't, but it'll do – it'll *have* to," he said.

I went down with him to the Atlantic Theatre on the day that he and Ben Nagle (the producer, who also had a part in the production) painted the big canvas flats.

"By God, E.J., I've got to hand it to you," Ben boomed when it was finished and they stood back to inspect it. "Abslolutely splendiferous!"

I persuaded my father to sneak me into the dress rehearsal. It was unbridled cacophonous chaos. There were dozens of bad-tempered interruptions occasioned by an increasingly manic Staf, who shouted, screamed, waved his arms, stabbed the air, tore his hair, threw the baton on the ground, stooped down, picked it up and threw it right in among the seats in the auditorium. Then he turned his back on the orchestra and stage and stamped his way up the centre passageway of the theatre muttering, "Ith-yots! Ith-yots! Ith-yots!"

Suddenly his eyes alighted on me, cowering and trying to make myself invisible in the gloom.

"Who-are-you? What-are-you-doing-here? Get-OUT!" he shouted, and I slunk away, terrified.

There was no possible way that *Die Fledermaus* would be ready for a public performance 24 hours later.

But it *was* ready, and it *was* put on, and it went without a hitch. There were deafening roars of acclaim and stinging, ringing handclaps, tears of joy and tears of relief and tears of pride when, after the breakneck finale, with Rosalinda (Auntie Winnie) asking, in song, for the whole company to join her in praising the reconciling power of King Champagne, Staf brought the orchestra's playing to a triumphant end with a great and truly extravagant flourish.

The audience was on its feet, and above the thunder of applause came the voice of Mrs Hawkes, the last of the Port of Cork's bumboat women, shouting, "Three cheers for the little Belgium!"

And she got them.

An unnamed critic in the *Cork Examiner* said of "the little Belgium": "Dr Staf Gebruers, who conducted, brought out the real beauty of the music." Of the man my mother had hoped wouldn't "make a hames of it", the critic said: "A tremendous amount of work fell on Mr Patk. Sutton as von Eisenstein." And of my Auntie Winnie: "Miss Winnie Sexton as Rosalinda left little to be desired."

When I read that "The scenery and lighting effects added much to the show," I felt that my dad's name was embedded in that word "scenery", because the prison scene looked great.

As for the broadcast, it was reported that "the reception was excellent".

"I said it before, and I'll say it again," Dingle, leaning against the bars at the camber across the road from the Soldiers' Home and Sailors' Rest, said, "Our putting on *Die Fledermaus* here in Cobh was, as far as the Corkies are concerned, a case of 'Here's up 'em all, said the boys of Fair Hill'."

Haunting Rocky

THE GANNETS ARRIVED from Bull Rock. That was how we knew the mackerel were in the harbour. The great black-backed gulls and the herring gulls were with us all the year round. You got used to their noise, their fighting over food, their scavenging, and their ability to stink your head or ruin your clothes by shitting indiscriminately from various heights. But the gannets, the biggest white and black sea birds around our coasts, only made their presence felt when the mackerel shoals came in.

Nux, occasionally Danny Murphy, Con Lynch and I spent hours watching them that summer of 1943. They stayed well out in the navigation channel, but they were a marvellous sight as they hovered, heads looking downwards, searching the tide for prey. Not that they had to do much searching when the mackerel arrived in summer shoals.

"Maybe they're choosy," I suggested when the subject came up. "You know, hard to please."

"And you honestly think they could pick just one particular fish from hundreds swimming in the tide 90 or a hundred feet below them?" Con Lynch said incredulously. "Pull the other one!"

"For God's sake belt up and *watch* 'em!"

Nux was irritated.

"The mackerel'll be in close soon," Danny Murphy said. "Tomorrow or the next day I'd say. And then ye'll be down the Deepwater, or out here on the Pier Head, or along at Lynch's Quay, with yeer rods, norsel, spinners, hooks and all the rest of the stuff ye'll buy in Cronin-Ba's or wherever. But look how the *gannets* catch fish. No rod'n line for them, just their beaks. 'They sow not, neither do they reap' – nor buy fishing tackle!"

"Hah-bleddy-hah! Pass the feather!" Nux said.

Danny giggled. Con and I joined in. Nux wasn't at all gruntled.

"Seriously," Danny said after a little while, "does any of ye know exactly *how* the gannet catches a fish?"

"With his beak, obviously," I said.

"Do you mean *in* his beak?" Danny asked.

"Yeah, I imagine so."

"No," Danny said. "He catches it *with* his beak."

"Murphy, boy, why are you talkin' in riddles?" Nux said. "All I want to do is watch the birds, and Nolan and yerself gabbin' away there non-stop about *how* the fekkers catch fish. *In* his beak, *with* his beak – who gives a cat's mulacka?"

Danny did one of his funny faces to me, and Con Lynch put his hand to his mouth to try to stifle a sputter. We went back to watching the dive-bombing exhibition.

A diving bird folded its wings back tight against its body, and with its long neck and pointed bill stuck straight out ahead of it, plunged down, streamlined and lethal, into the water from as high as a hundred feet. None of the ones we saw diving failed to come up with a mackerel.

Walking back in the pier, Nux moved close to Danny and said, "Awright, Murph, how *do* they do it?"

But Danny decided to play him along a little.

"How does *who* do it?"

"The gannets, of course, who else?"

"Do what?"

"Catch the – yerra, bugger off so if you don't want to tell me. See if I care!"

Murph, Con and myself burst out laughing. When we quietened down, Danny caught up with Nux and told him: it's on the way *up* that gannets get their fish, not on the way down. Having entered the water head first, they also came up head first, at speed, and with the sharp-pointed bill now pointing skywards, it acts as a very effective spear.

"Presto!" Danny ended.

* * * * * * * *

"A break! A break! There's a break comin'!"

Danny Murphy's prediction had been right. The mackerel came inshore with a vengeance two days after our last gannet-watching session on the Pier Head. The town was going to smell, eventually stink, of frying, fried and discarded mackerel now for days on end, and the woman who peddled fish wouldn't stand a ghost of a chance of selling anything at the doors. It wouldn't matter what she had – sole, cod, plaice, gurnet, hake or turbot. Molly Dorgan just might as well have shut up shop, and Clayton Love's, with Tossie in charge, go on broken time. No way would a woman of the house buy fish when her children, and probably her husband as well, caught and brought mackerel home by the dozen every morning, afternoon and evening when the mackerel were running.

A "break" was the name given to the sudden furious flurry of water when a shoal of them, chasing sprats, suddenly attacked from below in a feeding frenzy, and the terrified sprats fled to the surface like a living, heaving sheet of silver chain mail. The marauders, moving with astonishing speed, tore into the sprats from underneath, breaking them up, sending them into swirling turns. The little sprats perished in their thousands as the mackerel gobbled them up. The mackerel came close inshore because that was where the sprats came, seeking refuge, trying to stay ahead of their hunters. The cruel operation of nature's food chain handed us a few days of excitement every August.

The hardware shops made small fortunes from selling bamboo sticks and hanks of what we called norsel – light line to which we attached sinkers and hooks. The fellows who couldn't afford proper fishing rods used any form of stick. A length of bamboo fell between an ash plant or an old brush handle at the lower end, and a sophisticated affair with a patent grip, winding reel with quick release and brake, and fancy lead sinkers and spinners at the affluent end. But a five or six foot stick of any sort, an old rusty nut, a length of line, a thrupenny hook which you'd bait with a sprat, and enough room to squeeze your way to the edge of quay, pier or slip were all you needed when the mackerel were ravenous each August.

In the early part of the "season", when the "breaks" were small and sporadic, we followed them up the length of the waterfront from the eastern end of the town to about three-quarters of the way out the Water's Edge. At that stage, you might stand for the best part of an hour waiting for a bite and get not even a nibble. When the shoals really switched their attention inshore, though, there were times when you might spend ten or fifteen frenzied minutes constantly pulling wriggling, silver-bellied fish from the water.

The first one you caught each year was always the best because from hopelessly/hopefully holding a dead immobile stick, you suddenly found yourself holding on to something that jumped up and down in your hands. I used to look around to see if anyone was watching my success. Nobody ever was. They were having their own successes at precisely the same moment.

The fellows with the fancy rods and the expensive equipment never seemed to catch as many mackerel as us, for all their showy casts – which were totally inappropriate anyway.

"He thinks he's up the Blackwater fishin' for trout or salmon! You don't cast for mackerel – you just shove the

bleddy hook in the water and the mackerel'll do the rest,"
Con Lynch said. "Though personally I think the mackerel
must be awful dopes to go for hooks with bits of silver paper
on 'em when there's so many real live sprats there."

"Well, that's the way with some and more with others,"
someone four spaces down said.

That year, as always, I was frightened trying to get the hook
out of my first fish's gills. I hoped no one was looking at me
as I held him by the middle of his belly while he wriggled
frantically, his eyes starting to glaze over. Mackerel always
looked angry, and even though their mouths were small and
their teeth tiny, I didn't want to risk being bitten.

"Stun 'im!" Con said. "Hit his head a whack on the ground."

It seemed cruel to do that to a fish who was haring through
the water just seconds ago, full of streamlined speed. But
then again, the mackerel hadn't given a fig for the poor bleddy sprats, had he? And frying him at home wasn't exactly
merciful either, so I slid my hand back towards his tail and
whacked him hard on the ground, and he bled and died. I
tore the hook out of his mouth then and baited it once more.

That's the way it always was. From the first one on, the fear
disappeared as your hands became thick with scales.

On the way up King Street I saw John and Kevin Driscoll.
They had 55 between them. I had 11. We ate the whole of my
catch that night and didn't eat a single mouthful of mackerel for the rest of the year. Not that it stopped me from going
down again to fish every day while the mackerel were in.

The only thing I hated about it was the way some of the
bigger fellows indulged their twisted sense of humour by
coming up behind someone smaller who was standing right
on the edge of the quay or pier, pushing hard at the same
time as grabbing hold of gansey or shirt to prevent you from
falling in, but shouting, "Oh! Only for me you were gone!"

Twice I genuinely thought I was over the side. My heart
thumped with the shock and I went weak-legged. I had a
mortal fear of water ever since the day, a few years before,

when someone did it to my young brother John in the west camber. We were trying to scoop some of the sprats ashore to use as bait. The fellow who pushed John and let go ran away.

I stood petrified as John sank, went right under water, and when he came up his eyes were wide with terror in his round face, his mouth open, the water pouring down his throat. And then he went under again. Nobody around me moved. I could see he was going to drown. Surely someone who could swim would jump in and save him? He was little more than a baby! He was my brother . . . Someone? . . . Anyone? . . . No one! . . .

He came up for the second time, choking, thrashing wildly with his little arms. I knew what everyone in a sea town knows, what everyone who stood alongside me on the slip knew – if you go down for the third time, that's it, that's the end. You drown.

Nobody moved.

Before I knew it, I was in the water, having jumped. I was going down, seeing the faces above me through green water, losing my footing on the slimy surface of the main slip, panicking as I gulped in sea water, reaching out for John, thinking, Oh, God, *I'm* going to drown, too, and it's all my fault! O my God, I am heartily sorry and beg pardon for all my sins, and I detest them . . .

Suddenly my toes hit against something, and I stopped slipping and stepped up on whatever it was and straightened, pushing my head clear of the water. Two hands reached down and grabbed me by the shirt and held me. To my right I saw Tom Jago hauling John into the side of the slip by the hair, and then out of the water with the same grip. Then somehow both of us were standing on the slip, coughing and spluttering, John crying, me trying my best not to, and dreading that long walk up the hill to home.

* * * * * * * *

The peculiar thing was that, despite the fear, the terror, that the sea was able to exert on me when I found myself actually *in* it, I was still drawn to it. It was as though some gigantic magnetic force pulled my imagination and my physical body to it to stand and gaze at it, dream about it, talk about it, float in boats on it. I so envied my friends who were at home in it, swam and dived in it and didn't have any fear of it. Nux, I suppose, was chief among these.

He regularly swam off Whitepoint slip, a jutting concrete finger at the bend in the river opposite the highest part of Haulbowline Island. Because there was nearly always a swift current running there, only strong and competent swimmers entered the tide at that part of Whitepoint. Nux, young though he was, was both strong and competent. He joined the men and outswam most of them, apart from the iron characters with muscled bodies who swam slow, powerful crawls. They might outlast him, although they'd never outpace him.

Sometimes I arranged to meet him by the railway station late in the afternoon, and we walked out the Water's Edge, me with a book under my arm, Nux with a rolled towel containing his trunks. One of the additional attractions of accompanying him was that it provided the opportunity to look at a group of teenaged girls who also swam off the slip. They all seemed to have silvery laughter, long white legs and the beginnings of breasts, and Nux was the only one from our little group who actually got among them out there at the end of the slip. He pretended to ignore them.

Instead of hanging around them, he took off on long swims out as far as the *If*'s moorings and back. None of the girls would attempt that. They concentrated on diving nicely and doing exquisite backstrokes, placing their hands into the water with great grace. Nux didn't give a damn about grace.

One evening, when he went into the tide in a flat racing dive, instead of bearing left towards the yacht moorings, he just kept on going straight out towards the middle of the navigation channel where the current was strongest. To us watching him from the shore, his head in the water became smaller the further he went. While he was still in smooth water, we weren't worried, but as he approached the choppy part where the current was racing at full strength, we started to feel concerned. Only the town's strongest swimmers, fellows like Christy Ryan and the two Bunworths, Dick and Billy, ventured into that tide race – and then only in pairs.

"Hey! McCormack, boy, come back here!" someone shouted.

If he heard it, Nux ignored it.

It was a gentle time of day. The water close to the shore was glass-smooth and, because the day's twilight was introducing darkness, a deep bottle green colour. There wasn't even a hint of a breeze, and away to our left the first lights were coming on in the town. From the south, out close to the mouth of the harbour in Crosshaven, the music of Piper's Amusements came faintly over the water: the Andrews Sisters singing "Don't Fence Me In".

Nux's head was now only a barely seen dot in the water, and he was swimming straight towards Haulbowline. Everyone stopped talking. The swimmers got out of the water and stood on the slip.

One of the men put his cupped hands to his mouth and yelled, "McCormack! Come back here, you bleddy young eejit!"

The evening was so still that his shout went right across the channel and bounced back on echo off the rock at the butt end of Haulbowline.

"Where's his oul man?" someone asked.

"He's not here. He didn't come."

"He did. I saw 'im, but I think he left a while ago."

"Christ, will yeh look at yer man now, he's slap bang in the current!"

"Is his brother Dave around?"

"He is. He's over there on the seat in front of the castle, smokin'."

"Go over an' get 'im quick!"

Nux's older brother David came to the slip at a run.

"You better call that fekkin eejit of a brother of yours, McCormack, or else it's a dead body we'll be pullin' outa the tide in the mornin'."

Dave stood on the slip and shouted.

"Neil! . . . Neil! . . . Get back in here immediately . . . *Neil!*"

He might as well have been whispering for all the reaction he got.

I heard the noise of wood grating on gravel behind and to the left, and turned to see three men in bathing togs hauling Regan's punt across the gravel and down to the smaller slip near the castle. A fourth man came running after them carrying oars and rowlocks. They had the punt afloat in seconds and went straight out, rowing frenziedly.

We looked back out at the murderous tide rip. There was no sign of Nux in the quickly gathering gloom. Nothing was said. Looking at the men in the punt, you silently reckoned that the best they could hope for was to find the body.

And then in over the water came this long, drawn-out Tarzan's yell, and there he was, standing up on the red buoy, waving and dancing up and down!

I laughed out loud. No reason. I just felt like laughing. And John Driscoll did the same. And Tommy O'Loughlin picked up a flat skimming stone and threw it higher and further than anyone had ever done before. It zinged out of sight and came down into the tide with a beautiful "*Phitt!*"

Old Nux got a fierce bollocking in Regan's punt on the way ashore. But he told me later he didn't give a damn. That would put paid, he said, to anyone who thought they had a chance of beating him in the boys' junior section of any local swimming gala for the rest of the year.

It did, too. No one trained after that, and he won everything going.

* * * * * * * *

Having seen Nux's performance in swimming all the way out to the red buoy, I thought it was about time I learned to swim. But I wanted someone around who would be able to help me if I got into difficulties, someone I could be myself with and could talk to and was generally on equal terms with. Someone I could answer back. Someone who wouldn't give me all that adult guff like, "Now, what you must do is . . ." and "Under no circumstances should you . . ." And someone who was a good swimmer. Nux was all I needed. But when and where?

"If the weather is fine, we're going on a picnic next Saturday to Paddy's Block," my mother said on the Wednesday. "Daddy has the day off. You're to go down to Georgie Wood and book the boat."

Paddy's Block! That was the answer to when and where – provided Mam and Dad would allow Nux, and maybe John Driscoll, to come on the picnic with us.

"*Can* they?" I asked Mam.

"You'll have to ask your father tonight when he comes in," she replied.

"It depends on your mother," he said.

"If John and Neil come," my mother said, "remember, I'm not taking responsibility for them. They'll have to look after themselves."

"But will they be able to share our food?"

"Of *course* they will! What kind of a question is that?"

I told the lads at school on the Thursday morning. They were both delighted, and John Driscoll lit a candle to Our Lady Star of the Sea on the way home. He said a *Hail Mary* for fine weather.

The cost of hiring Georgie's clinker-built rowing boat was five shillings for the day. I was up very early on the Saturday morning, wakened by the sun streaming in the window. I got dressed quickly and went down to the kitchen where Mam was already busy slicing flat pans.

"Have your breakfast now quickly," she said. "I want you to run downtown to Darcy's and Dowling's for me. I've

209

made out a list of stuff for you to get, and I've put the money over there in Norma's rosary purse. For God's sake don't lose it."

Cold meats, heads of lettuce, cucumbers, tomatoes, beet-root, tins of salmon, and sweets were all on that list, and I was sure my arms were stretched longer than their normal length by the time I got back home.

My mother had started on making the sandwiches when Dad came into the kitchen and looked at the growing mound of food.

"Now, Mam, we're not providing for the whole of the army on Spike, you know!"

"Eddie, you have no idea how ravenous they'll be. Haven't I got our own small army of gluttons to feed?"

I went down with Dad to the camber to get the rowing boat and bring her up to the small slip alongside the Naval Pier where we tied her up to the railing. Then we went back up the hills again to collect the huge baskets.

The choice of Paddy's Block meant rowing straight out across the bank and through the gap between the eastern tip of Haulbowline and the north-west side of Spike. Paddy's Block itself was what Sully said was an isthmus ("No, no, no! Not an issmiss – an *isth-mus*, you bloody cawbogue!") but which Rowdy Ellis insisted was a peninsula. Anyway, it jutted out from the mainland east of Ringaskiddy and ended in a small strand across from Rocky Island. Regardless of what it was, it was where we were going.

It was a nicely remote spot where the women, if they went paddling, could allow their bloomers to show without having to feel ashamed or embarrassed, and boys could play cowboys and Indians in the gorse above the tide line. Sometimes you'd hear the curlews calling on some out-of-sight mud-flat as they waded in search of crabs, and on occasions I had heard army buglers on Spike practising their calls.

When the boat was loaded with adults, children, baskets of food, crockery, primus (just in case), kettle, teapot, towels and blankets, she lay so deep in the water that there were only four or five inches of freeboard.

We made slow headway, and the younger people were snapped at.

"Keep your hands out of the water!"

"Sit *still*! You're tilting the boat and making it difficult to row!"

"Behave yourselves or I'll turn the boat around and put you back on the slip again, and you can spend the rest of the day hungry and by yourselves!"

Finally, after wailings, crying, threats, slaps and fervent declarations that "we'll never do this again, never, *ever*! It's not worth it," we arrived.

Nux, John Driscoll and I jumped overboard and, up to our thighs in water, guided the boat in between the rocks and stones until her bow nestled on the edge of the strand. While the boat was being unloaded, Dad went off to find a comfortable spot to lie down in the sun and recover. There wasn't another soul on Paddy's Block that day, but Nux and John whispered to me that they were going off in search of a courting couple. "We might see them at it," they smirked.

I went along the shore a little way by myself and then climbed up the slope and sat on the top on the tough sea grass. A little breeze sprang up and blew my hair, making it stand up. It was good up there with the fresh smell of the tide in your nose. I lay down and pressed one of my ears to the ground and heard the whistle of the wind blowing through the grass. Then I sat up and looked off down to the shore and could see where the tide had already receded leaving the brown seaweed exposed. I was uneasy, melancholy and couldn't understand why . . . It came to me after a while – I was dreading asking Nux to teach me to swim. I couldn't face it, even over here.

The solution when it came was gloriously simple – just forget all about it, put it off, cancel it! I mean, I hadn't mentioned it to anyone else, so no one would be able to taunt me and say, "Yah, you're yellow for chickening out!"

I immediately felt better. I slid down the slope and looked across at Rocky Island, a menacing, threatening-looking place even under a high sun. It was overgrown, a knobby carbuncle of rock with a peculiar ridge across its middle. Nux and John Driscoll were further along the shore, making for where the family sat around the table cloths spread on the ground. The bleddy buggers! I thought, they're after the food already! I wonder did they find anyone "at it"?

They were already swigging lemonade and eating lettuce-and-tomato sandwiches and sausages by the time I got back, but their eyes were on the coffee cakes and Swiss Rolls.

Afterwards I moved across to my father and said, "Dad, could me and Nux and John Driscoll ever have a loan of the boat for a while?"

He looked across at my mother.

"Yerra, let them have it," she said. "They'll be all right."

I could have squeezed her.

"Right you are then," Dad said, "but be careful. No tricking around. And keep an eye out for rocks – I don't want any planks stove in. And remember, Bill, you can't swim yet!"

He didn't *have* to say that.

"Ah, Jaze, Mr Nolan," John Driscoll said, grinning impishly, "sure we'll save 'im!"

Although not a word of it had been spoken about between ourselves, the three of us knew where we were going to head for – Rocky. We rowed parallel to the shore until we reached the little headland, which we rounded, and as we did I said over my shoulder to Nux, "Are you sure you're game?"

"Game for anything, boy!"

When we cleared the headland we were in a tideway and had to row hard to cross it. I was experiencing a chill of fear already. The small island we saw as we got closer to it looked forbidding, unfriendly, alien. Rock-strewn, nettle-covered and full of tangled thorns, it rose out of the water with no sloping shores. We could see the remains of an old pier. If we were going to land, that was where it would have to be. It was just a skeleton of a thing, its decayed piles encrusted with blue mussels and giving off a sickening stench.

In close, every time we dipped our oar blades into the water, long cord-like sea weeds wrapped themselves around the wood, and it was a struggle to get the blades free of them.

"Dead Men's Laces," John whispered. "If any of us fell overboard here, we wouldn't have a chance. They haul yeh down and keep yeh there until you drown. 'Tis only then they release yeh."

I leaned overboard and caught one of the slim slimy tentacles and hauled it inboard, trying to snap it. It wouldn't break, just stretched and stretched.

John hit me a ferocious blow on the shoulder and shouted, "Get it out, leave *go* of it! What are yeh tryin' to do, get us killed?"

"What do you mean killed?" I said.

He blessed himself and said, "Jesus! Bringin' one of them things into a boat – cop yerself on! Don't ever bring one of those aboard a boat!"

Nux hadn't spoken since we were in mid-channel.

Eventually we manoeuvred the boat alongside the piles and tied the painter to a flaking iron stanchion. Nux climbed out first, pulled himself up on to what used to be the floor of the pier and teetered bum-tighteningly for a second or two on a plank that began to give way beneath him. He stepped off it just before it cracked in two and fell down into the water with a couple of splashes. Nux tiptoed his way in the rest of the pier with his arms spread wide like a wire walker.

I was next. I was very much afraid. John Driscoll pretended it wasn't anything, but his out-of-tune whistling gave him away. We stood at the bottom where the pier joined the island and looked up towards the top. The unwillingness to go up there was palpable.

"Well, we can't stop here all day like three spare mickeys at a weddin', can we?" Nux said. "Who's goin' first?"

"You," I said. "You're nearest."

"I will in me hole!" He pulled down the lower lid of one of his eyes, exposing the red inside rim. "Take a look in there! See any green?"

But his pride was at stake, and he reluctantly started the climb, me following, John bringing up the rear. It was a steep trudge up a diagonal. The side of the island we were on was in shadow, the huge hump of rock blotting out the sun. All three of us felt intensely cold. At first we didn't talk. And it was impossible not to keep on looking back down to check that the boat was still there.

I thought there was something evil surrounding us. I felt we were being watched, but not by living eyes. I wanted to turn and go back down.

"Ever seen rats, Billy?" John asked from behind me.

"No."

"I have. The cliff in front of our house on Rose Hill is full of 'em."

"What the hell did you ask that for? What made you think of rats?"

"I'm sure this place is full of 'em."

"Would rats attack yeh? Would they attack a human being?"

"Some say they would – but only if you trap 'em in a corner."

By now I was apprehensive every time I put my foot down. Suppose I stepped on one of them, on the belly of one, or on the head where the sharp teeth were.

"I once seen a grand little wire-haired mongrel bitch that was destroyed by a rat," John Driscoll said. "Went for the throat and tore it outa her."

Nux, up ahead of us, stopped and turned around. He had a piece of dried grass between his teeth, chewing on it.

"Driscoll, what did you say about rats?" he said.

"Great big vicious grey bastards!"

"Driscoll, I'm *warning* you!"

We carried on in silence, but why in God's name had I left

214

the sunshine of Paddy's Block? What was I doing in this God forsaken place? Why didn't we turn around and go back down and get to hell away from it? We should have stayed with the others on Paddy's Block. We weren't wanted here. We should go now or else . . .

I looked back over my shoulder to see if I could still see the boat. There wasn't a sign of her! She wasn't where we had left her. A scream started to rise in my throat and was about to burst from me when I found her again – the tide had turned her and pushed her further in under the piles.

A wind had risen since we landed and it was coming through the thorns with a whine. Summer had gone away.

We kept going until we reached the top, and then we stood on a narrow parapet looking down into two great pits which had been quarried out of the solid rock centuries ago. Up where we were, the wind was now howling, threatening to blow us off the ledge and down into those yawning holes. I looked around at as much of the island as we could see. There wasn't a tree or a habitation anywhere on it.

Nux kicked a small stone over the edge, and it took a long time to hit the floor of the pit.

John Driscoll screamed. He was the first to see the gigantic rat scurrying from where the stone had landed.

And then the gulls came. They swooped on us, screeching with hate, furious at being disturbed, at having their wild place invaded. We flapped and waved our arms hoping to drive them off, but they took no notice. Nux prized a stone out of the ground, revealing a mass of maggots. He threw the stone at the birds, and one of them, a dirty-looking gull with only one leg which it extended downwards, ducked left of the stone's trajectory and came in low and shrieking at Nux. It was terrifying.

We stepped off the ledge and turned to go back down the way we had come up. We slithered, half tripped, stumbled.

"Come on, quick! Let's get outa this place," Nux yelled.

John and I were close to crying, he saying "Jesus, Oh

Jesus!" and me saying, "It's haunted, it must be haunted – protect us!"

We got into the boat somehow, untied the painter and pushed with every ounce of our strength. Nux sat, his hands over his eyes so that he wouldn't have to look at Rocky as we left it, and neither John Driscoll nor I cared how many blisters we got on our hands as we savaged the water with the oars.

* * * * * * * *

The sun was still shining on Paddy's Block when we arrived back. There was no wind, and it was a warm and lovely afternoon.

"Ye're very quiet," my mother said.

None of us answered.

Gigli Couldn't Act

FOLLOWING THE TRIUMPH of *Die Fledermaus,* I spent an increasing amount of time thinking about music in general and singers in particular. That conversation I'd had with my father about the difference between the way Frank Ryan sang and the way Gigli sang and the exchange I had overheard between my father and my mother about Paddy Sutton and Frank Ryan stayed fresh in my memory.

It resulted (whenever the opportunity arose) in my taking down the classical records and the wind-up gramophone and playing the Gigli recordings. There were plenty to choose from, and I soon formed a little list of my favourites: "*E luceven le stelle*" and "*Recondita armonia*" from *Tosca;* "*Che gelida manina*" (of course!) from *La Bohème;* "*Donna non vidi mai*" from *Manon Lescaut;* "*O paradiso*" from *L'African* and "*Una furtiva lagrima*" from *L'Elisir d'Amore.*

I had no idea what the words meant, but the feelings I underwent as I listened to that glorious voice were emotional and profound, very different from the feelings I had experienced listening to the male singers in *Die Fledermaus.* In fact I don't think I had any particular emotional reaction in the Atlantic Theatre other than fierce local pride that our town had put it on.

When I went over my little list of favourite Gigli record-ings, I found that of the six arias, four were written by Mr Puccini. The other two were by Meyerbeer and Donizetti, composers I knew nothing about. But as my dad had been able to tell me so much about Mr Puccini and explain the dif-ferences between the way Frank Ryan sang and the way Gigli sang, I decided to see if he could tell me some more about Gigli.

I waited until one blustery night when the others had gone to bed and my mother had gone down to Harbour Hill to see Nan.

"So you've grown to love the great Beniamino?" my father said, pulling his chair up to the fire.

"Yeah, I think he has a lovely voice."

"That's exactly what he has, a lovely voice. It's a unique voice, really. But I suppose all voices are unique. No, all *great* voices are unique. I'd recognise Björling's voice immediate-ly, and Caruso's, and Tauber's. They all have their own indi-vidual characteristics."

"How would you recognise Björling's voice from Gigli's if they were both singing the same piece? How could you tell the difference if they're both tenors and both singing the same notes?"

"Well, there's no mistaking Gigli's voice, anyway," he said. "Björling – great voice, but hard, brilliant, no emotion. I don't think there's any beauty in it, nor any feeling. It always sounds to me like a mechanically produced sound, a *made* sound, as distinct from what I might call a felt or *experienced* sound. No, what I suppose I really meant was that Gigli has a uniquely *beautiful* voice. But tell me, did you listen to any of the others? Caruso? Tauber? McCormack? Björling?"

"No," I said. "There's something about Gigli's voice which makes me want to listen only to him. I suppose that seems stupid."

"No, it doesn't. Go on."

"Well, although I thought Mr Sutton was very good in *Die*

Fledermaus, I wouldn't go out of my way to hear him singing, do you know what I mean? And when I listened to him, I think I understood a bit better what you were saying before, about the difference between listening to Frank Ryan and listening to Gigli."

He laughed a small laugh and rubbed his nose vigorously.

"There's no comparison, really, between Paddy Sutton and Beniamino Gigli," he said after a while. "I'm not being deliberately unkind to Paddy when I say that, but it's a little bit like trying to compare a tricycle with a Rolls Royce. There's no common ground other than that they're both male human beings who have voices in the tenor range. One is the world's greatest tenor, and the other is an amateur who does his best."

"Remember you said before that Gigli has technical expertise?"

"Yep."

"And that it'd be too late now for Frank Ryan to get the training, even if he wanted to?"

"Yes."

"Well, where did Gigli *get* the training, and how old was he when he started? And how old is he now?"

My father held up his hand and said laughingly, "Whoa now! One at a time. He's . . . let me see – he'd be in his early fifties . . . Where did he get his training? In his own country, Italy . . . And how old was he when he started? He was just a boy."

"Wouldn't that have cost a fortune? Were the Giglis very rich?"

"No," my father said. "Very poor. His daddy was a shoemaker, and Beniamino was the youngest of six children. They had a very tough struggle to feed and clothe all of them. His parents couldn't even afford to give him a decent education, but luckily the church organist and choirmaster gave a helping hand. And then, when he was 11, because he was a very fine boy soprano, he was taken into the cathedral choir school where he stayed until his voice broke."

"What happened then?"

"What happened then was that he had to go out to work to help support the family."

He reached up to the mantelpiece and got down his slim little packet of Woodbines. He wouldn't smoke any other brand. He shook one out, tapped it with meticulous care to pack the tobacco tighter, folded a strip of paper into a long thin tube which he flattened, and lit the end of it from a glowing coal in the grate. When the cigarette was lit, he pressed out the flame at the end of the paper with his fore-finger and thumb, which he had wet with his tongue, and placed the paper strip leaning against the fender ready for further use.

"When Beniamino was 21 he won a scholarship to the Academy of St Cecilia in Rome, and the man who became his teacher, an old baritone by the name of Cotogni – Antonio Cotogni, I think – quickly realised that here was someone with an exceptional talent and a wonderful voice. The teacher got some of his own colleagues to listen to Gigli, and they all agreed that he reminded them of the young Caruso. Now that was a tremendous thing for them to say because, you see, Caruso was considered to be the greatest tenor who ever lived, and at that time he was going on 40. But Beni-amino had one great disadvantage. What do you think it was?"

"I haven't a clue," I said.

"*Try,*" my father said. "Think."

I tried to imagine the greatest disadvantage the singer could have. "He couldn't read or write?" I suggested.

"No, no, he was perfectly capable of reading and writing. No – he couldn't *act*. And for someone wanting to make his career as a professional singer in opera, that was a heck of a handicap. At least that was what was thought. But there was such beauty in his voice, and he sang with such . . . such pas-sion and sensitivity, that though he never did make any kind of fist of the acting, it didn't matter a toss.

"As he got a few years under his belt, his hair got thinner and his girth got bigger, so that these days he's a little roundy, half-bald man. But, my God, what a *voice*! You see, God gave Beniamino a great gift – not the biggest and loudest voice in the world, but loud enough. He was never what's called a *tenore robusto*, those fellows who can crack wine glasses with their lung power. Beniamino was kind of halfway between a purely lyric tenor and a dramatic tenor. But when it comes to singing of human sorrow, or joy, for me there's no one to touch him. Let me put it this way: when I asked you did you feel anything when you first listened to his recordings, you said – well, do you *remember* what you said?"

I tried to recall. "I think I said I couldn't describe it."

"That's right, you did. I asked you if you got a good feeling from listening to him, and you used words like 'beautiful' and 'sad' – am I right?"

"You are."

"Well, that's what Gigli's voice does: it says things which words, by themselves, can't say."

He leaned forward and picked up the poker, tapped and rolled a partially burned log, bringing the side with unburned bark on it into contact with the red embers. There was a crackling sound, and a small shower of sparks went up the chimney. Little patterns of sparks appeared among the soot clinging to the firestone at the back of the grate. My father eventually put the poker back in its place and said, "I think that's about as much as I can tell you about Beniamino."

"But do you like some things that he sings more than others?" I wanted to know.

"Oh, yes, of course. For a start, I don't think there's a tenor in the world who comes next or near him when it comes to singing Puccini's tenor roles, or Verdi's for that matter. I'm no expert you understand; I'm just saying what I feel, but there's other stuff I love to hear him singing besides operatic arias. Neapolitan songs, for instance.

"Like Caruso before him, he's very fond of them, very

attracted to them. Of course your music snobs look down on them – but not Beniamino nor Enrico. Some of it is fairly humble music, mind, but he turns to it with love and with his enormous, enormous talent, and when he sings "*Sorrento*" or "*Santa Lucia*" or "*Notturno d'Amore*", I swear to God, Billy, that although I've never been there, I can *see* the Bay of Naples, the blue sea and white sand and sunshine."

He was quiet for a minute or two, and I felt sure that in the silence he was away from that fireplace in that room on that rainy night in Cobh. Then he shook his head and somehow, eyes glistening, came back to Bellevue.

"What a gift!" he said. "What a gift."

"Does he ever sing in English?"

"Ah, yes, they *all* do. They *have* to have an English-language song or two in their repertoire."

"Did you ever hear him singing one?"

"I did, yes, and curiously enough it was a song written by an Irish composer – the chap who wrote 'The Harp That Once Through Tara's Hall's.'"

"Gigli sang 'The Harp That Once Through Tara's Halls'? I asked, amazed.

"No-no-no-no!" my father said. "As an *encore* he sang this song called 'When Other Lips . . .' or as he pronounced it, 'When o-their-leeps' – from the opera *The Bohemian Girl*, and *that* was written by the Irishman who wrote 'The Harp That Once . . .' – Michael William Balfe, a fair singer himself, who sang in the Italian Opera in Paris."

"And did Gigli sing 'When other lips' well?"

"Best I ever heard; the definitive version, you might say. I wouldn't ever want to hear it sung by anyone else after hearing him do it."

He glanced at his watch, and said, "Oh, be the Lord Harry, look at the time! Come on, let's go out to the kitchen and grab a cup of Nancy Lee, and then you'd better hop it upstairs to bed or your mother'll have ructions if she comes in and finds you still up."

As we went in the hall I said, "Dad, thanks for telling me about Beniamino Gigli. It was great."

"Don't mention it, son. Sure why wouldn't I? Isn't he the greatest tenor in the world? He's the man who sets the standards, the one by whom greatness among tenors should be judged. Like everything else in life, if the standards are right, you won't go far wrong. Now, fill up the kettle there like a good lad."

Too Young to be a Widow

I N THOSE DAYS the *Cork Examiner* used the anglicised form of spelling the name of our town – Cove, never Cobh. That was a policy which caused a certain element among the townspeople to say such things as, "Well, what the hell else could you expect from a shower of West Brits like the Crosbies? Them with their 'the Commander says this . . . and the Commander did that?' The Commander my arse! Who the hell does he think he is with his hoity-toity accent? And who the hell do they think *they* are?"

"The Commander" was Lieutenant Commander George Crosbie. He had spent a short period in the Royal Navy before joining the Irish Marine Service, eventually becoming OC Haulbowline. His posh, affectedly upper-crust, anglicised accent and mannerisms stacked the odds against his ever being treated with other than mild resentment by any locals who had even the vaguest republican sympathies. There weren't many of them in the town, but enough to make their presence felt. One of them threw a bottle of ink at the screen in Frennet's picture house one night during the war, right in the middle of a showing of an admittedly propaganda war film about a British tanker damaged in mid-Atlantic by

German gunfire. The name of the ship was also the name of the film, *San Demetrio, London.*

That stain stayed on the screen for years afterwards. I used to think it was a terrible insult to the men (including some from the town, among them Uncle John) who were serving in tankers. They were men who were liable at any minute to be burned to cinders or turned into flying pieces of lung and liver if their ships were blown apart in the red and orange roaring fireball which followed the explosion of a torpedo hitting a loaded tanker.

Uncle John was always on my mind, always in my thoughts. I was always praying for him: Uncle John who came smiling up the hill carrying gifts from America for us, his nephews and nieces; Uncle John who stood by the piano, one elbow resting on its lid, the other arm straight down his side, his hand in his pocket, his eyes closed, his head tilted back as he waited to start singing "Macushla", or "The Snowy Breasted Pearl", or "Gortnamona".

Nan and my mother and Auntie Jo (Uncle John had married Josie Cummins from Newport, County Tipperary) would sit side by side dabbing the moistness from their eyes, while my father sat alone, straight-backed on a straight-backed chair, serious-faced, looking down at his own interlinked fingers, the forefingers and thumbs meeting at the tips and forming a triangle.

Uncle John loved the songs that John McCormack sang, and when he had the time could easily be persuaded to sing "Kathleen Mavourneen", "Molly Bawn" ("This is for you, Moll," he would say to my mother), "Eileen Alannah" and "Love thee, Dearest, Love thee." Once, shortly after he got married, he ended his little drawing room recital by turning to Auntie Jo and saying, "And finally, for you, my darling, one of the loveliest songs I know. It's from the Irish opera *The Lily of Killarney* in which it's sung by a character named Hardress Cregan to the girl he loves, Eily O'Connor – 'Once My Heart With the Wildest Emotion'."

225

* * * * * * * *

Auntie Jo, gentle, smiling, beautiful, idolised my Uncle John, and he idolised her. At a time when hand-holding in public was a rarity, they held hands everywhere they went, and were unembarrassed. For a while there was a small stand-off from Josie Cummins by Nan and her daughters, though my mother took to her very quickly, warmed to her and looked on her as another sister. That formed a bond between them which lasted right up to Josie's death as a nun on the last day of October 1993.

She had a proud tilt to her head which was emphasised whenever she shook back her shoulder-length hair. And yet there was nothing of pride in her shy manner, or in her secret-smile personality. When she smiled openly, her eyes as well as her mouth were involved, and the quietness she carried about with her when Uncle John went back to sea was deep and impenetrable and suffused with longing. The times they spent apart were agony for Auntie Jo. She and Uncle had such a short time together – barely over a year.

On 2 August 1941 the first of what became known as the Russian convoys sailed from Iceland to Murmansk. Before the war ended, 40 of those convoys would have steamed over the horrendous route that took them north of the Arctic Circle where barely two minutes in the sea was enough to kill you.

As well as having to contend with lurking U-Boats, bombers, mines, and the threat posed by the battle cruiser *Scharnhorst* and her attendant destroyers, there were also the gales and blizzards sweeping down from the white polar wastes. There were mountainous seas so tremendous they caused even the biggest ships to pitch and roll furiously, so powerful they had been known to bend backwards the four-inch-thick armour of a ship's deck. It was a region where, for months on end, the sun never rose above the horizon. At other times, there were endless periods of daylight during which the sun never set, thus exposing the massed ranks of ships to the attackers.

226

During those vicious voyages, the decks, lifeboats, super-structures, masts, rails – every external surface above the water on the ships – became coated with ice so thick and so heavy that it endangered the stability of the vessels. It *had* to be hacked and chipped away. Even the spray froze.

The toll in tonnage sunk and lives lost was appalling, but the Russians were in desperate need of arms and other supplies; the convoys had to keep on trying to get through. By the time the last of the Russian convoys reached port in May of 1945, one in every eight of the ships that had set out had been lost.

Uncle John's first experience of being torpedoed came on one of these Russian convoys, in 1942. Off watch when the torpedo struck the tanker, he was one of a handful of crew members that managed to scramble into a lifeboat and pull clear before a second thunderous detonation tore the ship apart, and blew her out of existence. But before they were picked up by a rescue ship, he had seen some of his ship-mates die slow, shrieking deaths in the sea around him, had seen men writhing and roaring, dying from both drowning and burning because the sea was on fire.

"I'll never, ever forget it," I heard him telling Granda Jim and my father as they sat in the front room in No. 3, Harbour Hill. I was shut out from this "adults" talk, but I crept back downstairs and squatted, barely breathing, on the bottom stair across the hall from the room, hoping I wouldn't be discovered and sent out to play.

"They hadn't a chance," he said. "You could hear their screams, hear them calling out. And I saw some of them holding up their arms, black arms alongside black faces, black either from the oil or burned black, you couldn't tell which."

The frostbite that had already attacked his own toes and feet by the time the rescue ship got to their lifeboat gave rise later to concern that he might have to undergo amputation operations. Mercifully the doctors managed to save his toes and feet, and he was sent home to Cobh to recuperate.

He was very pale, his cheeks curved inwards, and his eyes seemed to have receded into dark hollows. A few times I saw Auntie Jo, sitting beside him, softly rubbing the backs of his hands with her fingertips in an oddly touching motion that suggested an attempt by her to soothe and comfort him, and at the same time to rub circulation back into his hands.

This was a very different Uncle John from the man he used to be, the man who, if you were his nephew or niece, he would sweep up in his arms and cuddle, and then spin wildly around before setting you down dizzy and laughing, and say with his mouth against your ear, "Now you be good and look after your mammy and daddy, won't you?"

"I will."

"What? I can't hear you. Surely you can answer louder than that?"

"I *will*."

"Good, good," he'd say, secretly pressing a halfcrown into the palm of your hand and closing your fingers around it. "Buy some sweets, and be sure to share them and, listen – are you *listening*? Say a prayer for your Uncle John, won't you?"

Those were the times when he'd hug my mother and say, "Cheerio, Moll, see you next time," and put his hands on my father's shoulders and look wordlessly into his eyes before giving him a brief hug, and then swing off down the hill smiling and glistening-eyed, waving once over his shoulder, not trusting himself to look back.

* * * * * * * *

When he died, it was my grandmother who heard the news first. It came over the air in an extravagantly posh English accent from a man born in Brooklyn of Irish parents. He was brought up in Ireland until his family moved to England. Kicked out of Mosley's Fascist party, he went to Germany, where, in 1939, he started broadcasting propaganda, abuse and threats from the studios of Radio Hamburg.

My grandmother was sitting in the bay window of her bedroom, looking out, as always, at the sea, the wireless on a small table beside her. Twiddling the dial looking for news, she accidentally tuned into Radio Hamburg to hear this pretentious voice saying, "Germany" (the way it came out was Chairmany) "calling."

She was about to move the tuning knob away from the station when she heard the sneering voice claim the sinking of more Allied ships in a convoy. The speaker named the vessels. The second one in his list was the tanker on which my grandmother's only remaining son, our Uncle John, was the chief engineer.

The owner of the voice was William Joyce, nicknamed "Lord Haw Haw". I detested him when I heard about him and have retained an abiding hatred of him ever since. It was not one whit lessened by his execution by hanging. I have never forgiven him for what his gloating announcement did to my grandmother that day in 1943.

The piece about Uncle John in the *Cork Examiner* following his death didn't come near capturing him as we had known him. COVE MAN LOST AT SEA was the single-column headline. It said he was "aged about 30", had gone to sea at 23, and "in less than five years qualified as a Chief Engineer".

It mentioned that he had been born on Haulbowline and educated at both the Cobh and Cork Technical Schools. He was described as "a very popular tenor and keen actor," who had taken leading parts in CYMS productions. That he had been torpedoed in 1942 was referred to, and it was pointed out that he was the second son of James Sexton and Mrs Sexton of 3, Harbour Hill, Cobh, and "the grandson of Mr P Sexton, J.P., a well-known merchant in Dungarvan". It ended by saying, "He leaves a young widow."

He also left a heartbroken mother and father, and sisters, and brothers-in-law, and nephews and nieces.

Nan took to sitting at her bedroom window, looking out to sea, a handkerchief pressed against her mouth, her head shaking from side to side, her body rocking gently backwards

229

and forwards. I often stood at that bedroom door looking in at her. I was unable to say anything, was, indeed, afraid to speak as I watched her in her misery and heard the disturbing low moans that came from her.

The eyes of my mother and of the older of my aunts were red-rimmed for weeks. My father became very quiet. His mouth was straight and thin-lipped. When he found my mother crying, he put an arm around her to comfort her, and we left them alone in these moments of anguished privacy.

Auntie Jo's face became long and drawn from grief, and her skin had a dirty grey-white appearance. Dressed all in black, she walked up to the cathedral every day and knelt alone for hours, praying, beseeching God, begging, imploring "Please don't let this be true, please, please, *please*, Sweet Jesus!"

I remember someone once saying, "A decade of *Memorares* always works. It'll get you *anything*. The Blessed virgin is fantastic."

Ten *Memorares* took a lot of concentration and staying power compared with ten *Hail Marys*, but I began to say a daily decade of them anyway – for Uncle John. "Remember, O most tender Virgin Mary, that it was never known that anyone who fled to thy protection, implored thy help, or sought thy intercession was left unaided. Inspired with this confidence, I fly unto thee, O Virgin of Virgins, my mother. To thee I come, before thee I stand sinful and sorrowful. O Mother of the Word Incarnate, despise not my petition, but in thy clemency hear and answer me. Amen . . . Remember, O most tender Virgin Mary . . ."

Auntie Jo, to me, was too young to be a widow. Widows were middle-aged or elderly women. It seemed all wrong.

She clung to two words in the official letter that came to her. They were in the phrase that said he was "missing, presumed dead".

"They didn't say he was *killed*," she said tearfully to me one day. "The letter just says '*presumed* dead' . . . I can't believe my darling John is dead."

She cradled my head in her arms and I could feel her body convulsing with sobs. Then after a while she calmed, pushed me out from her, still holding my shoulders, and looked at my face through eyes that were filling again. She bit her lower lip and said, "He loved you, you know. And you look *so* like him."

I didn't know what to say. She was an adult, and I didn't know how to comfort an adult, so I just remained silent. She took a tiny lace-edged handkerchief from her cuff and dabbed her eyes. "Always pray for him, won't you?" she said beseechingly.

I nodded.

Those *bastards*! Oh, those bloody, dirty, German bastards!

"Remember, O most tender Virgin Mary . . ."

* * * * * * * *

For a very long time, even when the rest of us had accepted the inevitable, Auntie Jo held on to the hope that, like other men who had survived torpedoings, Uncle John might still be alive somewhere, on an island perhaps, or in a prisoner of war camp, or drifting in an open boat.

Even after she entered a religious order and became a nun – she took his name as her name in religion, Sister Marie John – for years she held on to that slender hope. When eventually she had to accept that Uncle John was never again going to come home, she prayed for him and to him every single day, and kept it up for the rest of her life.

For her profession and final vows, she had a special chalice made. Into its stem were embedded her engagement and wedding rings. "It will make me feel closer to him at mass every morning," she explained simply.

She lived for the day when she would die "and we'll be reunited". But she would live on for 50 years, a devoted nun and brilliant nurse tutor.

Her goodness as a person was straightforward, simple, strong and deep. She had a way of taking both of your hands in her own and looking unblinkingly at you, giving you the whole of her attention. Her faith was awesome, but never intimidating, and in time she got her old smile back again. It was then she achieved serenity, and when her eyes sparkled you could see the girl she once was.

In 1993, before I entered the small bedroom in the convent part of St Vincent's Hospital in Dublin where her remains were laid out, I dreaded what lay ahead of me. I needn't have worried. Sister Marie John, Auntie Jo, Uncle John's widow, looked quite beautiful and at peace. Her expression was that of someone who had reached the blessed point of "letting go and letting God", and had then slipped peacefully and gracefully out of this life – to rejoin her "darling John".

Magic August Night

SUMMER MEANT, AMONG other things, new canvas shoes, mackerel, the regatta and Uncle Willie coming down from, as he laughingly put it, "Dirty Dublin". I can't remember him ever being in Cobh for Regatta Week. I think the reason was that he had to take his summer holidays in June or July. That suited my father, because they were the months that he, too, had to take his. It was a shame that Uncle Willie couldn't make it for the 15th of August at least once. He'd have loved it.

July and August were the two months during which the south coast towns held their regattas. We stated baldly, to each other if to no one else, that the Cobh Regatta was "the best in the whole of Ireland, boy".

In the long bright June evenings, the oarsmen came out on the waters of the harbours and the rivers that fed into them. They had all put in a day's work, and now they got down to serious training. Every evening the Whitepoint boat's crew rowed down to the coal hulk at the eastern end of the harbour. That was where the pleasure boat races would start. They practised that punishing pull from the hulk up past the Batteries, past the Holy Ground and the Baths and Lynch's Quay, past the North German Lloyd Pier, the Pier

Head, the Cunard White Star Pier, and then put in a backbreaking spurt to the finishing line opposite the bandstand on the Promenade.

They were competitive, hard men, stripped down to singlets and cotton shorts, and they were very serious and very intent on keeping out upstarts who wanted to gain a place in a crew. Whenever one of the younger brigade made an even temporary breakthrough, such as sitting-in as a substitute for someone doing overtime or away on a day's deep-sea fishing, he'd row till he nearly passed out from exhaustion and agony. The blisters on his hands grew big, white, soft, and water-and-pain-filled. When they burst, the flesh inside was red and raw.

The next day he'd show off his wounds with pride, and say, "See them? They're the badges of effort, boy! They'll turn into calluses, and get hard, and then you wouldn't be able to hurt me if you flogged me on 'em with a brass wire. But if you think *they* look bad, you shoulda seen me arse after the final row up to the hulk last night. I was *bleedin'*! Not that I'm going to show it to ye – ye can flog off!"

The Rushbrook boat, crewed by men who lived around Dock Terrace, did most of their training upriver along the shore that ran from Monkstown to Passage West and up into Lough Mahon. They had no intention of letting the Whitepoint crowd see their form.

Of course the clinker-built "pleasure boats" that featured in our regatta were a world removed from the smooth-sided, light racing shells that glided down the genteel stretch of the Thames at Henley. The boats in *our* regatta were tough, four-oared craft built for racing in seaways and tideways. We said they were for *real* men in *real* competitions – and if any of the oul lah-di-dahs questioned that, let him try a sustained burst from the hulk to the Naval Pier into a choppy ebbing tide and a west wind. *That'd* show them.

"Show them *up!*" Barney Cullen said. "None of your bleddy fancy sliding seats for our fellas. Those guys at Henley are fierce mollycoddled altogether."

Outfits like Whitepoint, Rushbrook and the Lee Boat Club had grainy black-and-white pictures on their walls showing the crews, or boats as they were called, which had competed down through the years. In many cases you could trace a family line of oarsmen through several generations of competition. They were very proud of that.

Regatta time was also the annual festival of sniping criticism. The regatta and its committee were criticised *before* it took place, *while* it took place, and long after it *had* taken place.

The committee would start holding regular meetings upstairs in the Town Hall, and people such as Lawrence Leahy, Tim Halloran ("the Count") and Pat O'Mahony proposed and discussed and seconded to their hearts' content. Mick Dolan, the *Examiner*'s local stringer, would occasionally get a few lines about their deliberations into "de paper". Whether he did or not, it didn't much matter because leaked details of what had gone on always got around the town anyway and were discussed at length all through the next day.

"Come 'ere, did you hear what that bleddy amadhaun stood up and said at the meetin' last night?"

"Who? Who're yeh talkin' about?"

"Who do yeh think? The bleddy runner-in of course! Jazus, that fellah only crossed the bridge yesterday, and he standin' up there and sayin' what they *should* do. 'Tis on'y the likes of 'im would have the neck! They should tell 'im to *piss* off, an' go back to where he kem frum!"

"Yerra, I dunno, sure the chap is on'y doin' 'is best. If summa the other luggawns on the committee on'y had the gumption to open dere mouts, it wouldn't arise at all."

The committee annually discussed and argued about such matters as whether or not there would be a fireworks display this year. It seemed immaterial to them that there was *always* a fireworks display.

"Sure for God's sake, isn't that what the regatta is for?" Mrs Wilson said. "Whoever heard of a Cobh Regatta without a fireworks display?"

"And they're proposin' to make a collection again this year for a fireworks display? What became of all the money they collected last year, that's what I'd like to know."

"Yerra, they *drank* it girl! Don't yeh know it? They spent more time in the Westbourne Bar on Regatta Day than they did in the Prom! Faith an' *I'm* not going to give 'em a brass farthing this year."

I overheard Skipper Regan and Jimmy Horgan, owners of two of the one-design yachts, talking by the camber the day the *Cygnet* was brought in alongside the slip to have her hull cleaned.

"I dunno will the new nylon spinnakers be here in time, hah?" Jimmy Horgan said.

"Personally, I wouldn't use one if 'twas given to me as a present."

"You wouldn't? Why not?"

"'Cos they still have to prove themselves."

"That's silly! They've proved themselves all over the world."

"Not here, they haven't; not in Cork Harbour."

"Uffa Fox recommends them very highly. He says they're the future shape of sailing."

"Yeh? And has he ever sailed in Cork Harbour, answer me that?"

"He has."

"He has in his arse. Southampton Water, that's about the only place the same Mr Fox has ever sailed."

"He *has* sailed in Cork Harbour, I'm tellin' yeh now."

"Sailed a one-design in Cork Harbour?"

"Oh, I don't know about that –"

"Hey! Youngfella," Skipper Regan interrupted, "what're you doing listening to a private conversation? Go on, bugger off!"

On the Saturday morning I walked up to the top of Bellevue because I'd seen Mick Long walking across the road from Queenie Meade's house. He was carrying his binoculars.

"Hello, Mr Long!"

He knew damn well who it was greeting him, even though he had the glasses to his eyes when I spoke. He knew, because only a few seconds before he had been looking at me through them.

"Huh? . . . Wha'? . . . Who have we here? . . . Oh, it's you, Billy. I never seen you comin' up the hill."

It didn't bother me that I knew he was putting on an act. In other words, lying. It probably wouldn't have bothered him, either, to know that I knew. But Mick prided himself in being in the know about what was going on, and if you wanted to get his views, you had to be prepared to put up with his mannerisms.

"Do you think the regatta committee will cancel the cruiser class race this year, Mr Long? Only a very small few of them turned out last year."

"Well, now, I don't know. You must remember the kinda day it was. There wasn't a breath of air for the Crosshaven boats to get halfway in the harbour, notta mind get to the start line. I think meself they'll have the cruisers down to be in it all right, but the *If*'ll probably walk it as usual.

"But that committee – sure, Christ Almighty, they're a bleddy joke, that's what they are, a *joke!* They couldn't organise matins in a monastery. I'll tell yeh what *I'd* like to know, and it's this: what becomes of all the money they collect every year? There's a few of 'em now on that committee, and I'll tell you for nuttin, *they're* not in it for the love of it. There's shag-all hanging by 'em. They'll get their whack out of it."

He was in full stride now, and seeing that I wasn't trying to get away, he lay the binoculars carefully on the ground by his feet to free his arms for the expansive gesticulations which were an essential part of his declamatory style.

"I see they're at the same bleddy stuff of wondering whether there should be a swimmin' gala this year, and would there be a greasy pole competition because there were some objections last year that it was too dangerous, and is it worthwhile havin' a punt race for the ladies, and what band should they go for for the Promenade. I mean it's the same god-damn shit every year."

"Mr Long, do you think our regatta is better than Cork's?"

"*Cork's?* Sure that's not a proper regatta ad all – a few lousy boat club crews rowin' up the most sheltered part of the river! Don't make me laugh. I suppose in the literary sensa the word – is that literary, or literal? Sure what the hell am I askin' *you* for? How would *you* know? *You* wouldn't know.

"Let me tell-yeh somethin' – this town gave a new meanin' to the word regatta, and ever since, all the other little piss-assed harbour towns up an' down the south coast – Kinsale, Youghal, Skibbereen, Glandore – have been tryin' to ape what we have here and, I might say, conspiciously failin'."

The whole town, even youngfellas my own age, held forth about the regatta. We were all experts. Tearing it asunder in advance was part of the great regatta game. Because the adults did it so whole-heartedly, so vehemently and so venomously, we felt fully licensed to do likewise.

The women on morning shopping trips downtown, and in doorways, and on the way to and from devotions at the cathedral, and sometimes as they leaned out of windows with their make-do turbans and snoods on their heads and their forearms bared for housework, sniped away unmercifully at the committee.

"Did you see the cut of 'em last year on Regatta Day? *Stocious*, girl, absolutely *footless*, maggoty drunk before the afternoon was even half over! Not a leg under them! And on the town's money – not their own. It'd sicken yeh."

On occasions Bishop Roche's name was brought into it. Ever since the time he stepped in and forbade the holding of the regatta dance when the 15th of August fell on a Saturday, he drew criticism. It didn't matter that his reason was that he didn't "want the boys and girls of the parish coming to mass late and in sin on Sunday morning".

The cooling Catholics and the critical Protestants didn't

238

hesitate to have their say, and they didn't mind what age the ears were that heard them. You'd hear comments to the effect that he was much too strict when it was remembered that there was a world war raging, and that the twentieth century would be already halfway through in a few years time, and that he had too much to say and was *given* too much of a say in how things in the town should be run. That it was about time someone stood up to him. But if someone *was* to stand up to him, it should preferably be a Catholic.

That year of 1943 the weather on Regatta Day was glorious. From early morning white sails began to appear on the sea far out by Roche's Point as the yachts from up and down the coast started to nose into the harbour. I ran all the way down the hills to The Beach after breakfast to see the local council workers putting up the flags and bunting in the Promenade. Mickey Glavin was scurrying around trailing great lengths of flex, stringing up rows of light bulbs, putting ancient-looking microphones in place, and all the time sucking on a Woodbine.

His voice could be heard on the loudspeakers: "Hel . . . o! . . . o! . . . esting one, two . . . ore . . . Can you . . . thing? Must be the fuh . . ."

The sound came through in fits and starts, Mickey's voice, whenever you heard it, sounding increasingly stressed as it boomed in loud and echoing for a couple of words here, a syllable there, followed by wild howl-around, feedback, then crackling, hissing silence.

I went into the Promenade and watched the last slats of the fireworks frames being nailed in place and thought, crumbs! Tonight the committee members in charge of the fireworks will be standing here in this very place where I am now, and there'll be Catherine wheels and rockets and cannon crackers ready to go off on these frames, and also from those earth-filled oil drums over there; there'll be detonations like thunder claps, and rockets will zoom up into the air making a slashing sound, and they'll burst into a million stars in the night sky and come down into the water among the anchored boats.

I stepped closer and reverently touched the frames so that I'd be able to hold that secret knowledge to myself when tonight came. Then I wandered away and slouched around the town, drinking in the large feelings, the feelings of breath-holding and expectation you have when you are waiting for something stupendous to happen.

I ate hardly any lunch. I wanted to be back down there on The Beach when the big red turf lorries, Ford's and Dodges mainly, rolled into town with the pleasure boats of Glandore and Whitegate and Kinsale and Waterford laid across the top and tied down.

The scraggly shawlies with their bold faces and straggly hair came off the train from Cork and walked up past the Yacht Club and along Westbourne Place, lugging baskets of fruit and boxes of sweets and chocolate bars, for which they'd charge at least one-and-a-half times what Mrs O'Brien or Pakie Neill or Bill Healy in the Top o' the Hill charged.

The rough-looking men who came with them – husbands, sons, brothers and brothers-in-law – pushed hand-carts or old prams on which were stacked folding roulette stalls and rickety shooting galleries where you'd get five shots for sixpence from old, rusty pellet guns.

By one o'clock the special trains put on for the day were emptying crowds into the town, and the high sing-song accents and voices of Cork were everywhere.

There were just a few small white clouds high up in the blue when the Butter Exchange Band got off the train and formed up outside the station. Men who had the day off and women with children in prams and swinging out of the skirts of their summer dresses stood in little huddles watching these Cork fellows in their dark-blue-almost-black uniforms which were ancient and threadbare.

There was one old man in the band who fascinated me. At least what he had done with his moustache fascinated

240

me, for he had obviously waxed the hair and then twisted and twirled it tight until it formed small thin spikes running out to left and right under his nose. He was a stocky man with a back as straight as if it were nailed to a plank. He adjusted the straps of a small drum which was slung to the left of his belt buckle, and when it was placed to his liking, he fished out a pair of sticks and rattled out a sharp paradiddle and a couple of rolls, then shrugged with obvious satisfaction and looked around. He caught my eye, and winked.

"He was a drummer boy in the Boer War," someone behind me said.

It didn't mean anything to me, but it sounded so important that I didn't even turn around to see who it was had said it. I believed it and, staring at the man, tried to imagine him as a little boy marching with troops into battle, beating out the rhythm for their steps. The problem was, I couldn't convert his 70-plus face into a youngster's. So I settled for thinking of a boy's small figure in the middle of men carrying guns, with smoke billowing over a foreign battleground, and shells exploding, and horses toppling over and kicking and flaring their nostrils and looking whites-of-the-eyes frightened, and soldiers falling down, writhing, the way they did in the films, clutching their guts, or holding a shattered leg, or just bleeding away from a shot that hit them in the chest, and screaming out, "Help! . . . Help me! . . . Please, for the love of God, someone help me!"

"*Errol!* Geh back from dat bleedin' wall or I'll swing for yeh, honesta Jesus, I'll *scrag* yeh!"

The shrill Coal Quay voice shrieking at full volume yanked me back from the daydream and replaced fantasy with Regatta Day reality. But once the frantic mother had run across the steps leading down to the tide and grabbed snotty-nosed Errol and shook him with brain-damaging strength, it was back to watching the Butther-a getting ready to march off towards the Promenade.

I had an idea – I'd walk along beside them, march in time with them, close to the drummer boy from the Boer War.

His face was set and stern now, and his lips were tight. They swung into a Sousa march, wheeled and headed towards Westbourne, me about three feet from the snare drummer, watching his hands and the blurring heads of the drumsticks, then his face, then the way he marched so proudly and purposefully, somehow distanced from all the other fellas in the band, ordinary Corkies who hadn't been where he'd been, hadn't seen what he'd seen.

Between the thump-thump-thump of the big bass drum, the blare of the trumpets and trombones, the oom-pah oom-pah of the bass tubas, the reedy singing of the saxophones and clarinets and the marvellous, rhythmic, machine-gun-fast playing of the snare drummer, I thought I couldn't stand it, I'd burst. It was a huge throbbing feeling. It was the day, and it was that man, and it was the fact that I was a boy growing up, but still a child.

When the band stopped playing opposite Darcy's sweet shop, the sudden silence made it seem as if the day had died, or at least come to a premature end. And in that moment, the Butther-a lost its magic for me.

The band members turned and walked off the road, crossed the pavement, and filed in through the cast-iron gates of the Promenade. They didn't have to pay, but everyone else did. Sixpence. Sixpence up to six o'clock, that is, because at the Angelus the Prom was cleared.

But my pals and I were too grown up now to fall for lashing out a precious tanner just to be on the Promenade during the afternoon when the only thing going on was the band recital. There had been a few years when being in the Prom was a dead loss. Mothers and fathers and young kids were all over the place, and all that was on offer were selections from Gilbert and Sullivan, the Savoy Irish Medley, the United States Medley and Thomas Moore's Melodies.

And nothing to see except kids pushing and tearing at

each other, and falling down and skinning their knees, and babies dirtying and stinking their nappies, and ice-cream-eating children making their faces grubby by rubbing mucky hands across them to wipe away tears or chocolate smears. Where was the gas in that?

"Buggar that for a barrel of straw!" Danny Dinan said to my mother. He had made the mistake of going in on one such eventful occasion. "Jesus, missus – excuse me now again for taking the Holy Name – but I was driven demented! *Never again*, I vowed, as long as my asshole faces downwards."

However, in 1943 there was a swimming gala in the tide and a greasy pole event. It was worth the sixpence that day all right, because I saw Betsy Love and Una Bunworth and Rhona James and Bunty Sullivan tugging their swimming togs up at the chest, and pulling them down at the tops of their legs and around the back to cover the cheeks of their bums.

Nux and Dave McCormack won the boys' races in the swimming gala. Christy Ryan fell the wrong way on the greasy pole, came down straddling it, grimacing, and everyone looking on said, "Ooooh!", and didn't laugh. I doubled over, feeling his pain, and me fifty feet away from him, standing on the Promenade wall. All that was worth the sixpence right enough, but if you stayed too long in the Promenade you couldn't get a proper feel for what it was like in the rest of the town. After the swimming gala, I left.

Westbourne Place and West and East Beach were crowded. Thousands of people had poured in by train, bus and car, and the place was jumping. You had to shoulder your way through.

"Apples! . . . *Tree* for a shillin'! . . . *Get* your apples and sweets! . . . Apples . . . *Tree* for a shillin'! . . . Whass dat, boy? You *could*, couldja? Well, shag off so, yeh cheeky little bastard, and *buy* 'em in de shop! . . . Apples! . . . *Tree* for a shillin'! . . . *Get* your . . ."

There was no sign of Nux, John Driscoll or any of the other lads, and I wanted to see some of the yacht races. I walked quickly along Harbour Row and up East Hill to the point where it levelled off before turning left and up towards Belmont. There was a group of men already there, looking back up the harbour.

The one-designs were out in midstream off the Prom, waiting for the starting gun. You could see the manoeuvring, George Radley, Jimmy Horgan, Skipper (or maybe it was his son Kevin "Houdini") Regan, the Roche's, all trying to get the jump on each other at the gun, all wanting to cross the line first when Count ("Spelled with an 'o' in it," Dingle Daniels used to say, and I didn't know what he was getting at) Halloran pulled the cord on the starting cannon.

The high sun flooded the harbour with light. Spike, round-edged and curvy, looked very green and benign. Haulbowline, lower-lying, a lot of it man-made, looked irregular and angular. And you could see distinctly the solid colours of the one-design's hulls – one all red, another yellow, another blue, another black, the last one white. They were a beautiful sight.

"Fifty years old, hah? An' just as good as they ever were."

It was Mick Long. He must have walked across from Bellevue. This time he had a group of adults around him, so I didn't count. I didn't care, either, but didn't adults know that children knew when they were being snubbed?

No one answered Mick Long for a few minutes. Then Stinger's father Tom Nash, a pilot, said, "What do yeh mean 50 years old? They're *60* years old."

"Oh!" Mick Long said. "I thought I read somewhere they were *50*. In fact I'm *sure* I read they're 50."

"I don't give a god-damn *what* you read – I'm tellin' yeh now, they're *60!*"

"Awright, Tom, I'll take your word for it."

"You have no alternative. It's a *fact!*"

"Awright, awright, I *said* awright, didn't I?"

"The problem with this town," Tom said, turning towards his companions, "is that some people don't mind talkin' through their arses and tryin' to sound intelligent at the same time. Can't be done. *Im*-possible!"

"Look here, there's no need to be offensive! I didn't come here to be insulted."

"No one asked yeh to come. We all have choices an' we all *make* choices. You can choose to stay here now, or leave. It's entirely up to you. But don't try to come the old sojer with us."

I didn't know whether to try to slip away unnoticed or stay and pretend I hadn't heard. Mick Long stood for a moment, stranded, undecided what to do next. Then he looked down at me and said, "Come on, Billy, we won't stay where we're not wanted."

He'd known all along that I was there. Now he saw my presence as a convenient facesaver for him.

"Leave the youngfella alone!" Tom Nash said. "Leave *him* outa this."

I don't think he knew who I was, but he wasn't going to let Mick Long get away with railroading me away from the viewing place.

"Do you want to go with 'im?" he asked me.

I was in a quandary. I hardly knew what to answer.

"I only just got here. I want to see the one-designs race, part of it anyway." I turned towards Mick. "So, if you don't mind, Mr Long–"

"Suit yerself!" Long said, shaking all his jowls in disgust, and tramped away down the hill.

"Good riddance!" one of the other men said, and we all turned our attention back to the race.

Mr Nash was the only one of the men I recognised, but it didn't matter. They got immersed in what was taking place down there on the harbour waters, and I loved listening to their talk.

"He was right, of course, Tom," one of them said.

"Who was?"

"Yer man, oul Jingleknackers. They're as good now as ever they were."

"Oh, I couldn't agree with yeh more."

"Beautiful lines, haven't they?"

"I wouldn't say exactly beautiful – attractive maybe, but functional definitely."

"Are we goin'ta start splittin' hairs now over bleddy words?"

"Now, lads, lads! Hold it! . . . What do *you* think, young-fella?"

"I don't know," I said, wishing I hadn't been asked.

"Come on, you must have *some* opinion. What d'yeh thin-ka the one-designs?"

"I think they're lovely."

"Good lad yerself! That wasn't hard, was it? Not like goin' upta the Dispensary to have a toot pulled? We'll settle for 'lovely' so . . . When *they* were built down in Baltimore –"

"Jazus, look at the *Cygnet*! Where the hell does he think he's goin'?"

"He's takin' a chance, Jim, that's what he's up to."

"I don't think it'll work. Look at Radley over there in the *Quereda*. He's held his nerve an' I reckon that if he maintains that course now for about another three or four minutes, he'll make the mark on this tack."

"Here, who's at the helm in the *Cygnet*? Is it Skipper or Kevin?"

"I heard last night it was goin' to be Ruby."

"Oh, Jazus, if 'tiz him, the *Cygnet* 'll walk it."

"An' what about Radley?"

"What about 'im?"

"He'd give Rube a bleddy good run for it."

"Who're yeh kiddin'?"

"I'm deadly serious."

"Talk sense, man! Ruby has forgotten more'n George and Willy put together will ever learn."

"Ah, for Jazus' sake –"

"Here, lads, lads! The language – for Christ's sake watch the fekkin' language, will ye? There's a youngfella present!"

246

I stayed with them until the first of the pleasure boats, which had come down the harbour from where their crews had put them into the water at the slip opposite English's butchers shop, made their start near the coal hulk anchored off Cuskinny Bay. A group of motorboats, including the guards' launch, accompanied them down and would accompany them back. It was the guards' launch that carried the "offeeshuls". And those fussy little men, legends in their own lunchtimes, stood up and waved their arms this way and that and bellowed through megaphones, "Clear the course! Will you *please* clear the course? . . . Hello! Will you *please* clear the course?"

"Ah, clear me bollix!" one motorboat owner was known to have shouted the previous year. I noticed his boat was down there again this time.

I ran down East Hill and along Harbour Row, past the Preaching House Steps, past Tommy Enright's barber shop and Ethna Rogers's house, down past Pakie Neill's and past the town's other barber shop, Tommy Jago's, past Mrs Poole's fish and chip shop (she'd make a fortune today), past Dick Nick's ice cream and sweets shop and around the corner to Lynch's Quay.

I could hear the shouts and cheers from along past the Customs House before I was halfway across the road. Here the crowd was thicker, and the men's shouts were mingled with screams of encouragement from women supporters.

When I reached the edge of the quay I could see the strain and the sweat on the faces of the rowers in the inshore boats. The coxes were roaring at their own crews, and some of the oarsmen had their eyes closed and their lower lips clamped by their upper teeth.

"Come on, Whitepoint!"

They were leading!

"Come on, Rushbrook!"

"*Pull*, Blackrock, *pull*, ye hoors!"

"Come on, Kinsale!"

"Ah, for Christ's sake, Glandore, what're ye upta?"

In each boat, the blades of the four oars knifed into the water in unison, the handles were pulled towards the oarsmen's chests in a long violent swing, the boat lunged forward, oar blades came out of the water together, were feathered, and swung back towards the bow to start the same movement, over and over again. I said a quick Hail Mary that Whitepoint wouldn't catch a crab, because Rushbrook were pushing them hard.

I ran back in off the quay as soon as the leading two boats passed, and tore along past the slip, the CYMS hall, the Labour Exchange and the North German Lloyd Pier.

A woman I bumped into as I tried to zig-zag my way out to the edge of the Pier Head said, "Ah, yeh bleddy little scut, yeh!" even though I'd said, "Oh, I'm very sorry, pardon me."

But I got to the edge just as Whitepoint, on the final killing couple of hundred yards, leaned into the stroke to stay ahead. Then the bowman in Rushbrook's boat faltered, caught a crab, and there was a groan of anguish from the Rushbrook supporters around me.

In an instant the third and fourth boats were up, level, and past Rushbrook, and the whole character of the race changed. It was impossible to lean out far enough to see what happened in that last stretch, and I could only stand there, enveloped by smells and noise, and listen to the speculation while we waited for the finishing gun, and then the announcement over the loudspeakers – if they were working!

Mickey's voice could be heard saying: ". . . esting . . . sting . . . One, two . . . ee . . . fi . . . ven . . . Ah the bleddy . . . again there, boy! . . . it . . . ah, bugger the bleddy thing!"

And then came the sounds of the finishing guns, two loud cracks, almost together, followed by roars and clapping and cheering.

All around me, but above me, I could hear the excited talk.

"They done it! They done it! I knew they would! I knew they had the measure of 'em."

"Don't count yer chickens!"

"Feck off!"

"A race isn't over until the result is announced, and if you
–"

"Attention, please! Attention, please! . . ."

From somewhere close by: "Hey! Whisht! Shurrup. I'm
tryin' to hear the effin announcement!"

"Ah-hah-yeh-boy-yeh!"

". . . the result of the . . ."

And then the arguments started.

"Dose shaggers of judges must be *blind!* How could *dat*
crowd have won it?"

"Dey won it fair an' square, *dat's* how dey won it."

"Cut right across our fellas' bows be the North German
Lloyd."

"No such ting!"

"A fix, a fuckin' fix, *dat's* what it was!"

"Get out yeh bleddy hoor's melt! Ye can't take it, dat's
what's wrong wit' ye!"

"Oh, yeah? Take *dat!*"

Following the punch, a Murphy's Stout bottle was broken
and brought up for use. That's when I decided to run.

"Guard! Guard! Over here!"

A blue uniform shouldered its way through the crowd. As
I escaped I heard one of the fighters saying, "Not at all,
Guard, we was only havin' a little friendly discussion about de
outcome of de race."

"Any more discussions of this nature, and ye can finish 'em
in the Bridewell or in the local barracks here," the guard
said.

I ran, full tilt, away from the place. This time I didn't stop
to say sorry to any one of the seven or eight people I nudged,
bumped into, knocked aside. I was scared stiff of violence,
and I didn't want to see blood.

When I got close to the eastern gates of the Promenade,
two crest-fallen Glandore men were coming out.

"I said it from de very beginnin', 'twas de biggest mistake ivir puttin' dat eejit in at number tree. He haven't de strinth. He didn't have it last year, and he haven't it dis year."

"To be fair to him now, Dinny, he did all right at Rathmore."

"Ratmore? An' what were we up aginst at Ratmore? Pigmies! Fuckin' pigmies. You coulda put your Julia in at number ber tree at Ratmore, and we'd stilla won, be Jazus. Don't *talk* to me!"

And so it went on, every race having its tragedies and triumphs, its arguments, its "I-told-ye-an'-ye wouldn'-listen"s. The pubs did a roaring trade, and the evening drew down loudly on a tumultuous town.

After tea, the stall owners lit their paraffin lights. Pellets pinged and whanged in the shooting galleries, pennies and threepenny bits and sixpences clinked on the roulette tables, three-card-trick men hoodwinked at speed, squatting wherever they could find a space, and the waterfront streets of the town became littered with orange peel, apple cores, sweet wrappers and dropped ice creams. The pubs filled up, and off-key drunks bawled maudlin come-all-yehs.

And then it was night. Magic. The fairy lights that Mickey had strung up in the morning went on all around the Promenade, and high up in the spire of the cathedral, Staf began to play the bells.

I stood by the old coffee stall listening, thinking of the small man from Belgium up there high over the town, playing music on a gigantic instrument that sounds like no other. Wouldn't it be terrible if, even for a minute, it went through his head that, while he was sweating and pounding the keys and putting his heart and soul into Gounod's *Ave Maria*, down on The Beach and in the Prom were thousands of Corkies who not only weren't listening, but couldn't care less? Wouldn't that be desperate altogether?

In an effort to make up for the ones who disregarded him, I stayed a little while longer. And what happened was even more stupid – I felt myself filling up. The bells always did that to me. And I thought, Aw *shit!* – this is Regatta Night, this is no night to feel sad.

"*There* you are! Where the hell have *you* been?"

The question arrived with the punch on the shoulder. Nux's eyes were alight with excitement.

"Congratulations! I saw you winning your race."

"Thanks . . . Listen, knackers, I've been searchin' everywhere for yeh. Come on, let's see what's goin' on."

You could feel the build-up towards the fireworks display which was scheduled to start at 10.30. We were wearing our best ties, and our hair was brilliantined, pressed into quiffs. Whenever we passed the young-ones from the girls' school, we cracked jokes and laughed and tried to appear very casual and blasé. We tried to click with the attractive ones, knowing full well that if any of the girls made a move, we'd have nearly died. They were pretty and giggly in their summer dresses, all looking a bit like Judy Garland in *Little Nellie Kelly*.

We met up with some of the other lads, and paraded through the throngs from one end of the town to the other. The yachtsmen from the bigger boats had come ashore, and they, too, were doing their parading, wearing their peaked yachting caps and blue blazers and white trousers, behaving like Admiral Muck, convinced they were the centre of attention.

"Gobshites!" Crab Walsh said of them.

Outside Darcy's sweetshop on Westbourne, it was Crab who stopped abruptly, spreading his arms, pushing us back from him. Looking upwards towards the roof, he suddenly pointed and shouted, "Don't! For God's sake *don't!* Don't jump!"

The crowd around us stopped in their tracks, stopped chattering, looked upwards.

"Who is it? Can you see anyone?"

"No."

"Oh, look – over there! Isn't that a head?"

"I can't see anyone . . . Oh, yes! There, look!"

Crab continued to shout, "Stop! Stop! Don't do it! There must be a better way!"

"Poor bugger!"

After a few minutes during which he remained silent while the crowed took up the "Don't jump!" chant, he grabbed Nux and myself by the sleeve and whispered, "Come on, let's get outa hear now and leave 'em to it."

When we reached the square, I asked, "*Was* there someone up there?"

"Nod-ad-all! I just did it for a bitta gazz."

Daisy Sullivan, Pappy's daughter, had decided to take the family rowing boat out on the water that night for the fireworks, and she had invited Mam, Dad, Norma, Margaret, John and myself and John Donovan to join her. So at ten-past ten I said so-long to Nux and the boys and went to the camber.

Dad and John Donovan rowed the boat out in the dark, and that in itself had a delicious feel of danger and adventure to it. We were all warned to sit still. The sounds of shouting and laughter coming off The Beach and Prom, and the competing sounds of recordings of Harry James and Glenn Miller and Benny Goodman and singers like Dinah Shore and Ella Fitzgerald being played at full blast on gramophones placed right next to microphones sent a frisson of excitement coursing through the veins.

The water off the Prom was full of boats – anchored yachts home from the day's races, motorboats, dinghies, punts, salmon yawls – some tied up alongside each other, others bobbing gently, late-comers trying to nose into an open space of water.

Then, without any announcement over the speakers, the first rocket whooshed into the darkness over our heads, and the show was on.

It was just the tiniest bit frightening, the suddenness of it all, and the shrieks that went up when the starburst happened, throwing its brilliant green and pink light over a wide area, showing us all the upturned faces, all the shadows and shapes on the surface of the water.

As the firework stars began to descend towards us, Daisy shrieked, "Oh, Mother of God! Eddie! Molly! It's coming straight for us! . . . Oh! . . . Oh! . . . Oh!"

Norma, alongside me, took it up, screeching at the top of her voice like all the other little girls in the adjoining boats. I nudged her hard with my shoulder and said, "For goodness sake will yeh keep quiet? You're making a holy show of us."

She kept it up, hands to face one second, face buried in small pudgy fingers the next.

John Donovan and my father laughed. Mam and Daisy eventually settled down to mild hysteria, but jumped every time a canon cracker exploded.

I was mesmerised by it all, and soon everyone else in the boat ceased to exist for me, and I was lost in a world of brilliant light and explosions and trails up the sky . . .

And I wanted it to last for ever.

Dad and Nijinsky

"A H, I THOUGHT I'd try to do something to reverse the flow," Dad said with a laugh one day when I asked him why he had left Dublin. Then he added, "Did you know that all the best jobs in the civil service are held by Cork people? Dubliners end up with just the junior jobs, or the menial jobs. Did you not know that?"

I said I hadn't.

"Oh that's a fact, I declare to me God," he said. "And do you know why?"

"No," I said.

"Because there's so many of them up there – Corkmen. When a Corkman goes to Dublin for the very first time and gets off the train at Kingsbridge, he takes the bus to O'Connell Bridge, finds a stone, throws it into the Liffey, and if it floats he goes home."

He left it hanging, lit a Woodbine, and walked away, smiling. After a carefully judged interval he came back to me.

"You think I was joking, don't you? Well, I was, but only a little. I'm dead serious about all the best jobs in the civil service going to Corkmen, and of course to some *other* people from the provinces, as well. And why does that happen?

Because they do better at exams, that's why. They get down to the books and study. In Dublin there's too many distractions – theatres and cinemas and dancehalls and God knows what else. But if you live in a provincial town or village, there's hardly any distractions. To get ahead you *have* to get your exams, and it's easier to *study* for your exams if you're not being pulled this way and that way by other things demanding your attention."

His handwriting was beautiful, full of flowing flourishes, with capital letters that were minor works of art in themselves, all curves and twirls, like grace notes in music. He read widely and deeply and voraciously over an astonishing range of subjects, retained most of what he read and knew more about more than anyone I ever knew. But he never brandished his knowledge, and he disliked know-alls. What he did like to do was *share* some of what he had learned, but only if by so doing he wouldn't be considered a braggart or a smart-ass.

During the years of my childhood, once I had got into bed he would come and tuck me in and lie beside me on top of the eiderdown. Then he would deliver a blaze of memory of things read and retained, and a burst of astonishment at man's courage and nobility and capacity to suffer. As I would lie there in self-forgetting attentiveness and profound concentration, he would bear me away with him in imagination with his wonderful gift of description, away, for example, to the South Pole with Captain Scott.

He brought men like Oates and Evans and Wilson and Bowers, as well as Scott himself, into that dark bedroom on Bellevue Terrace, so that I suffered through the blizzards with them, felt the cold, saw the crevasses, experienced their horror when the ponies had to be slaughtered for dog meat. I was with them when the sledges sank up to the handlebars in wet snow, and shared their despair when they reached the South Pole only to find that Amundsen had beaten them to it by a month. All of this because my father knew the details and was gifted with the generosity to share it and the ability to recount it and the man/child excitement to live it through the telling of it to a small boy.

On the night that he told me the story of Oates – stricken by frostbite, leaving the tent and saying, "I am just going outside and may be some time", and never being seen again – there was a catch in his voice.

"That was love, son," he said after a small pause. "Love and courage and a strange kind of nobility . . . The people who came in search of them found the bodies of Dr Wilson and Lieutenant Bowers and Scott a few months later. They were in the tent, which was covered in snow. The awful thing is that those men were only about ten miles from a food store when they died . . . Captain Scott kept writing in his diary up to the very end. The last words he wrote were, 'For God's sake, look after our people.' "

As he always did at the end of a story, he remained still for some minutes, unafraid of silence, the stillness broken only by the sound of our breathing. Then he got off the bed and in the darkness felt for my face with his fingertips. He leaned over, and I got the smell of Woodbines off his breath. He kissed me on the forehead and whispered, "Goodnight, son. God bless you." Then he slipped silently out of the room, closing the door quietly behind him.

* * * * * * * *

My father told me so much, and he never talked down, whether it was the suffragette movement he was speaking about, or Jack Johnson (the first black World Heavyweight Champion), or Mafeking being relieved, or the Hindenburg bursting into flames at New Jersey.

His account of the Wright brothers and their contribution to aviation history and Bleriot's flight across the English Channel and Alcock and Brown's flight across the Atlantic were infused with his own enthusiasm and that realism which is the true storyteller's gift, as were his descriptions of such sporting heroes as W.G. Grace and Paavo Nurmi and Jim Thorpe, and little Dorando Pietri's tragic run in the London Olympic marathon of 1908.

But it wasn't just heroes he told me about. He recounted the stories of the murderer Dr Crippen and the gangsters like Al Capone and Machine Jack McGurn.

In his corpus of knowledge were details he had read and absorbed relating to the St Valentine's Day massacre, Jack the Ripper's atrocities, the assassinations of presidents and other heads of state, the creation of concentration camps in South Africa, Chaka the warrior king of the Zulus ("What's an assagai, Dad?"), the battle at Rorke's Drift, the greatness of Madame Curie and the saintly medical/musical genius of Albert Schweitzer in his African hospital at Lambarene.

I think of my father now and I can still hear his voice in the darkness of the top floor front bedroom talking of Chaliapin and Toscanini and Al Jolson; talking of the battlefields of Flanders, of Ypres, and flooded, freezing, footrotting, lung-savaging, mind-destroying muddy trenches; of men with streaming eyes coughing their way to slow death from mustard gas; of the ten million people who were killed in World War I, and the scuttling of the German fleet at Scapa Flow in 1919; talking, too, of the white wastelands of the Arctic which Peary faced on his way to the North Pole.

Thanks to my father I was in the cockpit of the "Spirit of St Louis" with Lindberg in 1927, in the Sistine Chapel with Michelangelo, at the opera with George Bernard Shaw and in the desert with Laurence of Arabia. I was at poolside when Johnny Weissmuller set world swimming records and saw Emily Davison killed by the king's horse Anmer in the 1913 Derby.

On the night I asked him about ballet, he took a deep breath before he answered. Finally he said, "Well, it's a very complicated story, son, a hard one to unravel . . . Maybe we could start with a *person*, a man, the greatest male ballet dancer who ever lived, and who, God love him, is in a lunatic

257

asylum in Switzerland now as we talk. But tell me, why do you want to know about ballet?"

"One of the boys at school had a picture of a man ballet dancer, and he said it was only old pansy stuff and that the men who did it were cissies."

"And did you believe him? Do you think he was right?"

"I don't know," I said. "That's why I asked you."

"Did he have any other pictures?"

"One – of a woman ballet dancer."

"And what were these dancers wearing in the pictures?"

"The woman was wearing a little feathery hat and frills around her shoulders and a gauzy skirt which was spread out on the floor around her and things that looked like wings."

"And the man? What was he wearing?"

"Very tight trousers, like ladies' stockings. He looked very strange."

"Strange? Strange in what way?"

I wasn't sure how to put it. I was sorry I had brought the subject up. I wished we could drop it.

"Well, one of the boys said the dancer must have had a hanky or something pushed down the front of the trousers because . . . because . . ." I couldn't finish it. My face felt as if it was on fire. I was glad the room was dark.

My father got off the bed and walked across towards the window where he opened the shutters and looked out into the night. Eventually he came back and sat on the bed, leaning against the headboard, and started to tell me about a man I'd never heard of – Vaslav Nijinsky. He said he was "maybe the greatest male ballet dancer of all time". He told me of a small cutting from an old yellowed newspaper he (my father) had found under the lino in one of the rooms in his parents home in Dublin.

"I kept it for the descriptions," he said. "A critic who had seen some of Nijinsky's performances said that in his leaps 'he had defied gravity'. I wish I had that cutting now to show it to you, but someone stole it years ago. I never got it back.

258

I think the same critic said about Nijinsky that he found him 'terrifying in his muscular energy'. There's great power in that, isn't there? Nothing cissyish or pansyish or nancy-boyish about that."

My father had never seen Vaslav Nijinsky, but he was able to describe his slanted eyes, his short thick-set body, his awkward manners, his long, limp, flat-lying hair. "He was a shy sort of a lad, didn't say much, maybe didn't want to, maybe *couldn't*."

Nijinsky, he told me, was born in Russia, but both of his parents were Polish, both of them dancers, his mother a devout Catholic who had Vaslav baptised in Warsaw several months after his birth. He was their second child, their second son. The first-born was named Stanislas. After Vaslav the Nijinskys had a little girl, Bronislav.

"I'd say now that their mother was a woman marked for tragedy. Stanislas fell out a window one day in Warsaw when he was only a child, landed on his head and never recovered. He'd been brain damaged by the fall, poor little lad, and he got worse, and eventually he became so violent that he had to be locked up. Didn't the father up and leave them, walked out, went off with another woman.

"But you know, there's an old Chinese saying that while you can't stop the birds of sadness from flying around your head, you can certainly put the kibosh on any ideas they might have of building nests in your hair. Mrs Nijinsky got on with her life. Got hold of a house, and took in lodgers."

My father described how the young boys and girls from the Imperial School were often given small walk-on, non-dancing parts in productions at the Maryinski Theatre, and they were expected to stay together in the special room on the fifth floor which was allocated to them.

"But Nijinsky was a little divil," my father said. "He used to hide himself backstage and watch from the wings, and do you remember me telling you about the great Russian bass Chaliapin?"

"I do," I said.

"He was young Nijinsky's big hero. The boy couldn't take his eyes off him."

The more my father talked, the more Nijinsky changed from being just a name into a person. And although I had no knowledge or ideas of what Warsaw or Moscow or St Petersburg looked like, I was easily able to summon up images of yelling Cossacks riding their horses through streets and squares, charging into the crowds, slashing and hacking with their swords – and drawing blood from the forehead of the shy young boy with the massive thigh and calf muscles and the sallow complexion and lank hair and awkward open-mouthed manner.

It banished the images of Fred Astaire with his long jaw, patent leather hair, patent leather shoes and white tie and tails, dancing across the flyblown, blotchy screens of Paton's or Frennet's picture houses; and Gene Kelly of the throaty voice and boyish grin and open-necked shirt; and Donald O'Connor, Ray Bolger, Jimmy Cagney, Mickey Rooney – Hollywood stars all of them. And the few looked-down-upon local fellows who went to Nita Murphy's classes to learn hands-and-arms-severely-down-the-sides traditional, kilted, Irish step-dancing, to yowdlee-dow music provided by fiddles, accordions, thumped pianos and unimaginative metronomic rhythm produced from side drums and wood blocks.

Ballet was something else. Suspect. Effete. Remote. Classical, for God's sake! As Dicky Dan said, "That stuff is only for go-boys," and although we didn't know what he meant we agreed with him simply because it sounded about right. But here was my father already giving it new dimensions for me, new meanings, de-mystifying it, making it more accessible – and all because he spoke of it as being about real people in a real world, and related what he knew in language I understood.

"He was a most tremendous dancer – a tremendous *athlete.*" (My father always pronounced "tremendous" as if there were a *j* in it instead of a *d*.) "And what an actor! When Sarah Bernhardt saw him in *Petrouchka*, in which Nijinsky danced the part of a puppet made out of sawdust and straw, she said she felt afraid, because she felt she was watching the greatest actor in the world. So when I hear the kind of rubbish trotted out by your school companions, and by a lot of adults, too, may I add, I feel very irritated. And then I think to myself, sure what the hell would they know? It's pure ignorance on their part."

"You know you said Nijinsky is in a lunatic asylum now – is that because he's old?"

My father gave a short laugh.

"No, no, his age hasn't anything to do with it. What gave you that idea?"

I said it was because I had overheard him and my mother talking about someone they knew who had become senile in his old age and had had to be put into the County Home. I just wondered if it was something like that had happened to Nijinsky.

"Ah no, nothing like that," my father said. "Sure Nijinsky is only . . . let me see now . . . born in 1890, that'd make him only what? . . . 52 . . . No, he was locked up years and years and years ago. And you know, one of the tragedies of the whole thing is that he danced in public for barely ten years."

He spoke of the sadness of exile, and said that an even greater sadness was that he got "mixed up with someone who ruined his life. When you're a bit older, you'll understand better what I'm trying to tell you. You see there are many people who believe that Nijinsky would have been far better off if he had never met the person who introduced him to the world outside Russia, Mr Diaghilev."

My father left a long silence during which he dragged deeply on his cigarette. In its glow I caught glimpses of his head shaking as though he were perplexed. After a while he said, "These are not nice things to be talking about, and I don't want to explain them; there'll be time enough for that.

261

But, when he left Russia in 1911 with Diaghilev's company, it was the last time he ever saw his native land."

My father paused again, for an even longer period, and when he resumed talking, his voice was different, quieter, husky. "In September 1917 he disintegrated. And he was only 27."

He got off the bed and walked once more to the window where he stood in silence. When he came back, he sat on the edge of the bed with his back to me.

"A very terrible thing happened to him," he said. "His wife's family had him forcibly put away in an asylum. It's where he still is, remembering nothing, staring, lost. He might as well be dead, because in a way he *is* dead."

He stood up then, touched me on the forehead with his fingertips and went out of the room very quietly. I didn't hear him going down the stairs. He probably stayed on the landing outside the bedroom door because, after about half a minute or so, the door opened again and he came in.

"Are you still awake?" he whispered.

"I am."

"Something I forgot to tell you – Nijinsky's wife never gave up hope. Hope is very important. Maybe the most important thing in the whole world. Without it, you're lost. Romola never gave up hope, even long after the specialists told here there was nothing they could do for him. She used to take him out of the asylum occasionally and take him on visits to the theatre to see ballet performances. She hoped it might cause a breakthrough into his locked mind, remind him of who he was, what he had been.

"He just sat there, staring straight ahead. No reaction. That's the way he still is. One of the living dead . . . Say a prayer for him."

I did. Many. For a long time afterwards.

Questions but No Answers

I HATED THE word "corpse". It made me afraid. I'm not sure whether it was death itself that terrified me, or dying. I knew – of course I did – that we all have to die, but references I had heard to there being a "death rattle" just before death scared me, as did the idea of someone not wanting to die, but *having* to die anyway. ("He had a very hard death, missus, God love him, he didn't want to go at all.") All of this was overwhelming. Believing in hell made it worse. Made me almost whimper.

So I went to benediction in the cathedral as often as I could, because at benediction the sacred host was out on the altar in the glittering golden monstrance, in full sight of the congregation. You could gaze at it, realising that it was the body and blood of Our Lord Jesus Christ under the appearance of bread, and think about that, and be filled with the wonder of it. There wasn't an opportunity to do that at mass, at the consecration, when the priest, taking bread in his hands said in Latin:

. . . Who the day before He suffered, took bread into His holy and worshipful hands, and with eyes raised towards heaven, unto Thee, God, His Father almighty, giving thanks to Thee, he blessed, brake,

and gave to His disciples, saying: Take, all of you, and eat of this, FOR THIS IS MY BODY . . .

He genuflected, then raised the sacred host to be seen by the congregation. That was the only point at which you actually saw it, and you had to bow your head immediately in adoration and strike your breast as the altar boy rang the bell three times.

But as soon as the singing of "*O salutaris hostia*" began at benediction, I knew that I could do some of my best and most deeply felt personal praying, wrapped in a small cocoon of holiness. There were interruptions of course when, because of the responses you had to make to the priest's recitation of the Litany of the Blessed Virgin, your thoughts got sidetracked.

Some of the words in the litany I just didn't understand. "Mother inviolate" for example. And "Mother undefiled". But along with everyone else in the church I said the response, "Pray for us".

Tantum ergo Sacramentum veneremur cernui, "Down in adoration falling, lo, the Sacred Host we hail" . . . When that was sung, my eyes stung with emotion, and, crying on the inside, I asked God to help me with all my puzzlement and worry over death, dying and the dead.

But the questions continued to surface, remaining unasked and unanswered, sinking into the subconscious for periods and then coming to the top again and again and again.

Why do *good* people have to die? And *young* people? And *babies*? And people who are *innocent*? How does God allow it? *Why* does he allow it?

"It's God's will." "It's the will of God." What did that mean? That God really *wanted* these things to happen? All that pain? All that ugly death? Did God really *want* all that inflicted on people?

It was all very well the cruel-faced Dönitz ordering his U-Boat captains, "Be hard. Think of the fact that the enemy in his bombing attacks on German towns has no regard for women or children." But what had Nan or Auntie Jo or my mother ever done to the children and women in those towns?

How come submarine commanders on both sides in the war were known to have machine-gunned survivors who were struggling in the water or cowering in lifeboats? How could they *do* that?

And how could the captains of U-Boats carry through Dönitz's orders about attacking rescue ships as they stayed behind to pick up survivors from the choking, oil-slicked sea? But they did, and sank some of them, sending them to the bottom with the loss of everyone on board. Were those U-Boat captains ever haunted by the sight of floating blood which turned the sea red? Ever tormented by the screams of the dying which they would have heard if they had been on the surface?

I thought of the *Irish Pine*, neutral and crippled and pathetic, wallowing in heavy night-time seas on the lonely, rain-lashed Atlantic. I thought of Struckmeier switching his periscope to full power and looking at her, seeing clearly her badges of neutrality, the tricolours on her sides, the lights all on, the word ÉIRE floodlit.

I thought of him lining up his helpless, unarmed target and giving the order to fire, and counting the seconds, timing the torpedo's run; and then watching the explosion tearing a great hole in this "enemy". And I thought of him then giving orders for the course he wanted steered and taking his U-Boat away from that spot, leaving the scene where the *Irish Pine* had gone down. I thought of the crew of the *Irish Pine*, those men who were never seen again. I thought of the grief of their families.

And when I heard later about Struckmeier himself being killed, I thought: serves him right, the dirty bloody murderer.

I thought about Prien's bravery in going into Scapa Flow, but I didn't give a damn about him and all his crew being

265

depth charged into eternity by the destroyer *Wolverine*. Granda had admired Prien and defended him, had pointed up his acts of chivalry. So what had changed Prien? What had changed *in* him?

And why?

How could chivalry live side-by-side with the coldness of the committed killer? How had he continued to keep on looking at men dying horribly, and remain unmoved? He had sunk 28 ships (165,000 tons) and sent many hundreds of men to their deaths. Some had ceased living in an instant, fragmented in gigantic orange explosions, incinerated in massive fireballs; but some had died terribly, and slowly. From the bridge on the conning tower of U-47 he had watched them. Was he touched in any way by what he saw?

Did he believe in God? Was Hitler his god? Was Prien ever *afraid*?

When *Wolverine*'s patterns of depth charges exploded close to Prien's boat, causing her to buck and shudder in the heaving depths of the Atlantic, causing her pressure hull to creak and groan like a moaning whale, rupturing pipes and blowing out her lights, did Prien stand looking upwards, steadying himself against the boat's violent movement, hearing the churning screws of the destroyer, the pinging of her Asdic? Did he stand, sweaty-faced, waiting for the next pattern? Did he feel frightened?

Did he experience a terror of death? Was it for him the ultimate horror of life? Did he meet death with fear and tears – or did he face it unflinchingly? Was he loath to die? Had he *learned* to die? Did he cry out? Did he think of the faces of any of the men he had killed? Did he *scream*? Did he shriek – to God, or to them – "I'm *sorry*! Oh, Christ, I'm so *sorry*! Forgive me!"?

Questions, questions – and no answers.

I hoped the final minutes were terrible for "The Bull of Scapa Flow". But I couldn't understand.

On nights when the wind blew from the west, I could hear

266

the clock bells in the cathedral striking every quarter of an hour. I lay in the dark bedroom thinking of the stricken hearts below in Harbour Hill. Nan and Auntie Jo, indeed all of us, were trying, unavailingly, to deal with the wounds of loneliness.

I thought, too, of the ferocious ocean, and of those who were trying to cling to life on it, struggling and hoping to survive. Some of them were lucky, men like Michael Minihan and the 33 others who made up the crew of the *Irish Oak* when she was torpedoed one Saturday morning 700 miles west of the Fastnet.

The 34 crew members of the *Irish Oak* were fortunate to be picked up by the *Irish Plane* eight hours after their ship went down. Michael Minihan was the oldest of the survivors. He was over 70. Originally from Limerick, he had spent 47 years of his life in the USA. When the *Irish Oak* was targeted by a U-Boat, Michael felt his life was about to end. Instead, he and his companions were rescued and were landed in Cobh. I felt very glad for Michael Minihan. Auntie Jo found in their rescue another reason to hope that Uncle John might turn up.

But I was lost and caught up in a maelstrom of emotions and puzzlement. There were so many contradictions I couldn't cope with. The case of Joachim Schepke was just one more. Granda Jim had mentioned him. In his short war, the captain of U-100 sank 39 ships. Seven of them were from convoy HX72. He got all of them in a four-hour period in September 1940. He was another German hero, another of Dönitz's aces. He was 29 when he was killed three days before my birthday in 1941. By then he had accounted for 159,130 tons of shipping, and God knows how many men.

U-100 was on the surface on the night of the 16th of March, and Schepke was on the bridge. Part of the wolf pack attacking convoy HX112, U-100 was on the surface because she had been damaged by depth charges from the convoy's escorts. From almost two-thirds of a mile away, the radar on the destroyer *Vanoc* picked up the presence of the surfaced

267

U-Boat, and the ship's captain immediately changed course and raced at full speed, 30 knots, to ram the submarine.

Schepke could see her coming. He could actually hear her, because his diesel engines, which gave U-Boats like his their surface speed of 17 knots, which allowed them to manoeuvre quickly and steal away in the darkness, were out of action, and he was running on the virtually silent and much slower electric motors. Now he was trapped.

He could see the great, rearing, roaring, foaming, white bow wave of the onrushing destroyer coming straight at him. He shouted to his crew. Some of them jumped overboard.

The *Vanoc* thundered towards U-100. Nearer, nearer, nearer. Thousands of yards dwindled to hundreds, then to feet, then inches . . . the impact was tremendous. Metal crashed and tore across metal as the destroyer's bows crunched into the U-Boat's hull and then up on, and into the conning tower and bridge at the precise point where Schepke was standing.

The last sighting of him was his body bloodily crushed and squashed into the periscope standards as the wrecked submarine was driven under the destroyer never to be seen again. In the seconds before it happened he must have known he was going to die, must have known *how* he was going to die. Was he scared? Did he pray? Was he sorry – about *anything*? Did it hurt? Was there awful, searing, blinding, pain?

The words "I hope he was in agony" formed in my mind, but deeper down I knew, or felt, that I didn't fully mean it, not 100 percent, because there was a small obstinate spark of pity for him that just wouldn't go out. Alongside the serve-the-bastard right thought was another which said: the poor bugger.

* * * * * * * *

In Cobh poor old Alex Telfer, who wasn't all that old, collapsed and died on the floor of his office, James Scott & Co., overlooking the slip near the GPO, and the 22 years he had spent on the Urban District Council were cancelled out in an instant. "Poor bugger," Dinny Twomey the jarvey said. "He wasn't a bad sort, the Lord've mercy on him."

Up in the Mansion House in Dublin, a Cork girl named Patricia Cowhie (who, as a grown-up, would marry Christy Ryan and come to live on Bellevue Terrace) won the All-Ireland Minor Dancing Championship for girls under 12.

And at a special court in Cobh, before District Justice S.P. Kelly, B.S., a Scottish ship's master, Alexander Smith from Arbroath, was fined £2 and ordered to pay £7-10s expenses for failing to obey an order to "bring his ship to halt". He had been warned by the firing of a gun "under order of the competent Port Authority".

"Poor bugger," was Danny Dinan's comment. "What did they think he was going to do? Invade the Great Island? Jesus, missus, they'd make yeh die, honest to God, they would. Ah, leave me alone, don't *talk* to me."

Serious things and trivial things, all jumbled up together, and me struggling to understand, trying to find a pattern that made sense – and failing. And becoming confused and bemused. And causing my mother to say to my father, "I don't know what's the matter with him at all. He's not himself."

"Ah, he'll be all right," my father said. "He's just coming through the shadows."

"The shadows? What shadows are you talking about?"

"Well, strictly speaking it's the shadow, *singular*," my father said. " 'The valley of the shadow of death.' He's obsessed with death at the moment. He's trying to deal with it, trying to cope with it. A lot of people go through that sooner or later. He'll come out of it."

I wished that I could be as certain as my father sounded. I thought I had emerged from "the shadow" when I was able to contemplate, in May 1943, the reported death of an old (80) man named Patrick Beirne, who was the last survivor of a group of people claiming to have witnessed an apparition

269

of the Blessed Virgin at Knock, County Mayo, on Thursday August 21, 1879. He had been only 16 years of age at the time. Thinking about him and his passing away didn't leave me feeling morbid or vulnerable at all, or questioning why he had to die.

All óf us had heard about Knock and the famous Knock shrine. We had been told how, although all the witnesses had been soaked through by the rain, the actual place where the apparition was said to have appeared remained dry. Witnesses had been questioned and cross-questioned by Church authorities who wanted to make sure that the claims were authentic and that after that, Knock became a place of pilgrimage. Most of us knew people who had visited it and prayed there for "special intentions", or who had taken the sick and crippled there seeking a cure.

And now the last of the witnesses, Patrick Beirne, was dead and I contented myself by trying to visualise what it must have been like to see the Blessed Virgin. For me to be able to do that instead of concentrating on Patrick dying was like a breakthrough.

Maybe I had come out the other side of "the shadow" at last. I hoped so.

But what happened at Ballymanus was never something I could put completely out of my mind. Again the war, and the things that men *did* in war, the devices they were prepared to invent and use to exact the maximum force and destruction against "the enemy", were at the root of what took place in the small, peaceful fishing village in County Donegal not far from Annagary.

When a mine floated ashore there one Monday evening, it was an object of curiosity. A considerable group of men and boys gathered around it, touching it, prodding it, examining it, talking about it. One man, standing well back, shouted a warning to them, told them that what they were doing was very dangerous, that they should get away quickly because it could go off at any minute. They just laughed at him. But

Lieutenant Dunleavy of the Marine Coast Watching Service knew what he and they were looking at, and he kept on shouting warnings.

And then it happened. John Roarty and James Rogers were bending over the mine when suddenly it was as if the entire beach exploded, as if the earth had cracked open releasing terrible force and ear-shattering noise. Chunks of rock and pieces of bodies, arms, legs, hair, together with scraps of jackets and jerseys and shoes, were blown up in the air, and tumbled over and over, and then fell spinning back down.

Carnage.

Eighteen men and boys died in an instant. Some of them were as young as 15. The oldest was only 33.

For a while no one knew what to do. There were bodies and bits of bodies everywhere. People screamed and cried and collapsed, became numb and dumb, and then wild-eyed and distraught. The area had to be searched and bodies had to be identified, which was an awful obligation because in some instances what was left was unrecognisable.

The coffins were eventually taken into the local hall, which was to have hosted a farewell dance for the lads a few nights later. Most of the 18 had been due to go off to England shortly to work. Instead, relatives and friends from the village and from the townlands sat in a vigil for the dead. The emotion, the mourning, were beyond description.

"Out of the depths I have cried to Thee, O Lord: Lord hear my voice," the priests leading the Prayers for the Faithful Departed intoned.

"Eternal rest give unto them, O Lord," they said towards the end. And those who were there said the customary response: "And let perpetual light shine upon them."

"May they rest in peace."

"Amen."

"O Lord, hear my prayer."

"And let my cry come unto Thee."

Oh, the war, the rotten war. I couldn't make sense of any

of it. I couldn't cope. I just cried and cried and said Acts of Contrition.

I was 11, and still walking in the valley of the shadow of death.

Out of the Shadow

I T WAS ONE thing to read or hear about, or see in the films, ships that were attacked by aircraft, but another to actually be close to one, to stand near the edge on the Deepwater Quay and look down on one and see what had been done to her. "Janey Martin, boy," as Barney Cullen said, "that was *amazing*."

And nobody ever thought that the first air-attacked ship we'd see would be the battered and rusty and dirty little *Kerlogue* – battered and rusty and dirty from the seriously punishing runs she repeatedly made across and back the Bay of Biscay, carrying filthy cargoes like coal.

Fellows who were interested in ships and shipping became good at guessing a ship's tonnage. Mostly it had to do with your perceptions of her length and how much water she drew and her overall size. When you'd been lucky with a few guesses which came close enough to the real statistic, you would look at a ship and say something like, "Three, three-and-a-half thousand tonner, I bet." Or you might contradict someone else, saying, "Aw, don't be such an eejit, boy, eighteen hundred tons is as much as that one is." And if your guesses continued to be close, you'd feel that you really had a good eye for this sort of thing.

But none of us came even near guessing the *Kerlogue*'s correct tonnage. It was hard to believe it when we were told: 354 tons gross.

She was a 142-foot-long, diesel-engined coaster, owned by the Wexford Steamship Company Ltd, and said to be a bitch in a seaway. They owned two other coasters at the time – the 440 tons *Edenvale* and the *Menapia*, a 900 tonner.

At 4 o'clock on the afternoon of 23 October 1943 the *Kerlogue*, loaded deep (her freeboard was only about a foot) with a cargo of coal, was on a voyage from Port Talbot in Wales to Lisbon in Portugal, and was butting her way south. Suddenly two fighter aircraft came at her in a screaming attack dive, guns blazing. Cannon shells ripped and tore across the tiny ship, slamming into the bridge, screeching as they ricocheted off metal, splintering wood wherever they struck it, bursting human flesh, causing blood to spurt, bone to break.

For the men on the *Kerlogue* the next 20 minutes were frightening and violent as the two planes banked and dived and mercilessly raked the little ship, climbed, banked, came round again, and repeated the strafing. They kept on doing it until suddenly they flew off towards the north and disappeared.

By then the ship's bridge was destroyed, her radio transmitter and compass smashed into uselessness, her two lifeboats wrecked, her hull holed and her engine-room pierced. *Kerlogue* was taking water, and Captain Fortune (compound fractures to both of his legs) was lying unconscious from shock and blood loss. Three other members of his small crew were seriously injured – Second Officer Samuel Owens (chest wounds), Second Engineer James Carty (back wound) and Able Seaman John Boyce (injuries to his legs).

Kapitanleutnant Rolf Struckmeier wasn't the only one prepared to attack a neutral ship, nor were the Germans the only ones who did it. The planes which attacked the *Kerlogue* were RAF Mosquitos.

The coaster was 130 miles south of Ireland at the time. Denis Valencie, first officer of the *Kerlogue*, took over command of the stricken ship and decided to head back for Cork Harbour. A couple of hours after the attack, another aircraft came on the scene, but this one, slower and more sedate, a Sunderland flying boat, circled the ship instead of attacking. Because *Kerlogue*'s wireless was in fragments, Valencie's only way of communicating with the flying boat was by Aldis lamp, the hand-held electric lamp with the finger operated mirror behind the lens, used for sending signals at sea. That Valencie knew Morse code and could send it was borne out by the Australian pilot of the Sunderland. His official report stated that he had identified the ship as "Eire merchant vessel *Kerlogue*" which "flashed SOS" and requested the plane "to escort them as they had been attacked by aircraft, and needed medical assistance for injured crew".

That Australian airman replied to Valencie on *Kerlogue* that escort could not be given, and he resumed his patrol.

The damaged ship with its three seriously injured crewmen (Captain Fortune would be a cripple for the rest of his life) arrived off Cork Harbour just before dawn on the following day. An Irish naval launch which had gone out to rendezvous with her went alongside and put a doctor aboard. He carried out emergency medical treatment on the injured men, and the launch escorted battered little *Kerlogue* in past Dog Nose buoy and Spike Island, around the Spit light, and then up past the Holy Ground, the harbour office, the North German Lloyd Pier and the Pier Head, past No. 10 buoy and the Promenade, and in then on a slowing, slanting run to the Deepwater Quay where she tied up. The injured men were immediately taken away to hospital.

"Fekkin' lousers," Nux said.

"Who?" I asked.

"The fekkin' RAF, who else?"

"Ah, that's a load of bollix, McCormick boy," someone close by said.

"Why is it a load of bollix?" Nux wanted to know. "Isn't it what we heard? That it was R–A–bloody–F planes that attacked her?"

"Well, we don't know the circumstances."

"Ah, circumstances my hole!" Nux said, walking back towards the *Kerlogue*'s stern. "They *did* it, and they're nothing but a bunch of fekkin' lousers as far as I'm concerned. And I hope Dev does something about it."

What De Valera did about it was to stand up in Dáil Éireann and make a statement in which he told the house that the ammunition discovered on the *Kerlogue* (pieces of cannon shells were found among the coal when the ship's cargo was being unloaded at Cobh) was of British origin, and that he had communicated this fact to the British authorities. They, in turn, admitted that the attack had been carried out by RAF planes, but they insisted that the vessel had *not* been identified by the attacking aircraft as Irish.

Somebody lied.

When the official record of the two Mosquito pilots' attack on the ship was examined, it revealed this peculiar entry: "Sighted, and attacked with cannon, *1,500 ton* merchant vessel flying *French* flag, and word *EMPO* clearly discerned on starboard side – the word *FRANCE* also on bows. The vessel, *which returned fire with cannon* without effect, was left circling with smoke issuing from it. Also a quantity of oil was seen surrounding the vessel and drifting away."

The italics have been inserted to emphasise the dubiousness. Anyone claiming to mistake a tiny 354 ton ship for a vessel five times that tonnage needed further training, eyesight testing, or a re-education in what constitutes truth – in this case possibly all three.

The Sunderland pilot, coming across the damaged ship two hours after the Mosquitos had shot her up, apparently had no difficulty in identifying her as the "*Éire* merchant vessel *Kerlogue*". So much for the Mosquito pilots' claim.

And as for the allegation that *Kerlogue* "returned fire with

276

cannon", this, about a small, unarmed, neutral ship which continually sailed out of convoy, criss-crossing the German U-Boat routes from the Biscay bases out into the Atlantic, is so preposterously untrue as to be incredible. But it is what the relevant British authorities insisted. They said *Kerlogue* was off course, and that therefore they would not accept responsibility for the attack. However, they were prepared to make ex-gratia payments to the injured men!

"They're bloody lousers, I don't care what you say," Nux said to all of us, and went walkabout on his own. When the others drifted off, too, I stayed on, looking at the *Kerlogue*, trying to picture what it must have been like out there 130 miles to the south.

I thought of noise, fear, disbelief that this was happening. I thought of men wondering if they were going to die. It was all too much, so I turned around and walked along past the Yacht Club and along Westbourne Place and up the hills to home.

The *Kerlogue* was patched up in Cork Harbour, repaired and made seaworthy once more, and a 59-year-old master mariner from Dungarvan, County Waterford, Thomas O'Donohue, was signed on as captain. Captain O'Donohue, it turned out, was one of those rescued by the *Irish Plane* when the *Irish Oak* was torpedoed five months earlier by U-607. You'd think he might have accepted that as some kind of sign for him to quit the sea before his luck ran out. After all, he was almost 60 and taking over a small workhorse of a ship expected for the foreseeable future to continue crossing the U-Boat routes, alone and unprotected, can't have seemed the most promising of his options.

Four days after Christmas, and very early in the morning, when they were between three and four hundred miles south of the Fastnet and bound for Dublin, Captain O'Donohue must have wondered if he was in for a rerun of what had happened to Captain Fortune a couple of months previously. Two planes came into view, but this time they were German – Focke Wolf Condor bombers.

The captain and crew of the *Kerlogue* prepared themselves for the worst. Not that there was very much they could do other than get the lifeboats ready for quick launching in case they had to abandon ship. The men on the *Kerlogue* waited.

The bombers went round and round in big sweeping circles, getting lower all the time, but *gradually*, not in a threatening or hostile way. Slowly it began to dawn on the crew of the *Kerlogue* that they weren't going to be attacked. Puzzlement replaced apprehension as they realised that the bombers' crew were trying to pass a message.

When eventually communication was established, Captain O'Donohue was requested to bring his ship about and go to the south-east as quickly as possible. The obvious urgency and the way the request was made prompted Captain O'Donohue to change course straight away.

At about 11am, he found out why the bombers had sought their help. For some time he had been aware of what looked like small bits of flotsam in the water dead ahead of the ship. Now he found out what the "flotsam" was – *people*, men, some in uniform, some in what looked like underclothes, all of them struggling to remain afloat. He could see them on all sides, rising and falling on a sea that was becoming rougher by the minute.

As the *Kerlogue* drew closer to them, O'Donohue and the others on deck could *hear* the men in the water; there were shouts and occasional screams, and it quickly became obvious that a number of the survivors were in a bad way. Their shocked faces looked weak and exhausted among the grey slopes of water. Some of them were badly burned. Out beyond the periphery of the first small group, some bodies were floating, face down, shoulders up.

The situation was desperate. Using all his skill as a ship handler, Captain O'Donohue brought *Kerlogue* as close as he dared to the first knot of survivors, easing the heaving ship to within reaching or at least heaving-line distance. Then, with careful urgency, the crew of the *Kerlogue*, some with boathooks, some leaning out dangerously, arms extended, began to haul in and lift the survivors out of the sea. Most of the men in the water couldn't help themselves. They were spent. Their hands were blue-white and shrivelled from immersion in the sea. There were cuts and bruises on faces and foreheads, which looked sore from wind and salt spray.

At this stage the *Kerlogue*'s crew had no idea what nationality the survivors were. It wasn't important. They were Germans. Drenched, dripping and shivering, they lay where they were put down as they were brought aboard, unable to move.

The *Kerlogue*'s crewmen, involved in a hazardous operation, were racing against time. The sea was getting up, and O'Donohue was all the while mindful that unless he exercised the greatest care, it would be easy for a man in the water to roll under the hull of the *Kerlogue* and be trapped there, or cut up by the propeller. Hauling and lifting the survivors aboard was exhausting work.

Back and forth across the survivor-strewn sea, Captain O'Donohue took *Kerlogue*. Hour after hour they kept it up. On board the ship the number of miserable survivors grew. They lay or crouched, hunched against the sides of the hold, sprawled across its top covering, squeezed into the already cramped wheelhouse, taking up every square foot of space. Their clothes were soaked and already beginning to smell.

O'Donohue instructed his crew to put the worst-off of the injured into his cabin, and there, in between manoeuvring his ship, taking her to where his eyes told him to go or to where frantic voices in the lonely sea called him, he and the ship's greaser, Garret Roche, did what they could for the badly wounded. It was rudimentary first aid, not enough to save the life of one man who had suffered horrendously from all-over burns. The best that could be hoped for was that his last hours were fractionally freer from pain.

With the light beginning to fade as the afternoon wore on, the temperature dropped. It became bitingly cold. Two more survivors died, probably as much from exposure and hypothermia as from anything else they may have suffered.

Even when night came down, the *Kerlogue*, with as many lights rigged as could be found, kept up the search. Eventually at about 9 o'clock Captain O'Donohue decided that he and his men could do no more. They were almost crippled from fatigue. The ship was crammed with men they had fished out of the sea, well over 100 by O'Donohue's quick head count.

Hoping to God he wasn't leaving anyone behind out on the edges of the search area where their despairing shouts would be lost on the wind and in the vastness of the ocean, he turned his ship and set course for Cork Harbour.

One of the survivors came to him and said he was the senior German officer aboard. He identified himself as Lieutenant Commander Quedenfeldt. He formally requested Captain O'Donohue to take the survivors to one of two French ports on the Bay of Biscay – La Rochelle or Brest.

O'Donohue politely but firmly said no, he intended going to Cork Harbour. Quedenfeldt accepted the decision without demur.

The *Kerlogue*'s skipper made contact with Valentia Radio, and passed on details of his position, course and ETA of his impending arrival with his shipload of rescued German survivors. His transmissions were also picked up by Land's End radio in Britain, and from there the British authorities were informed. The British reaction was a series of orders, masquerading as requests, to Captain O'Donohue. These were broadcast from Land's End radio, instructing him to proceed immediately to Fishguard to land the survivors.

But Captain O'Donohue, an Irishman in command of an Irish ship flying the Irish flag and sailing out of convoy, made up his mind that he would maintain his course. His primary objective was to reach land as soon as possible so that the men he had rescued could receive the medical attention they so obviously needed. When Land's End radio resorted to

280

repeating the orders/requests every 30 minutes, he dealt with it in the most effective way he knew: he switched off the radio and continued steaming towards Cork Harbour.

(That action would earn him a blistering, insulting attack from the senior Royal Navy officer at Fishguard. That individual not only berated O'Donohue for not landing the Germans at the Welsh port, but said that the *Kerlogue* had got what she deserved when the RAF planes attacked her in October! Other Royal Navy officers subsequently apologised to the Irish skipper for the boorish behaviour of their colleague – a "desk sailor".)

During the long cold night, the crew of the *Kerlogue* did what they could for the survivors. Every spare scrap of dry clothing, blankets, sheets, towels, even rags, anything that might help to ward off the chill, hot drinks, and food until it ran out, were given to the freezing, wounded Germans.

Shortly after first light on the last day of the year, Captain O'Donohue asked Lieutenant Commander Quedenfeldt to organise a roll call. This revealed that three of the survivors had died since being picked up by *Kerlogue*. It was decided to bury them at sea.

Captain O'Donohue stopped the ship for the sad little burial service which was conducted by the senior German officer.

Tennyson's lines seemed to hang over the ship:

Sunset and evening star,
And one clear call for me
And may there be no moaning of the bar
When I put out to sea.

The three bodies were slid overboard, consigned to the depths of the sea from which they had been plucked just hours before.

That left 165 survivors alive on board the *Kerlogue*. Another man, Engineer Lieutenant Adolf Braatz died during the day. It was decided to bring his body ashore for burial.

Late in the night *Kerlogue* arrived off Cork Harbour. It had been hours since she picked up Roche's Point light and the lightship at Daunt Rock. Now the flashing pinpricks of light from the inner harbour buoys could be seen and, in beyond them, the lights of Cobh scattered along the waterfront and up on the hill.

Kerlogue didn't have to come into the harbour unaccompanied. She was met by an Irish Naval Service MTB near Roche's Point. A doctor and other medical personnel were put aboard her. The *Muirchú* escorted her into the harbour.

At 2.30am on New Year's Day, 1944, she again tied up at the Deepwater Quay in Cobh. The news of her arrival spread quickly through the town, and in no time at all men and boys, women and girls flocked along to the Deepwater Quay to stand and stare down at the haggard unshaven faces of the Germans who stared dumbly back.

Grey army lorries from Collins Barracks in Cork drew up, and Irish army soldiers wearing thick green uniforms and carrying heavy Lee Enfield .303 rifles "guarded" the survivors as they were transferred from the ship on to the trucks. It was an opportune occasion for the officious and the solicitous.

"Look at 'im, the 'Great I-Am', he'd turn your stomach," John Magill's aunt said of the officer in charge. "I'd hate to be waitin' on the likes of that fella to defend me if the war ever came to this town."

"Sure isn't it here already?" her companion said.

"Yerra, girl, they lose the run of themselves whenever there's a bit of excitement," another woman said, and they folded their arms defiantly across their chests and planted themselves in prominent positions close to the lorries.

The officiousness was swamped by the waves of sympathy and pity released by the sight of the vulnerable-looking, hollow-eyed men who came off the deck of the *Kerlogue*. They were dishevelled and pale and cold. A few of them looked frightened. The ones who were physically weakest, as well as the injured, had to be helped on to the quay, and then up

282

into the lorries. Engineer Lieutenant Adolf Braatz and Petty Officer Weiss had to be *carried* ashore – Weiss because he was dying, Braatz because he was already dead.

For me New Year's Day didn't seem like New Year's Day at all. That was two of them in a row that had none of the old thrill and joy you felt on the first day of a new year. The previous one had been made grey and cheerless by the shock of the harbour tragedy. This one was again marked by death.

Somewhere in Germany mothers and fathers, maybe wives and children, sisters and brothers, would one day (if they survived the bombings) learn that people they loved and missed were buried in Ireland, in Cobh, in the Old Church graveyard.

They wouldn't know that people from a town they'd never heard of walked behind the coffins of men they never knew; wouldn't know that those same townspeople joined in the Prayers for the Faithful Departed that were recited at the graveside, said a decade of the rosary for the repose of the souls of the newly buried and shed tears when the army bugler played the Last Post.

They wouldn't know, either, of the emotional turmoil of a boy who was afraid of death and hated it, and who hated all Germans for a long while after the death of his smiling uncle because he thought all Germans were guilty of murder.

They wouldn't know that when he looked into some young faces on the deck of the *Kerlogue* on New Year's Day, 1944, he didn't see enemies – all he saw were boys like himself, just a little older. But just as confused.

And they wouldn't know that that night he went to his father and said, "Dad, I've come through it."

"You've come through what, son?"

"The shadow, Dad."

"There you are," my father said, cradling my head. "Sure I knew you'd be grand."